Trac

A Sou

...is Prewitt

Also available in audio book everywhere

All the happiness.

Ellen Morris Prewitt

Visit the author's website at ellenmorrisprewitt.com

Cover by Novagiant Media at novagiant.com
Cover photograph by Elli Morris stills & motion at ellimorris.com
Cover model credit: Goldie the chicken

ISBN: 978-1975914677

For more TRACKING HAPPINESS, tune into "Ellen's Very Southern Voice: Novels Told Write" podcast on Stitcher, iTunes and Google Play or wherever the finest podcasts are aired.

Dedicated to Tom, my stalwart love

TABLE OF CONTENTS

CHAPTER 1: Why Would Big Doodle Betray Us?

To understand how I wound up on a train hurtling across the top of the United States, you have to go back to that Saturday morning in Ruth Ann's Cut and Curl in downtown Edison, Mississippi. Ruth Ann could handle up to seven heads in her tin-shack beauty shop, but that morning only my best friend Erick and I graced her chairs. Erick was getting his curls blonded for a visit home to see his folks, and I was waiting on a trim. My hair was a mess where I'd gone at it with the manicure scissors. Marrying your childhood sweetheart only to discover he was a philandering horndog and divorcing him six months later, it'll derail you like that. Erick had been there for me through all my troubles. We'd met a year back in that very beauty shop when I complimented him on his gorgeous skull. Most people don't know to admire the skull, but my grandmother Pooh taught me different.

"Train leaves Jackson at five this afternoon." Erick's head bristled with aluminum foil. "You should come with me, Ms. Williams. We'd have fun together, riding the train."

'Ms. Williams' was Erick's nickname for me, after gravel-roads country singer Lucinda Williams, who is from Louisiana, not Mississippi, but pointing out such a distinction to a man from Minnesota was just being picky.

"Don't tempt me." I would just about chew barbed wire to get out of town. The downward turn in my life had begun when my daddy died almost exactly two years earlier. Then the marital mistake, which the whole town knew about. My mother couldn't quit harping on that disaster the way she did, even though she herself had taken up with a denture-chomping hayseed who owned his own tanning bed. Leaving all that behind might restore my sanity.

"You could meet the fam." Erick's head bobbed as Ruth Anne yanked another sheet of tinfoil into place. Even with his head done up in foil, Erick was Roman-god beautiful, with a long, regal nose and his dancer's body. Before moving to Edison, Erick had been a famous ballet dancer. He came to Mississippi for the International Ballet Competition held in Jackson every four years. God knows why he decided to stay. "Mom and Pop and the twins formed an oompah band. They're in a fierce competition with a rival oompah band. They call themselves the Tuba Whos."

"Now you're just lying." I could listen to Erick talk about his family all day long—they were Polish; they drank whiskey dotted with maraschino cherries; they farted out loud and laughed and farted again. "You're family is so much more fun than my stick-in-the-muds."

"Call Mary Martha," Erick said, referring to my boss at Sinclair's Temps employment agency. "Tell her you won't be available to work for a couple of days."

"Rita Rae would have a fit if I took off for Minnesota." I could hear my mother now.:'You're going where? On the train?'" As it is, she's—"

"Now, that's just not right," Ruth Anne interrupted. She pointed her dye brush at the television running silently in front of us. "Airing our dirty laundry on national TV."

Images of the pimply drug-dealing chicken clerks from the local Chicken Palace appeared on the screen.

If I'd seen those boys ducking into the backseat of the cop car once, I'd seen it a thousand times. The nightly news couldn't leave the drug scandal alone, which hurt my heart. After all, my dad had helped launch the Chicken Palace Emporium into modern-day fast-food chicken fame. Every town in the Southeast with more than five thousand people had a Chicken Palace.

"I know y'all love your Chicken Palace down here, but why is the national news covering this?" Erick, not being from Edison, was somewhat removed from our goings-on.

The screen switched to a twenty-foot tall cardboard cutout of Big Doodle Dayton in his original chicken suit. Early on, Big Doodle had made his own chicken costume for his Chicken Palace commercials, a white Elvis jumpsuit and an oversized paper-mâché chicken head—Big Doodle was very crafty for a Southern man.

"That's the annual Chicken Palace Convention in Chicago." I fluffed my smock as Ruth Anne started in on my hair. "My dad went to the convention every year before he died. I love Big Doodle," I added because it was true. When I was a little girl, Big Doodle had been my co-conspirator—he helped me make a chicken angel costume for the Christmas pageant one year. He was Daddy's best friend and running buddy at the Air Force Academy before they both returned to Edison to get into the chicken business, my daddy a grower, Big Doodle a seller. I hadn't seen Big Doodle since he'd moved away from Edison years ago, but I still held him firmly in my heart.

"Bend your neck," Ruth Anne ordered, and I complied. Her scissors feathered against the nape of my neck, trimming up the mess. I had bailed on my marriage so quickly, I'd had no choice but to move back in with Mother. Now I woke up to Clyde Higgenbotham hollering in the shower about some guy shooting Billy—*pow*! It was a miracle I had a hair left on my head.

"What do you know?" I heard Erick say. "The chicken man himself. Looking very unhappy."

"Big Doodle in person? Not the cutout?" I dared not look up—Ruth Anne would poke you with the scissors if you fidgeted.

"In the flesh."

I stole a peek. The most successful man to ever come out of Edison scowled, his face drawn up like he'd been sucking on an underripe persimmon.

"Turn it up," I ordered.

Ruth Anne pointed the clicker at the screen.

" ... the local Chicken Palace," Big Doodle intoned, inclining his big head toward the camera—you'd expect a man as short and round as Big Doodle to have a small head, but he had a big ol' truck head. "To reassure our eating public, we are hereby severing all ties with the Edison Chicken Palace. Our local investors have failed us, and we must move on to what matters, such as the unveiling of our new Big Doodle Triple Gizzard Stack Sandwich."

Big Doodle disappeared, replaced by a news anchor who joked about the *fowl* mess at the little Southern town's fried chicken joint.

Ruth Anne clicked off the TV. She laid her hand on my shoulder. "He didn't mean it, hon."

"What?" Erick asked.

"He's blaming the local investors for the drug scandal. My dad was the only local investor at the Edison Chicken Palace. All those years ago, when Big Doodle wanted to open a second CP, Daddy loaned him the money."

Erick squinted at the TV. "That hardly seems fair."

"It sure as hell does not," I agreed.

"Being as how your daddy is dead," Ruth Anne said.

"I meant because my dad would never have anything to do with drugs." I glared at the darkened TV, willing Big Doodle to reappear and explain himself. "I can't believe Big Doodle's talking bad about my daddy when he's not around to defend himself."

"Must have forgotten we were down here listening." Ruth Anne scratched her head with the handle of her scissors. "What did he mean, 'sever ties' with the CP? How can we have a Chicken Palace without Big Doodle?"

"Oop. Oop. Oop." I quickly untied my smock. "I gotta go. Mother's at her book club meeting."

"You afraid those snobs will be mean to your mama?" Ruth Anne asked.

Edison's snootiest would have a field day over this latest Watkins family disaster. My mom would be upset if she learned about Big Doodle's accusations from one of them. Even worse, what if Big Doodle did sever ties with our CP? At one point, all the CPs in Mississippi had bought their chickens from my dad. Only the Edison CP still did. Sonny Floyd, the man who was buying Daddy's business from us, relied on that contract to pay the note. If Big Doodle severed all ties with the CP, my mom might wind up in the poor house.

"There's plenty of time to change your mind and come with me!" Erick called as I sailed toward the door.

"Love your heart!" I twirled and blew him a kiss. As I left, I avoided my reflection in the mirror—my half-trimmed head had to look a mess.

*

I found Mother with her elbow propped on the check-out desk at the library. She was outfitted in her navy suit with the red squiggles on it. Over the years, as Daddy's business had taken hold, Mother had transformed herself from a sew-your-own-clothes type of woman into a ladies-who-lunch gal. Her membership in the Clandestine Readers Book Club was very important to her.

"Why'd you do that to your hair?" Mother asked when I walked up.

Mother was a *why* type of person. Why do you stay so bony? Why do you dress like that? *Why* did you marry that son of a bitch? This last was wailed on our front porch when I arrived home from the justice of the peace to tell her I'd gotten hitched.

"I need to tell you something." I tugged her away, not wanting to talk in front of the Book Club members.

Kim Stratton—who'd been in community college with me—sauntered past the counter wearing a sleek beige dress and a saucer-brimmed black hat.

"What's she doing here?" I asked of the woman who represented everything I was not: sophisticated, voluptuous, and a really good speller.

"It's a book club/fashion show." Mother glared at my hand clamped onto her arm. "What is it, Lucinda?"

The Book Club ladies had taken up all the adult tables. Every one of the members was pushing eighty, except for Mother and one black-headed lady who stared at us like we might be her excuse to bolt. "Here." I dragged Mother into the children's section with its bitty tables. A pudgy little girl seated at the end of the table studiously ignored the adults invading her territory.

Mother kept her eye on the fashion show until I told her Big Doodle had appeared live from the convention. She ran a Greta Garbo hand through her used-to-be-red hair. "Restored" she called it. Mother was rightfully proud of her looks, her only odd feature being her chicken legs. Of course, the chicken legs might have been what attracted Daddy to her—one never knows what brings one's parents together.

"Big Doodle is blaming Daddy for the drug scandal at the Chicken Palace."

"Tell me this is an April Fools' joke." Mother threw her hands in the air, and cried. "April Fools!"

At Mother's outburst, our table companion—not more than ten years old—cut her eyes toward the circulation desk as if she intended to report us to the librarian.

"*Sorry*," I mouthed to Miss Junior Librarian and returned to Mother. It *was* April Fools' Day, but, "It's not a joke. I saw it on TV."

"That's Bennie Dayton all over." Mother and my grandmother Pooh were the only people I knew who still called Big Doodle by his real name. When Mother, Daddy, and Bennie had been in high school together, for reasons never shared with me, Bennie had been tagged with the nickname "cock-a-doodler." As a little girl, I'd shortened it to Doodle and added the Big. The name stuck—Big Doodle with his round body and giant head sort of resembled a chicken.

"That man is something else." Mother was working herself into a snit. "Blaming your father for his problems but not coming right out and accusing Bill by name."

"You'd think he didn't even care about the Edison CP anymore," I said.

'Well, it has gone to pot."

Mother wasn't alluding to the drug scandal. After Big Doodle moved away and focused on his vast empire, the original Chicken Palace with its tacky red-and-yellow paint job had been left to limp along as best it could. The picnic tables sagged. The concrete under the benches was splattered with years of spilled milkshakes. The drive-thru chicken no longer clucked, "Lay your order on us." It was pretty pitiful.

"Big Doodle was reading from a sheet of paper, Mother. It was a formal announcement."

"What kind of 'announcement'?" Mother squirmed in her chair, trying to force a more domineering pose. Seated as we were in tiny tot chairs at a tiny tot table, this wasn't easy. Her legs were crossed at an odd angle, and her pantyhose had mashed her kneecaps bloodless—Rita Rae was not a happy camper.

"It's bad, Mother."

"How bad?

"Big Doodle said he was gonna sever ties with the Edison CP."

"Sever ties? What does that mean?"

"Maybe the chicken contract? After all, if Big Doodle would talk bad about Daddy, no telling what he might do. I have a good a mind to march straight up to that convention and give him the what-for. His best friend, his *benefactor*." I checked the rise in my voice. "Erick invited me to go on his trip to see his folks in Minnesota. The train passes right through Chicago. I could go up there and make Big Doodle take back what he said."

Mother stilled. "Yes, you could."

"What?" My mother—who'd adopted Clyde Higgenbotham's belief that anything worth visiting, owning, or even knowing about could be found right here in Mississippi. M-i-crooked letter-crooked letter-dotted letter-crooked letter-crooked letter-dotted letter-humpback-humpback-i. State Flower: Magnolia. State Capital: Jackson—she was encouraging me to leave the state?

"He would listen to you," she urged. "Bennie has always been fond of you. Remember your chicken angel costume?"

"I remember you made me take off my red chicken comb. Said chickens had no place in church."

"Be that as it may, y'all were close. You could tell him Bill had nothing to do with these *allegations,*" she said low-voiced then shivered. "I'm guessing he'd remember you."

"Sure he would," I said, offended. "I called him not too long ago."

"You did what?"

"I called him." This was kind of true. I had called Big Doodle at Chicken Palace Emporium Headquarters in San Francisco to offer my condolences over the drug scandal. Unfortunately, I'd gotten a little lost in the automated phone maze, but I left a message expressing my regrets about the unseemly developments across town. "At the time, I didn't know he was sullying Daddy's name."

"Well, there's the difference. You could take the train, tell Big Doodle he's mistaken. Have fun with Erick and his family." Her face clouded. "As long as you don't haul off and fall in love with an ice skater or someone else equally inappropriate."

"An ice skater?" I envisioned myself wrapped in the arms of a skinny man executing a perfect triple twist. "Why would I fall for an ice skater?"

"Oh, you know." She waved a hand at my thick-headedness. "Men wearing masks and all those pads."

"I'm not falling in love with a hockey player, Mother." I had no intention of taking relationship advice from a woman who'd moved a rube into her house for no discernible reason other than she needed boinking now and again, and in a small Southern town, "now and again" wasn't proper. "Besides, what inappropriate choices have I made other than Stirling?"

"You chose Stirling *inappropriately* twice."

"Okay. Granted, I did do that. But lots of folks give love a second chance."

Mother raised her eyebrows. "You spent four years in community college staring through a secret mirror while your fellow students played Chinese checkers."

"That was one class, and it was important research," I protested, causing Miss Junior Librarian to put a finger to her lips.

"You refused to bring any of your college boyfriends home," Mother plowed on. "Afraid of what your dad and I would think. You won't wear anything that remotely flatters you, and here you are at age twenty-five without a friend to speak of. "

"That's not true. Pammy's my friend," I said. Pammy was a high school pal who now conducted home spas for Glamor Galore.

"Yes, there is crazy Pammy ... a woman with a pirate tattoo and a police record."

"Pammy doesn't have an actual record. Plus, Mary Martha's my friend."

"You can't count your boss."

"Erick's my friend, that's a fact."

"A man whose last name is an astrological sign."

"His last name is Gminski. He uses Gemini because it's more fun."

"He's from Minn-e-so-ta." Mother glanced at the fashion show, where Kim Stratton preened in a new outfit. Kim's eyes were exotic with heavy liner, her sleek hair nipped into a bun at the nape of her neck. The deep vee of her shift showed off a double strand of pearls and cleavage I couldn't conjure in my dreams. Every man in Edison, Mississippi loved Kim Stratton.

"Kim Stratton would be a nice friend for you," Mother said.

I sighed. "Mother, I'm never gonna be Kim Stratton. Be thankful I have Erick as my friend. He doesn't remember me as the dorky kid with the pet chicken. He says I'd be fun on a train trip with him."

As I said it, I realized I'd talked myself into joining Erick on his trip. I could ride the train, visit another state—I'd never been out of Mississippi, except when Daddy and I flew to St. Louis for a Cardinals baseball game on my Sweet Sixteen birthday. It would be fun to go somewhere other than Jackson. Don't get me wrong. Jackson had health food restaurants with soy sauce in bottles instead of plastic packages, and Jackson had used bookstores with announcements for Reiki healing classes where you could tear off a slip of paper and go to the public library and research exactly what a Reiki healer was and then show up to be healed to your heart's content. But riding the train into the unknown North …. If I were lucky, while I was gone, Mother would lose interest in my romantic failures. If I were really lucky, I'd arrive back at the house and discover Clyde had vacated the premises, picking up his portable tanning bed and rolling it off to Arkansas to hunt for diamonds or something.

When I relayed my decision to Mother, I threw in the fact that Erick would be auditioning his world-saving idea at a contest at the gigantic Mall of America—Mother loved to shop.

I must have laid it on too thick, because she chirped, "I could come with y'all!"

Erick would kill me if my joining him meant Rita Rae showing up with twenty pieces of luggage in tow.

"Of course, Erick says the mall's not very well insulated," I explained while Miss Junior Librarian flounced in her chair and popped open another book. "When you take your clothes off in the dressing room, your *be*hind goose-bumps."

This wasn't true. I'm sure the Mall was perfectly insulated. I was playing my "the North is cold as hell" card. It's a conversation we have often in our household. "Can you believe they eat ice cream up North?" Mother would say. "That Ben and Jerry's is up there somewhere. Cold as it is, and them making ice cream."

"You're probably right," She sighed. "Besides, Bennie Dayton might be thrown off by my presence." She patted her hair.

I blinked. Mother and Bennie? But I wasn't about to go there, not when she'd decided to stay home. Rita Rae might berate me for my yes-I-want-my-dolly, no-I-don't-want-my-dolly decision making, but guess who I got it from?

"Try not to get distracted, Lucinda. Sometimes your exuberance makes you shoot before you aim. Focus on making Bennie change his mind. When you return, we can talk." Mother gave me a significant look.

I couldn't think of one part of my life Mother hadn't already talked to death, a fact I was about to mention when I saw the sadness in her eyes. It was the same sorrow I felt whenever I thought about Daddy.

"Don't worry, Mother. I'll sort out Big Doodle, and everything will be fine." I reached to pat her hand, but she was scooting her chair from the table and straightening her skirt. She flashed a smile at Miss Junior Librarian, who'd given up any pretense of ignoring us.

I leaned in the child's direction. "The Mall of America has big ol' rollercoasters inside the mall," I singsonged. "Most awesome thing in the *wor-eld*."

Miss Junior Librarian lifted her nose in the air and slowly returned to her book.

Didn't matter. Soon everyone in Edison would be talking about Lucinda Mae and her amazing trip to Minnesota.

Quickly, I kissed Mother good-bye. She, in turn, told me to be careful, put toilet paper on the toilet seat, and refrain from giving my phone number to strangers—everything except the actual words *I love you*. That was okay. I knew what she meant. Besides, I was off on a train trip.

*

Once, when I was in the fifth grade, we put on a school play. All of us children were dressed in black-and-white convict stripes with real chains wrapped around our ankles. We formed a conga line and shuffled across the stage to "Jailhouse Rock." Why this passed for a good idea in Edison, Mississippi, where a full third of those on stage would end up in real convict hardware, I do not know. Only little Stevie Barnett, who went by Critter, grew up to actually kill someone. But still.

Before that reality set in, I was exhilarated to be on stage, my hands clasped around Jimmy Evers's skinny, wiggling waist. As we sashayed to Elvis, the notes climbing higher and higher, the possibilities of the world opened before me. For the first time in my life, with all those eyes glued on my shimmying dance, I believed what my daddy always told me: I could be anything I wanted to be.

The train roaring into the station gave me the same *whoosh!* of excitement. It made me believe I could ride it to a place where there was no more *no* in my life. Whatever my heart's desire, I could step onto the unfolding steps, and it would be mine; grasp the handrail, and I was in business. If only I had the courage to approach this roaring lion that was settling down and making nice as a kitten, I could be off on a grand adventure and no one and no thing could stop me.

That is, unless I got stuck behind a yakker.

"She shows up in her lace mini-skirt and stilettos." The woman in front of us had one foot on the steps, but she'd gotten to the good point in her story, and she wasn't budging.

"Coming to my house to tell me Larry was bopping her. Sixty-two years old and wearing red stilettos. If she wants his sorry ass, she can have him."

Her own sorry ass was front and center on the steps, her questioning face looking down at her companion who was as stuck as the rest of us. Erick was behind me, probably being his usual cool-as-a-cucumber self. Erick had danced on stage with the best ballet dancers in the world, competing with men from Sweden and Brazil and Russia—not only competing but making it to the semi-finals of the International Ballet Competition before a dastardly French judge eliminated him. He was the best-looking man to ever hit town, although he did have a little bit of an underbite. Ask me, the underbite made him look aristocratic, like someone had made a faux pas and he was going *eek!* but trying not to let them see he'd noticed.

He must have been going *eek!* now because I heard him sigh. The conductor finally held out his hand for the lollygagging woman's ticket and barked, "Heads up, sister girl!"

The yakker, whose hair had been home-permed to the crispy stage, shoved her ticket at the conductor with an exaggerated "Excuse me." But she got her butt off the step, and the conductor motioned to me. "Your turn, sister girl. This train's about to take off."

"We're going on an adventure," I told him, almost the same way two years ago I'd blurted out to strangers that my daddy had died. Then I'd go on and on about how he'd loved his chickens and treated them with kindness before it was the thing to do. That was grief talking. This was different.

"An adventure, you say?" The conductor swiped a magic marker across my ticket and handed it back to me. "Hope you're not disappointed."

After Erick peeled off to his berth, I was lugging my overnight bag and lime-green tote and knapsack best as I could, when the lights flickered and I realized we were underway. Who would've thought, me riding the famous *City of New Orleans*, leaving Edison, Mississippi, in my dust, hurtling toward Yazoo City and Greenwood and Memphis and beyond?

The train lurched, and I wobbled, my baggage pulling me off kilter.

"Careful," a passing conductor said. "Train takes some getting used to."

Outside the window, I caught a glimpse of Mississippi slipping by: industrial buildings running with rust, a row of shotgun shacks baking in the afternoon sun. At one of the houses, a man sat on his front porch, leg stretched, heel propped, watching us pass. In the front yard of another house, a washing machine tilted and red geraniums spilled from its mouth. The April breeze ruffled the fresh leaves of the trees, and honeysuckle crawled all over barbwire fences. "Bob wire," I had called it as a child, the same way my Southern world had turned my bedside dresser into "Chester drawers." Two teenage girls on a side street ran toward the train, arms raised, waving. I wanted to wave back, but my heavy bags wouldn't let me. So I whispered, "Bye, bye, Mississippi," as the girls slowly faded from sight.

*

Thankfully, even with my late ticket purchase, the train had a berth available in the sleeper car. *Sleeping car* is a misnomer because you can stay in your berth even when you aren't asleep. The name of the baggage car is misleading too, because the average person riding the train—that is, anyone not carrying something oversized, such as a coffin—carts his or her luggage with them down the narrow hallway into their sleeping/non-sleeping berth.

I wanted to make the berth mine, so I unpacked my suitcase. No computer because my laptop had been hijacked by a virus that parked me on a site where I could only apply for a home mortgage or buy a car. Plus, technically, the laptop belonged to Stirling, my ex-husband, and I didn't want anything on the train to remind me of him.

My transistor radio I set on the small table beside the bed. Pooh had loaned me the old-timey radio so I could listen to the Cardinals games. Pooh and I had been St. Louis Cardinals fans since she'd been laying my bottom on the changing table, insisting she was only tackling the messy job because she believed I'd amount to something one day.

My only other gadget was a pink cell phone given to me by Pammy to replace my broken phone. (Pammy had lots of phones, and I wasn't gonna ask why.) I'd run into Pammy this afternoon when I went to the grocery store for some toothpaste for the trip. She was dressed in her usual Goth get-up. The two of us had spent our high school days watching old black-and-white movies and dying our hair purple while we dreamed up scenarios where a rock star would wander into town and, after stomping around complaining about how true shit boring Edison was, he would run into Pammy and me, melting all his angst.

Nowadays, Pammy made a killing leading Glamor Galore spas. Women gazed at her tattoos and piercings and could not believe she had such perfect skin—Glamor Galore must be a miracle! I told her I was going to visit Erick's Polish family in Minnesota, and she'd told me about some trouble she'd had with the Polish Women's Association in Jackson. They'd gotten drunk and "out of hand," whatever that meant in Pammy's spa world. She'd forced the pink phone on me: "Girl, you're gonna need it."

My sleeping/non-sleeping berth all set up, I called Chicken Palace Headquarters. I wanted to tell Big Doodle I was on my way to the convention so I wouldn't arrive and say, "Hey, Big Doodle! It's me, Lucinda!" and he'd have a blank look on his face and I'd be embarrassed. After leaving a message, I surveyed my new quarters. The tucked-away bed, the stainless-steel sink, the humongous window with its clacking-by scenery—it was delicious.

I might not have fallen so hard for my new berth if I hadn't recently been forced to share a basement bathroom with two pulpwood haulers. I know, I know: you don't just marry the man; you marry the family. And all newlyweds have to start at the bottom, but I hadn't known the bottom was going to be the Kenny family's moldy concrete basement with pipes that rattled and rolled like small animals were having sex inside. Years before, when I was in middle school, I had made out in that basement with Stirling—spelled with an *i*, not with an *e* the way you spell *sterling silver*, more like silver plate, not the real thing at all. Who would have guessed our teenage make-out site would turn into my married house of horrors where Stirling's brothers—singing and burping, bumping into furniture and hollering curse words—gravitated night after night to the basement bathroom like drunken college boys weaving toward a pine tree. The worst offender was Stirling's older brother, who I called Jack-O for the crazy way his eyes rolled around in his drunken head. It wasn't very nice to make up names for your brother-in-law, but brushing your teeth over a sink where you later learned Jack-O, drunk as Cooter Brown, had unzipped his pants and peed—it can make a person ugly like that.

Someone knocked on the door of my berth.

Erick. Eager to go exploring.

CHAPTER 2: First Time on the Train

Erick wore black leather pants and a white t-shirt. He'd rolled the sleeves of the shirt. Erick enjoyed channeling Elvis Presley, his hero—he knew all about my turn in "Jailhouse Rock."

I didn't feel rightly attired.

"Wait a sec," I said and flew through my suitcase.

I emerged in a fluffy skirt that clamped my waist then billowed. The skirt was bright red, vintage, in some sort of puffy material. I wore it with a thin black belt because the belt showed off my skinny waist and the skirt hid how bony the rest of me was. Mother was right about that: I was bony. Let me tell you, when your childhood dentist looks in your mouth and says, "You know you got bones in there?"; when your doctor in the sixth grade feels something in your tummy and pokes around and around and finally says, "Well, I'll be— that's her backbone," you remember all your life.: *I am a bony chick.*

"Ms. Williams, *that* is a skirt. Perfect belt."

That was my Erick—he appreciated accessorizing.

As we walked the aisle, Erick told me how glad he was I'd decided to come along. "Even if you're not actually here for me," he added.

"Oh, I am. In Chicago, I'll make Big Doodle take back the ugly things he said about Daddy. He'll feel so bad he'll probably use the closing ceremonies of the convention to announce Bill Watkins had nothing to do with the drug scandal. Then you and I will go to the Mall of America where I can jump up and down and make a fool of myself when you win the million dollar prize."

A Daily Prayer

Strengthen me this day, O Lord
For all that lies ahead.

Keep me in Your care always
And grant my daily bread.

Instruct me in Your paths
As I put my trust in You.

Show Your love through all I say
And everything I do.

Forgive me in Your mercy
Whenever I am wrong.

Wash my heart of sin and guilt
And make my spirit strong.

Make me glad to lend my hands
To all who are in need.

Help me to relieve their pain,
And may they soon be freed.

I offer You my thanks, dear God
For all You've done for me.

Hear my prayers and raise me up
To closer with You be.

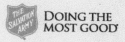

"What will you do if can't sweet-talk Big Doodle into doing what you want?"

"Let's not think about that." I clamped Erick's arm tighter, both for reassurance and to guard against the swaying of the train. "My mother practically made me take a blood oath I would succeed at this thing."

Our first stop in our train tour was what the conductor called the "buffy." To get to the buffy, you went down a flight of stairs. This was a revelation to me: trains have stories. Same thing happened on our Sweet Sixteen trip to St. Louis when my dad and I stayed in a hotel. They messed up our reservations and upgraded us to a room with a spiral staircase that disappeared into the ceiling. The entire stay, I kept walking up the stairs then back down again, amazed you could walk through a hotel ceiling.

The buffet counter reminded me of the snack counter at church camp, but better stocked. An adorable plastic-sealed package held a small can of tuna fish, crackers, a knife, mustard, and mayonnaise. A rose, creamy pink, nodded in a vase on the counter.

The clerk behind the counter pointed at his name badge. "Sampson. What can I get for you two?"

"Just a Coke." I resisted the tuna—we would be eating supper in the dining car before too long.

"One Coke coming up." He snagged a Coke from the shelves and slid it onto the counter, assessing my red, swirling skirt.

"Nice skirt," he said. "You make it?"

Good Lord, no, I almost blurted out. That wasn't the image I wanted to convey: Girl from Mississippi in Homemade Skirt. But I could tell Sampson meant it as a compliment. "No. I could never make something as complicated as this."

"Made my vest." He puffed out his chest. Jazzy salsa dancers strutted across the sparkly print.

"Well, you've got the touch."

"Train lets us accessorize." He tapped the rose vase. "Gotta make it your own any way you can."

I cut my eyes at Erick. "Erick appreciates accessorizing. Plus, he's a famous ballet dancer."

"And Lucinda enjoys embarrassing me," Erick said.

"That's what friends are for, right? Let me fix that for you." Sampson popped open my Coke and poured it into a plastic cup then handed it to me. "Where you guys headed?"

"Minnesota. My family." Erick made his *eek!* mouth.

Sampson raised his eyebrows. "Bet I got me a family just like that."

Figuring they could use alone time, I swept up my Coke. Pivoting, I mouthed to Erick, *"He's cute."* Out loud I said, "Love your heart."

"Love your heart too," he replied. "Even if you do remind me of my mother sometimes."

Playing matchmaker wasn't my normal style—too high of a risk for error—but I wasn't wild about Erick's boyfriend ("Not my 'partner,'" Erick said. "We're not running a dry cleaners together.") James, who everyone called J.J. was too abrasive for me. He was a fight promoter, a job that took him all over the southeast. J.J. was cut, I'll give you that, but otherwise I don't know what Erick saw in a man who spent his time encouraging people to get in a small cage and beat each other up. Not to mention that when Erick and J.J. were off, J.J. was on with Little Davey, the inept manager at the Chicken Palace. Little Davey carried beef jerky in the pocket of his CP uniform like a redneck chicken management engineer. Who would ever hook up with Little Davey?

As I wandered from the buffet, it occurred to me the train might turn out to be similar to the bus station in Edison, where ladies of the night plied their trade. Or the gas station where you could buy heavily grooved condoms from the machine hanging on the bathroom wall. A temporary place with hit-and-run sex. Sex on a train would probably be more civilized, less cheesy, since it's hard to treat someone as a one-night stand when you're stuck on board together. Sex on a train had to be at least a two-stop stand.

I'd arrived at the dining car.

A man seated at the first booth glanced up when I entered.

"Not open yet." He tapped his ledger with his pencil.

"Can I look around? First time on the train."

"Be my guest. Leave your drink here." He pointed his pencil at the table then returned to work.

The dining car did not disappoint, with white tablecloths and silver salt-and-pepper shakers. I ran my fingers along the crisp cloth. It reminded me of my first grown-up date with Stirling. It was late summer, and Stirling was home from traveling around Europe, which I later learned meant screwing his way across the continent. At the time, Sterling was counting out his change, telling the clerk how euros made it so much easier to get around. He was wearing Italian loafers with tiny tassels and a grownup business suit. When he asked me out, I thought, why not? Sterling and I had broken up in the tenth grade when rumors of him and a large blonde made me throw up in the lunchroom trash can. But there he was, being sophisticated, you know.

He took me to the finest restaurant in Jackson—one with white tablecloths and a front closet with jackets for men who showed up in shirtsleeves. Stirling told me all about his trip to Europe, and I told him about this book I was reading, *Journey to the End of the Night.* I'd found the book at one of my garage sales. I love garage sale paperbacks—for half a buck, you can try anything. Sometimes I scored, like with this writer, Louis Something Celine. At first, the plot was confusing, and I had to keep flipping back and forth to figure out what I'd just read. Then the excitement took hold, and I fell in love.

Needless to say, not too many folks in Edison, Mississippi, were fond of Celine—hard to press someone to your bosom if you've never heard of him. So imagine my surprise when Stirling told me he was a fan. Later, after Stirling bragged he'd made it all up, I could see where he'd mostly gazed earnestly at me while I prattled on about the blessing of exuberance, the thrill of running pell-mell into the future. At the time, the gin martini coursed through my veins (I can't do gin; it makes me crazy), and I revealed more and more of how the book made me feel. Stirling gazed at me as if I was the wisest person in the whole world. All the grief and confusion from Daddy's death lifted, and I shivered with the possibility of being happy again. Even in light of Stirling's later massive sexual betrayals, whipping out his pink penis and poking everyone in sight like a human fucking gerbil, it was probably his pretending that night to share my deepest feelings that hurt me the most.

At the end of the dining car, I turned and walked back to the front. Declining my now-watery Coke, I mashed the big red button and stepped through the heavy sliding door into the rocking section that tied one car to the next.

The small space was kind of like a dash between the thoughts of the train, less connected than the regular train. It was open to the elements somehow—I could feel a breeze, see through the flooring to the track running beneath me.

The door screeched open, and a man side-stepped into my space. He was concentrating on the automatic door sliding back into place—feeling the handrail to steady himself, watching his footing—and hadn't seen me yet. When he finally got his bearings, he was going to look up, and I'd be embarrassed, caught spying on an intimate moment between him and the train.

Instead, he began flapping his coat pockets, looking for something. It dawned on me: he had come in here for a smoke. Which, of course, was illegal.

He glanced up, cigarette clasped between his fingers. I swear he could've been a movie star, someone from one of my old black and white films. Steel-blue eyes, well-defined jaw but slightly pudgy cheeks, a former tough guy who wasn't so tough anymore—someone who oh so needed a fedora. His blue eyes looked right through me, making me feel like I'd left the house that morning without my panties on.

Erick might have had Sampson, but I had mine.

CHAPTER 3: The Movie Star

"I've Got Mine" was a game Erick and I played. We had quit while I was married—Stirling didn't think the game was seemly. But before that, whenever Mary Martha placed me on a job in downtown Jackson, Erick would drive the forty-five minutes from Edison, right past the auditorium where he'd suffered his cruel loss during the International Ballet Competition, and meet up with me. We'd scout out a spot, open our bag lunches, and play.

The rules of the game said that by the end of the lunch hour, each player had to have made a pick. You could only choose once, the risk being that, after you'd called yours, a much cuter guy would stroll by. We'd then decide who'd made the better pick. Erick usually won because he was more patient and dedicated— sometimes, he followed his guy down the street. I tended to swing right out of the box—high ball, outside ball, whatever—like a a rookie baseball player just called up to the bigs.

Could be I was doing it again. The man caught in the passageway with me was drop-dead gorgeous, but prudence suggested I wait a bit, scout out the competition.

I was not prudent. I stared.

The Movie Star—my pick—eyed me up and down and asked, "You looking for a customer?"

Okay.

I tend to dress a tad…flamboyant, but there was nothing sleazy about my outfit. Well, rhinestones on the black top, but they were small, and rhinestones were in fashion again in a kind of retro way.

"Rhinestones do not a hooker make," I told him.

He placed the unlit cigarette between his lips—no wedding ring, I noticed—and motioned to my skirt.

"Cigarette girl. All you need is a tray. You know, from the movies."

"Oh."

The train was rocking, my fluffy skirt swaying. My kitten heels skittered on the grooved floorboards while I wildly wondered what to do next. Should I smile slowly, as if he'd said the most clever thing in the whole world, or ooze out a remark so bombshell sultry he dropped the cigarette from his mouth? I was considering his accent—he'd pronounced you, "yous," with almost an *s* on it, so he might be from New Orleans—when a quite large woman tapped on the glass behind him.

Before you knew it, she was in the rolling space with us, and we were trying to maneuver to get out of each other's way, and then he'd re-pocketed his cigarette and was gone.

Oh, well. It was a train. He couldn't get far.

As I stepped into the next car, a funny noise burped from my lime-green tote. It was the cell phone. I had a premonition: I was not yet out of Mississippi, and my mother was calling.

Sure enough, when I answered, Rita Rae was saying, "Lucinda Mae, you need to know."

That was the way Mother always prefaced bad news: I don't like dropping a rock on your head, baby, but you need to know....

"Know what?" It was best to go ahead and get it over with.

"The *allegations* are growing."

"Growing how? Did they find pot plants in the Chicken Palace restroom?"

"It's not funny, Lucinda. We've misunderstood the situation. The druggies have taken over Edison."

"Druggies? Edison doesn't have any druggies." Except for Stew, the guy who lived out past the interstate exchange, the only person in town known to succumb to the crystal meth craze, but Rita Rae didn't need to know that. "Those clerks were high school boys slinging weed. Losers with no adult supervision, thanks to Little Davey, who couldn't manage to make a cow give milk."

"It wasn't only those poor, misguided youths at the CP. They're part of a drug ring that spreads throughout the Chicken Palace Emporium system."

"What the hell are you talking about?" I grabbed a seat back to steady myself against the train's rocking.

"That Chicken Emporium stinks worse'n bat shit at a Halloween party."

Clyde had taken control of the phone. I could imagine the two of them standing in the kitchen, shoulders touching so they both could hear and interrupt each other as need be.

"We're in the middle of a real shit storm." Clyde was talking in that nasally voice he used when he wanted to sound important, like at the supper table when he was spouting off Learning Channel wisdom. "Law enforcement are crawling all over the CP, looking for evidence on the drug ring. And Stirling's getting married."

"Don't tell her that." Rita Rae was back on the line. "She can only take so much. You wouldn't believe what they're saying about your daddy now."

"Who's saying?"

"Newspaper. Online." Clyde again, a real I-told-you-so tone to his voice. Clyde was at his most obnoxious when the topic was small-town politics. Clyde's dad had been a state legislator. Never mind that after the man had died, they discovered the old coot had another family over in Jackson. Mother claimed that mortification didn't count because Clyde "wasn't from that other family."

"*The Clarion Ledger*'s been quoting inside sources saying your daddy was the linchpin king behind a goat-doping, chicken-smuggling scandal."

"Daddy? A goat-doping scandal?" I flashed on an image of a goat sitting on a stool, arm braced for the illegal shot that would make him a better mountain climber. "What does that even mean?"

"Focus, Lucinda." It was my mother. "They're saying Bill ran a drug ring out of the Edison Chicken Palace, and Bennie Dayton isn't raising a finger to stop this malicious talk."

"Ol' Bennie practically called Edison a rogue operation," Clyde added. "'Whatever the local investors were up to shouldn't reflect on the good name of the Chicken Palace Emporium,' blah, blah, blah."

"They're calling Daddy a criminal? Are you sure?" Mother and Clyde had a tendency to exaggerate ("They're closing the I-20 exit to Edison! Traffic's being re-routed to Bovina!" When the only thing that was happening was a re-paving). It was best to ask twice.

"You got your work cut out for you, little lady, dealing with that Bennie Dayton. Your mama is counting on you to clear this mess up. Everybody in town is believing your daddy was a criminal. People'll believe anything they read on the Interweb."

He paused. "The scandal could improve attendance at the museum, though." He was referring to Big Doodle's Chicken Palace Emporium Museum located off the highway exit. The museum featured memorabilia commemorating the Chicken Palace story, such as the Ride-a-Rooster—a big, bucking chicken whose name took on a whole 'nother meaning when us kids hit middle school. "That crappy museum might finally outdraw the Tomato Museum in Bovina."

At that, Mother snatched the phone and launched into a garbled explanation of the "biggest drug ring in the Southeast"—something to do with goats imported from Jamaica, smelly chicken parts, and a tractor-trailer distribution system—until I said goodbye, trying to remember as I hung up: did someone say Stirling was getting remarried?

*

It took me a while to get internet reception, but I found the *Clarion Ledger* article Clyde was talking about. The "inside sources" blaming Daddy for the drug ring weren't named, but who could it be other than Big Doodle or one of his minions?

I sighed—my job had suddenly gotten much harder. I needed to somehow remind Big Doodle of the good ol' days in Edison. Me, chasing his chicken Prophet around the front yard. Him, chasing my chicken Peck. The "Fearsome Foursome"—two humans and their chickens—had been captured in a semi-famous photograph, which now hung in the Chicken Palace Emporium Museum. I needed to get that photo in front of Big Doodle. He'd remember how close we were, and his heart would soften.

I checked my watch: 6:04 pm. The Museum would be closed. But a closed door never stopped my friend Pammy.

"Hey, girl." She picked up on the first ring. "Strange seeing that number pop up on my screen, since it's my number. Whatcha doing?"

"I need your help, Pammy."

"I'm on it. What is it?"

"Can you go to the Museum and get a photograph for me?"

"The Museum is closed by now."

"That's why I'm calling you, Pammy. No one else could do this."

"No problem. What photo do you want me to steal?"

"We're not stealing it, Pammy. After you use it, we'll return it." I had to make these particulars clear— Pammy could be...enthusiastic.

"Gotcha. So tell me which photo."

I described the Fearsome Foursome photo: Big Doodle standing, my arm encircling his waist, the two chickens posing nonchalantly at our feet.

"I know that photograph! It's my favorite Museum artifact. That one chicken is wicked."

"That's Prophet, Big Daddy's chicken. He was a Naked Neck. A very rare type of chicken."

"Looks like a crazy person shaved its neck."

"Yeah, a naked neck on a chicken is not a pretty sight. But that chicken was sweet, sweet."

"What am I supposed to do with the Naked Neck photograph?"

"I need Big Doodle to see it before tomorrow morning?"

"Big Doodle is in Edison?"

"No, he's in Chicago at the Annual Chicken Palace Convention, but the convention usually has its own website. What about snapping a picture of the photo and sending it to him through the website contact page? Mark it urgent or something so they'll get it to him straight away."

"Okay. I'm good to go. You having fun?"

I hated to disappoint Pammy—she always wanted more for my life than I did. "Not yet, but good times are right around the corner, I'm sure. Let me know when you've sent the photo."

"I got this covered. You concentrate on having fun." The phone went silent.

A family passed me in the train's narrow hallway, the mother and daddy leading with two little boys waddling behind. I watched them disappear. Outside the window, trees ticked by. I was alone on a train, barreling away from home under the cloud of a scandal. I was suddenly overwhelmed, afraid I'd taken on a mission I couldn't handle.

I touched the corridor wall, steadying myself.

Irrationally, I wished my grandmother Pooh were with me. When life got to be too much, which it did all the damn time these days, Pooh would pull out her ceramic bowl and beat up a batch of Katherine Hepburn brownies—so named because they were made using

Katherine Hepburn's very own recipe. As soon as the brownies emerged warm from the oven, we'd go sit outside on the glider under the pecan tree and snack on the gooey goodness, Pooh telling me, "Don't you forget, Lucinda—men enjoy a good brownie."

Pooh wasn't a fan of Big Doodle—she called him "the old goat," possibly a slur related to the Genuine Curried Jamaican Goat dish, the only non-chicken dish on the Chicken Palace menu and actually imported from Jamaica. Go figure—maybe Big Doodle visited Jamaica and fell in love with the national dish. Anyways, Pooh always claimed Big Doodle hadn't properly compensated Daddy for helping launch the chicken chain, and she was quick to point out when all the Mississippi Chicken Palaces except the one in Edison dropped Daddy as a contract grower. "No One Here Is Mean to Our Chickens" was my Daddy's free-range chicken-raising motto. Big Doodle supported the philosophy in the company's early going but drifted away from it over the years. It upset Daddy something fierce to know chickens across Mississippi were suffering to supply Chicken Palace customers, but he wouldn't let a bad word be said about Big Doodle, because they were friends.

I was leaving home for only the second time in my life while the bottom was dropping out of things back in Edison. I could have used some reassurance, like the gentle glide of Pooh's glider and the seat cushions that smelled a little moldy—but porch mold, not dank, wet-socks-and-dirty-underwear basement mold. Wherever Pooh had traipsed over the years, the glider had followed, from her front porches to beneath Mother's pecan tree. I guessed when Pooh died, I'd have to lug the glider down to the cemetery and set it up over her grave. Pop a brownie in my mouth, sit…glide.

I had a bag of those brownies somewhere in my suitcase.

Such was the comfort I could dredge up for myself: chocolate, my grandmother, and a smelly glider.

*

Ten minutes later, Erick joined me in the club car. The car's swivel chairs were designed for observing the landscape, so they faced the windows. Every so often, whoever decorated the train had stuck a little table on the floor, its large base a suction cup, its tiny top shaped like a tiddlywink. Erick had covered our table top with a printout from the Mall of America website describing the *Your Idea Can Save the World!* contest. He shuffled through the sheets as if he'd lost a page then sighed with relief. His nervousness reminded me I was not the only person in the world with worries.

Peering over his shoulder, I asked, "Does your invention have anything to do with being a short order cook?" Erick worked the graveyard shift at the Edison Diner. His boss always gave him the short end of the stick, a disservice he took in elegant stride, probably on account of being a ballet dancer.

He fluttered his eyelashes. "What did you have in mind, Ms. Williams? An egg timer that slaps the customer when he asks if his order is ready yet?"

I envisioned the little timer waving its hands while it squeaked, "I'm ready! I'm ready!"

"That's a fabulous idea. I'd love it."

"It sounds like something you'd love, it does indeed," he mused as he flipped a page and studied a chart. "You're gonna love my invention."

"I am?"

"You are."

"Are you gonna tell me what it is?"

"Nope. You'll have to wait."

"What will you do with the million dollars when you win?" In the thick air around us, folks had nodded off, snoring, their heads at funny angles against their padded chairs.

"I don't have to win the grand prize, only get to the finals."

"Okay. How will you get to the finals?"

Erick ripped opened a package of Juicy Fruit. After offering me a stick, he unwrapped his gum and chomped down. Sweetness filled the air.

"I've already made the first cut, on the application."

"Look at you!" I slapped his arm.

"The next step happens at the mall on Tuesday, with you of course."

"Of course."

"They'll conduct an interview. Then we wait while they decide if we make the next cut."

"That's nerve-wracking. How long do you wait?"

"They make their decision while we stand there. If I do make it—"

"Which you will."

"—they'll tape the semi-finals over the next several days. All the semi-finalists have to tape an explanation of their invention. You can go with me to that too."

"Cool."

"Then the two finalists are announced live Saturday night during the show. That's the group I have to be in."

"The final two?" That sounded like a tall order. "How many made the cut on the application?"

"Eight hundred."

I bit my tongue. "And what's special about being in the finals?"

I waited. Erick played life close to the vest, and I didn't want to pry. He was so private, I didn't understand how he was going to handle being on a rowdy game show where they might make him act the fool. I'd never seen Erick act the fool. I might as well try to imagine Rita Rae traipsing to Walmart in her nightie: impossible.

After a moment, he said, "That French judge, the one whose scores tanked me in the IBC?"

"Yeah." The judge had given Erick such low marks that the near-perfect scores of the other judges hadn't been enough to keep him in the competition.

"He made a remark about my dancing. Something uncalled for. If I can make it to the finals and get on TV, I have a chance to make up for that."

He returned his attention to the pages spread on the table. The corners of the sheets were crimped and several sections were highlighted or underlined. Some even had little exclamation marks. "I have to make sure I do everything right."

He was so intent, studying and re-studying, my heart went out to him.

"I know your idea can save the world. Everyone will love your heart same as I do."

He glanced up, his eyes serious. "I'm counting on that, babe."

The conductor in his navy uniform and bellman's cap strolled through the car calling out, "*Ya*-zoo City! *Ya*-zoo City!"

"*Ya*-zoo City!" I repeated softly.

They said everything on the train twice: "Good evening, good evening. May I have your attention please, may I have your attention please." The repetition was a lot better than the airplanes with their "cabin pressure" and "oxygen mask" and "flotation device" rigmarole.

Erick was thoroughly absorbed in the contest rules, so I eased out of my chair.

As I approached the door, the conductor tipped his hat, so I asked him how he came to conduct on a train. "All in the family," he said and told me how his great-grandfather worked for the railroad, cutting ice from the Great Lakes and shipping it down South where everyone was sweltering in the heat, dying for a block of ice. Seems a physician from Florida figured out how to produce artificial ice and that was the end of the natural ice business, the loss of his great-grandfather's job. The great ice-cutting saws stilled, the picks hung empty over the frozen lakes. In their place, the turbines chugged to life, producing man-made ice.

When he asked me why I was riding the train, I told him I was on a quest to save my family from a cruel, empty-hearted businessman who had us in his sights for reasons we could not fathom.

"My goodness," he said, and I felt guilty for blurting out a brain fart of frustration over a scandal that made no sense.

"Actually, it's probably not that bad," I admitted. "Things have pretty much gone to crap back home, but that's the way life has been for a while. Who knows? Maybe the Universe will surprise me and send happiness onto the train."

"Trains will do that," he replied. "They sure will."

Our stop in Yazoo City was quick. The brakes squealed, the train hesitated for a second, and *whoosh,* we were off again. I was back at the table with Erick, casually studying the Mall of America brochure when my Movie Star walked by, turning sideways every now and again so he could shimmy past cattywhompus chairs.

I nudged Erick.

He glanced up. Staring fixedly at the guy, he whistled, low.

I had made a good pick.

CHAPTER 4: A Real Scandal

"He's mine," I told Erick.

"It's a crying shame he can't be mine. Such is the luck of the gene pool."

Erick was talking in a world-weary tone while he flitted glances at the man, who had paused to examine a magazine left in one of the chairs. Even without the cigarette dangling from his lips, he still had the 1940s movie star I-am-so-good-looking aura about him.

He appeared to be about ten years older than I was, thirty-five or six, maybe—although he could have been as old as forty. Things get fuzzy around forty—it's hard to put your finger on someone's age then.

"Find out where he's going," I said to Erick. "And how old he is."

"Going?"

"Find out how long he's gonna be on the train. What's his destination?"

"Are you sure you're ready to get back in the saddle, Ms. Williams? The ink is hardly dry on your divorce decree."

"The signature isn't a real signature made with an ink pen. It's a stamp. You can tell by running your finger across it."

Erick stared at me, his eyes twinkling.

"What?"

"Nothing." He pressed his lips together as if to suppress a smile.

"I did one of those things, didn't I?"

"You did."

"What was it?"

"You don't need to know. It probably wouldn't be as cute if you did."

I'd lost track of the conversation. "What were we talking about?"

"Whether you should be getting involved with someone so soon after your divorce."

"Right. The answer is yes. When your husband has humiliated you with every chick in town, it is imperative to get back in the saddle as soon as possible. Otherwise, you might come to believe you're as sexually worthless as he treated you. Which is not healthy. All things being equal, I should get involved with someone else, pronto."

"As you wish." He stood.

Erick kept his hand—his foot?—in ballet by teaching classes in Jackson in exchange for free time in the studio, and he hadn't lost a smidgen of his physique. Six foot three, chest muscles pushing through his white t-shirt, biceps bulging from the pegged sleeves, black leather pants hugging everything in sight—you could not miss Erick.

The man rolled the magazine in his hand as Erick approached.

"My friend and I were wondering." Erick nodded at me.

I stifled the urge to yelp.

"You know where this train goes after Chicago?" Erick adjusted the waist of his leather britches.

"This train here is the *City of New Orleans*. In Chicago, it turns around and heads back to NOLA. If you wanna go on further, you catch the *Empire Builder*." The man slowly rolled the magazine in his palm. He could've had a gun in an ankle holster, wouldn't surprise me.

"*Empire Builder?*" Erick squinted like he didn't trust the man, never heard of such a thing as an *Empire Builder*. Erick had worked community theater in Jackson. He did misdirection well. "Where's that go?"

"St. Paul. Then on to North Dakota, I think. But no one goes past St. Paul."

"That where you're getting off? St. Paul?"

"St. Paul is my stop." He lowered his eyelids, a snake about to strike. "Tell your friend that. Tell her I'll be on the train with her to St. Paul."

Of course, I could hear every word he was saying, so he'd just told me himself—told me his destination and told me he knew I'd sent Erick over to find out.

As the man walked to the front of the car, sliding open the door and letting in the rat-a-tat-tat clacking of the wheels, and passed from sight, I couldn't help but notice with approval how squarely shaped his butt was.

Only much later did it dawn on me to wonder how the man knew where I was headed.

*

Erick knew all about the *Empire Builder*. We would arrive in Chicago in the morning with just enough time to scoot the couple of blocks to the convention center and confront Big Doodle. Then we'd hop on the *Empire Builder* to St. Paul. Each train had a name. As the Movie Star said, our train was the *City of New Orleans* because it originated in the Crescent City. Seemed to me they should change the names when the trains turned around. Call it the City of Chicago when it leaves that station, but they didn't. You made your reservations by the name of the train. "One Superliner

Bedroom on the *City of New Orleans*, please," not "Jackson to Chicago." The point being: the Movie Star and I were following the same route.

Erick was aloof, tracing the route to Chicago on a train handout. He was quietly miffed at the Movie Star since the man hadn't bought his casual "we were just wondering" routine.

"Who wants somebody easily fooled?" I asked.

"Who wants to be made a fool of? Do a favor for a friend," he humphed, trying to act peevish.

I hugged his neck and gave him a peck on the ear, which caused him to raise his eyebrows, but he let me get away with that kind of thing because he knew what I'd been through with Daddy dying then the Stirling fiasco. Of course, everyone in town eventually knew about my terrible marriage—we only have about two thousand people living in Edison, all told. But Erick knew particularly about my husband's horn dogging because my no-good husband took his women to eat at the diner where my best friend worked.

When I'd told Stirling Erick said his lunch dates looked mighty suspicious, Stirling said, "Of course they look suspicious. I'm writing a book about sex addicts. Those women, every one of them: hopeless addicts."

I believed his story because right after we got married, Stirling announced he wanted to be a writer. I was a ball of wifely support. After all, our love had caught fire over a book—why wouldn't I want Stirling to offer such happiness to others?

To make his dream come true, Stirling went to a writers conference in Jackson. After that, I would find him in the basement with his eyes closed, stroking the arm of the recliner, chanting, "I am a *good* writer."

When that didn't work, he tried drawing circles on a piece of poster board and labeling them: "Bear," "Smokey the," "College Roommate," "Old pizza," "Ants." But he didn't know what to do with the circles, how to make them connect into something that mattered.

He turned to sex.

He knew what to do with that.

By the time I stumbled upon Stirling and the truck-stop waitress—Stirling glancing up like a little boy caught on the jumbotron at a baseball game: startled, squirming, but mesmerized by the picture he was presenting of himself—we had traveled far indeed from that day at the Chicken Palace when Stirling had fitted his Italian loafers beneath the concrete bench, causing me to believe I was in the company of a man who'd figured out how to be both sophisticated and eat a Chicken Palace Barbecued Rooster Special. Looking back, I wonder if either of us had been seeing the other. Me, I was searching for the innocence of youth, before Life burst in and stole my daddy from me. Who knows? Maybe Stirling was worn out, too, jaded from his sexual jaunt across Europe. Maybe he saw in me our earlier time together. Maybe I didn't live up to his expectations either.

And now he was getting re-married.

Antsy, I called Pammy.

"Girl, I was about to call you. The Fearsome Foursome is winging its way across the interwebs as we speak."

"You got it? You sent it?"

"I did, and I did. The Convention website has a big ol' friendly "Contact Us" page. BTW, did you know that Museum is alarmed? Who would have thought it? But when Cecil Everett Clay showed up, I suggested he overlook the B&E in exchange for a date."

Poor Cecil Everett Clay. He was the manager at the Museum. He probably never dated 'cause he couldn't stop talking about chickens.

"Thank you, Pammy. For sacrificing your Saturday night for me."

"No sacrifice. Cecil Everett and I are going to the Banging Heads concert in Jackson. In fact, I better sign off. Time to get dressed."

"You think Big Doodle's gonna get the photo?" Sending a picture on a corporate website wasn't exactly the most direct form of communication.

"Oh, he'll get it."

"Why?" I asked, wary. Belatedly, I remembered a truth about Pammy. She was the Energizer Bunny: wind her up and she kept going and going and...

"I gave the photo a title."

"What title?"

"The Fearsome Foursome: Big Doodle and the Naked Chicks."

*

The train idled at the Greenwood Station, an old-fashioned brick building so cute you'd think we'd landed in a quaint English village. I half expected Miss Marple to emerge at any moment and announce she'd solved the case. Old lady snooping around, always bringing up sex—I loved Miss Marple.

Instead, a woman pulling a suitcase on wheels halted and lit a cigarette. Her bronzy hair flipped on the ends, and her creamy brown skin glowed in the sunlight. When the conductor motioned to the woman's cigarette then pointed at the station, she turned on her heels, sashaying a few yards down the platform. Tilting her chin, she took a drag on the cigarette and blew smoke at the conductor. Not three feet from the conductor, a white man was smoking, but the conductor said not a word to him.

"Things are bad back in Edison," I told Erick, who was intent on the woman and the conductor, waiting to see what happened next.

Erick tapped on the windowpane. The conductor, who was sauntering toward the smoking woman, halted. Erick spread two fingers, pointed at his own eyes, then pointed at the conductor. I had no idea what was going on, but the conductor glanced toward the train as if he was considering returning to his spot by the door. Instead, he folded his arms against his chest, standing his ground.

"You're not interested in the chickens, are you?" I couldn't blame Erick. Only folks truly from Edison thought Big Doodle and the Chicken Palace Emporium were as fascinating as a pig riding a bicycle—which we had at the Mississippi State Fair.

Erick looked at me sideways. "That's not true. What do you think is the world's most famous polka song?"

I considered. "Do polka songs have names?"

"The Chicken Dance."

"You're kidding."

"Every polka party you go to, there's a ring of little kids dancing, all flapping their wings. It's a standard."

"I'm worried about the scandal, Erick."

Erick swiveled his club chair to face me, giving me his full attention. "Tell me exactly why this is bothering you. Is it your family's history with the place? You don't even eat there."

"No. Bad association."

"Ahhh, right. Stirling."

"Not only that. Big Doodle dropped my daddy's philosophy about being nice to chickens. He kept buying Daddy's chickens for the Edison CP because of his history with Daddy, but he didn't mean it anymore. I personally don't see the point in being in business with chickens if you're not gonna be nice to them."

I glanced out the window as the woman dropped her cigarette and ground it under the toe of her high heel pump. This caused the conductor to take a step in her direction.

"So what's the big deal here?"

"The conductor is mad at the woman for smoking," I explained. "Plus, I don't think he cares for her for some reason."

"I know what's going on out there." Erick pointed at my head. "What's going on in here?"

We were knee to knee. My fluffy skirt brushed his leather pants. "It isn't only the Edison Chicken Palace. They're saying the whole system is involved in a drug ring run from the Edison site." I chewed my thumb. "They're talking goat doping."

"Goat doping? What does that even mean?"

"I'm not sure. Something to do with the goats imported from Jamaica—weed, Jamaica, smelly chicken parts moved on over-the-road trucks, you know."

"And tell me again how your dad was involved with the CP?"

"When Big Doodle didn't have the wherewithal to open a second store, Daddy scraped together the money from his growing business. That's where the little biddies are raised until they're full-weight chickens and ready to go for processing." That was the hardest part for Daddy, letting his chickens go—he hated move-out day. He loved move-in day, when the new batches of biddies arrived. He would stand in the pen with his goofy straw hat; the biddies would swarm his legs. "Daddy didn't know if he could afford to let go of that much cash—he and Mama were poor young-marrieds eating tuna casserole every night. But Big Doodle needed help, so Daddy made it work."

"Huh. If your dad was an investor in the chicken chain, why aren't you rich?"

"Not the chain. The Edison CP."

He tapped my knee. "I wondered what you were holding back, Ms. Williams."

"They weren't just business partners, Erick. They were friends."

"Friends, but he took your dad's money and didn't give him an interest in the chain his money financed?"

"That's what Pooh says, but if you ask me that's twenty-twenty second-guessing. No one knew the Chicken Palace Emporium would turn into the big deal it did. Big Doodle could've been doing my daddy a favor, giving him a piece of the bird-in-hand, so to speak. Now 'anonymous sources' are saying he was head of the drug ring."

"Who? Your dad?"

"Yep."

"And people believe that?"

"Clyde says they believe anything online." I glanced out the window. The woman who'd been irritating the grumpy conductor flashed her ticket at him and boarded the train. Her small, round suitcase bumped up the step, the plastic bag on her arm swinging.

"My daddy always said that, for all his business success, Big Doodle was a tad flighty, but he's got to know how hurtful he's being. It's hard to believe he would turn on my daddy that way. Turn on us." I let the possibility of such treachery sink in.

"Don't take it personally, babe." Erick arched his back. "He's probably just pointing the finger at someone other than himself."

I was mulling this over—was Big Doodle that much of a chicken shit that he couldn't handle the fallout from his own scandal?—when the smoking woman entered the club car. Spying Erick, she paused and pointed a long, red fingernail at him.

"I saw you in that window. You watching out for me, baby?"

Erick, ever polite, stood when she spoke to him. The woman let her eyes slide over his well-built frame. She tapped the front of his shirt where the Elvis button announced, "Wave if You Knew The King."

"Precious heart, do you know what year Elvis died?"

"August 16, 1977." Erick's eyelids were at half-mast, studying the woman who in turn was studying him in a way that had nothing to do with Elvis.

She slid her fingernail across her ruby-red lips. "Then you know anyone *old* enough to have known the King ain't *worth your time*."

I pointed to the small cardboard suitcase she pulled behind her. The cover of the case was red and bumpy as snakeskin. I would've used it as a pocketbook if it had been mine. "Is that your suitcase or your pocketbook?"

She narrowed her eyes at me, telling me to bug off—can't you see this here boy and I are busy?—as clearly as if she'd drawled it out loud. I might have arrived on the train with Erick belonging to me and nobody else, but it wouldn't stay that way.

The woman introduced herself as the Bruised Magnolia. She had an act; she'd appeared on Broadway; she was headed to Chicago for a gig. As she flirted with Erick, she swung her plastic bag, releasing the distinct smell of fried chicken. I thought I heard Erick say, "Finding a reason to harass you, it's the oldest chicken trick in the book." But it was probably the fried chicken smell. Your mind did that to you. Taste, touch, smell, a few other things I hadn't figured out—they'd take your logical brain to the mat every time.

The woman giggled, the chicken smell spread, and my mind returned to the chicken-and-potato-salad picnics we had every Saturday when I was little. Mother and I would set the table on the deck of the ranch house, Mother carrying the plates, me the forks for the potato salad. After lunch, I'd crawl beneath the red cedar table and wedge myself into the spot where the legs crisscrossed to form a cradle. One time when I was lodged in there, Daddy found me, sniffling. The deck was damp with rain, and I was picking at the cedar, staining my fingernail red, when Daddy crouched down.

"What is it, punkin?" His face was hidden until he poked his head beneath the table. "You crying?"

I told him about the girls in my class who'd been teasing me about my family. "Ugly things," I said when he wanted to know what they'd been saying. "Laughing at Poppa Dean not looking before he crosses the street, just steps into traffic, paying no never mind to any cars barreling down on him. And how Pooh's face turns all rubbery when she sings in the choir until she looks like that Scream mask from the movies. And how we have a chicken for a pet instead of a dog like a normal family."

"Come here." He motioned with his fingers.

I unfolded myself and sat in his lap on the wet deck.

"What about Peck?" He arranged my arms so he could hold me. "Do you enjoy her?"

I nodded. The chicken followed me around the yard, her bright eyes shining.

"Do you like Pooh?"

"I love Pooh."

"Does her face turn rubbery when she sings in the choir?"

I sat up from where I'd been leaning against his chest. "Does it ever! She could be in the Rapture or something." I opened my mouth, stretching it into a long, narrow O.

"She does indeed. And Poppa Dean never looks before crossing the street. Honey, people can say bad things about you or your family or whatever they want. Sometimes what they say is true. It's up to us to see the good in people we love. So tell me, what do you love best about Poppa Dean?"

That was easy. Poppa Dean had a switchblade collection he kept on Pooh's sewing table. When Pooh was busy in the kitchen, Poppa Dean would let me paw through the knives. My favorite was no bigger than my pinkie, but the blade *pinged!* open same as the big knives. Poppa Dean would let me click open the baby knife as many times as I wanted, the blade glinting free.

"His pocketknives," I said, proud as all get out.

"That's my girl." Daddy hugged me. "Now let's get up off this wet deck."

Anyone who thought my daddy would be involved in the drug trade had lost their mind. He loved Mother and me too much to do such a thing. More importantly, he searched too hard for the good in life to ever willingly mess it up. For an uninformed Big Doodle Dayton to be dragging his name through the mud was almost unforgivable.

Erick clapped his hands, nodding at the Bruised Magnolia.

"You leaving?" The corners of her mouth turned down.

"Duty calls," he said, and I didn't know if he had pressing business or he had to go to the little boy's room.

Without Erick, the Bruised Magnolia was not interested in me, so she continued down the club car. I explored a bit, see if I could spot the Movie Star. I found a chick with a tramp stamp who kept bending over a lot, a businessman whose conversation with his train mate made him sound as hollow as a corked bat, and a wild-haired professor type who kept saying "Bi-*zan*-tium," but no Movie Star.

If I knew Edison—and I did—a bonfire of gossip was erupting right now over Daddy's supposed involvement in the chicken scandal. I might blame Mother and Clyde for turning every twitch of a dog's butt into the biggest calamity since the Yankees overran Vicksburg, but guess who they'd learned it from? In the coming days, the good folks of Edison would idle their shopping carts in the grocery aisle, tut-tutting over the Chicken Palace, and before you knew it, the preacher would be in the pulpit denouncing the whole Watkins clan as a band of liars and chicken thieves. The situation was way worse than when Louisa Jennings made a big deal out of Pooh naming her dog Ikie. Louisa told everyone Ikie must be one of Pooh's old boyfriends 'cause there had never been an Ike in the Watkins family. In truth, Louisa had been mad because Pooh's Kathryn Hepburn brownies beat out Louisa's Jezebel Tarts at the church bake-off. I could hear Louisa now: "I always *knew* Bill Watkins was too good to be true." The other old bats would purse their lips, gleeful to learn the truly kind people in town were just as big of shits as they were.

Outside the window, telephone lines buzzed with unknown messages. Cows in the fields chewed unknown cud. An unknown town passed by, showing us its backside. No answers to give. Didn't even want to say hi.

*

For dinner, I added my turquoise elbow-length gloves to my red skirt and black rhinestone top. When we entered the dining car, a young girl with a bright blue bow in her hair said, "Keen." Everyone else stared at me the way they do when you've got a hole in your pants.

Erick and I headed toward an empty table by the window, timing our lurches so we didn't topple into anyone's lap. After we ordered, Erick took a call that must have been from J.J. I sat with my gloved hands demurely folded in my lap—elbow-length gloves did that to you, calmed you down, even if the gloves were turquoise. I followed my own, un-corralled thoughts.

I thought about my dad and the St. Louis Cardinals he loved so much. Pooh's transistor radio wasn't working, and Erick had agreed to dismantle it for me. When Erick first moved to Edison, he fixed up an old house two blocks from the diner, a great old place with lots of windows and a front porch. His friends helped, but Erick did all the rewiring himself. Until he worked his magic on the old radio, I was bereft of the Cardinals. We were at the very start of baseball season, a crucial time with the Cardinals taking on the Cubs, and I had no idea how they were doing.

My dad taught me to love baseball. How to keep the scorecard, who was a star and who was a utility player. Our trip to St. Louis for my Sweet Sixteen had been to see home-run king Mark McGwire play in his last season with the Cardinals. First at-bat, "Big Mac" McGwire hit a home run into Big Mac Land. The next day, we took our ticket stubs to McDonald's and got free cheeseburgers. Later, McGwire got caught up in the steroid scandal. With the troubles at the Chicken Palace, I wondered if scandal was going to taint everything my daddy had taught me to love.

The woman from the train depot sashayed in and sat at the booth across from us. She opened her box of fried chicken, which I don't think you were supposed to do in the dining car, bring in your own food. The fried chicken was not, I noted, Big Doodle's chicken. The salty smell of the chicken overwhelmed the other food smells in the car, but it couldn't beat out the woman's gardenia perfume. She was sporting a red tube top and red hot pants. She was smacking her lips and saying, "This is gonna be delicious."

Everyone in the car was not looking at her.

She removed a chicken wing from the box and pointed it at Erick then at her table. Erick crossed the aisle, inclining his head for me to join him. I scooted onto his side of the table.

"Thank you, precious." The woman flashed me a fake smile. I suspected she would've been happier with Erick snuggled up beside her in the booth. My suspicion was confirmed when she laid down the wing, cleaned the corner of her lips with her magenta fingernail, and asked, "You two *together* together or are you just traveling together?" She assessed me like I might be a thin man in drag, not very filled out even with the fluffy skirt.

"We're friends."

"Hmmmmm. You got a boyfriend, honey?" she asked Erick.

When Erick said, "I'm working on something else right now," I wondered if he might mean Sampson.

"You said you'd perform on Broadway?" I asked. "Erick's a performer too. He's a world famous ballet dancer."

"Where you dance, sweetie?"

"I'm not dancing right now."

"How can you be a world famous ballet dancer and you don't dance?"

"It's a long story."

"One you don't share?" She brushed chicken crumbles from her cheek.

"Not easily."

"Erick's going to win the Mall of America invention contest," I interjected. "He's already made the first cut."

"I know that contest." The Bruised Magnolia studied Erick. "They got some sure-nuff goofy people on that show. Why you appearing on a contest thinks a talking doorbell can save the world?"

The waiter brought our meals, fresh salmon that stunk up the table. But the roasted potatoes were crispy, and the Bruised Magnolia was entertaining. She reminded me of Mary Martha Sinclair, my boss at Sinclair's Temps. Mary Martha didn't care what anyone thought of her, either. You went to lunch with Mary Martha and people stopped by your table to say, "You are the most beautiful woman I have ever seen." On Mary Martha's corporate papers, it didn't say *President*; it said *Light of the World*. When you'd been with Mary Martha's company for six months, you got a lava lamp.

All these different people on the train, it was fun. Not at all like living in Mississippi, where I swear everyone was from the same gene pool. The train was a fruit basket turnover: everyone topsy-turvy, arms flailing.

I was beaming at the Bruised Magnolia, who was coaxing Erick into accepting a wing from her, when I remembered the drug scandal. Surely Mother was handling the fallout okay? Or did she need me there with her? Edison gossip could be pretty brutal.

Family did that to you. You might snip at one another, but let someone else chime in, and they were apt to draw back a nub.

"Turned the goat into a *mule*," I sighed.

Erick and the Bruised Magnolia glanced my way.

I smiled an apology. "Reminiscing about home. You know, right when you thought no one was paying attention to the goat, turns out to be the centerpiece of a mind-blowing drug scandal. And, yes, it actually does come from Jamaica."

They stared at me like I was loony tunes, and maybe I was. Mother was perfectly capable of taking care of herself—one zinger from her would put Louisa Jennings in her place. Of course, Clyde would be there to offer whatever support Clyde offered. Plus, if anyone said something ugly in front of Pooh, she'd come out swinging. Pooh might be the spitting image of a Southern grandmother, with her lumpy waist, bunned hair, and flabby arms, but she could rumble if she needed to. My family was fine. I didn't have to run home and take care of them.

I let a tiny sigh escape.

"Go ahead." Erick set down his drink. "Tell it."

CHAPTER 5: The Other Side of the Moon

"I'm sad for the Chicken Palace," I admitted.

"A chicken palace?" The Bruised Magnolia snapped her fingers at a waiter and ordered a glass of wine. "Where a chicken is king or something?"

"That would be the museum," I corrected her. "Cecil Everett Clay talked Big Doodle into founding the museum when everything in Edison was dead as roadkill. Then Cecil Everett got one of the civic groups in town to staff it with volunteers—"

"The GivingHands Social Club," Erick offered.

"Look at you!" I slapped him on the arm.

"I've been through the museum." Erick lifted a shoulder.

"A museum? With stuffed chickens?" The Bruised Magnolia wrinkled her nose.

"Mostly chicken memorabilia donated from Big Doodle's private collection. They've even got the terrarium that displayed the biddies at the CP, before Daddy decided the chicks didn't cotton to that. Plus the costume from Big Doodle's early commercials. Cecil Everett had wanted a 50,000 square-foot museum shaped like a heart—'We love Big Doodle!'"—I threw my hands in the air—"but that was just dreaming."

"It's a cinderblock building on Center Street, painted bright yellow." Erick filled in the gaps in my story.

"Yellow in honor of the chickens," I added. It was kind of sad, really—the happy yellow building, Cecil Everett Clay sitting on a folding chair outside the door, waiting for tourists to show up. Sometimes a group driving from Jackson to the gambling boats in Vicksburg would see the billboard, take a detour to the chicken museum, but they never visited twice. "The Learning Center my Daddy talked Big Doodle into adding didn't make it, either. No one much cared to learn about humane chicken processing methods."

"Wait." The Bruised Magnolia halted her wine glass midair. "Did you say Big Doodle's chicken? As in Big Doodle's Chicken Palace Emporium? Serves all things chicken: chicken wings, chicken fritters, chicken on a stick. Nothing but chicken."

"Yes, that's it." I nodded eagerly. "Although they do have the now-infamous goat. I can't speak for the rest of the Southeast, but no one in Edison ever ordered the goat. If you ask me, they should be investigating why that crazy goat dish was on the menu in the first place."

"I read an article about him." The Bruised Magnolia swept a strand of hair from her eyes. "He used free-range chickens before it was popular. No hormones, that kind of stuff."

"Exactly. Daddy was growing those healthy chickens, and Big Doodle bought them from him. He stopped after the Chicken Palace chain got so big, except for the Edison site, of course."

"Not anymore." She sniffed. "Article said he's out of the free-range chicken business. Canceled his last contract. 'Cause of the drug scandal."

"What? Are you sure?"

She sipped her drink. "Pretty sure."

I slumped in my seat. "That was my daddy's legacy."

I'd been afraid this might happen, but I couldn't believe Big Doodle would really do such a thing. Yes, there'd been the glitch recently with the Christmas cards Mother sent to Big Doodle's mansion outside of Denver, which was rumored to have its own bowling alley, plus a collection of miniature horses Big Doodle let roam at will through the house, pooping where they may. The last several years, the cards had come back "Return to Sender." But I'd always blamed the post office for that snafu.

"It's so unfair. If Big Doodle had stayed with Daddy's methods of chicken management, this whole scandal wouldn't have happened."

"How so?" the Bruised Magnolia asked.

I was trying to make my explanation as short as possible yet wanting to include the relevant, important details, but when I began to describe how raw chicken parts are stinky, both from their natural odor and the antibacterial agents processed chickens were dipped in, causing a truck-bed full of raw chicken parts to smell as strong as a short trip to sulphuric Hell, Erick said, "Lucinda."

"Too much chicken information?"

"A little. While we're eating, you know." He made his *eek* mouth.

So I sat quietly as we chugged toward the state line. The Bruised Magnolia reminisced about Christmas in Mississippi—stapling Santa streamers to the wall, shooting mistletoe from the trees with a shotgun. Erick kept up his end of the conversation by describing his family's tradition of using maraschino cherries to make Rudolph noses on their candy cane reindeer. I wasn't in the mood to join in, and Erick must have sensed it because when I excused myself for the evening, he offered his cheek for a kiss good night.

"Love your heart," I said.

"Sweet dreams," he answered. "See you on the other side of the moon."

*

Before going to my room, I stopped at the buffet to get a toothbrush—I was a terrible packer; if I didn't forget my toothbrush, I forgot my pjs. As I made my way to my berth, purchase in hand, someone behind me whispered, "Pssssst!"

The Bruised Magnolia crooked her finger at me. The rocking of the train was knocking her skinny behind against the wall.

"You think Erick likes me?" Her eyes were forlorn.

"I'm sure he does. Why would he not?"

"You left, he dropped me like a hot potato. Is it cause I'm Black?"

I smiled. "What do you think?"

Her mouth formed a pout. "It'd be easier than him not liking *me*."

All I could do was repeat what Erick had told her earlier. "He's working on something, that's all."

Executing a lazy half turn, the Bruised Magnolia rolled against the wall, watching me over her shoulder. "He's lost me. I'm off this train in the morning."

Her gazed trailed off as she ran her fingers along the wall, slowly disappearing down the corridor.

*

Opening the door to my berth, I felt the train shudder to a stop. Outside the window, a neon sign glowed in the darkness: *Memphis*. Too bad we were arriving in the city at night. In the daytime, Erick could have at least glimpsed the hometown of his hero, Elvis.

Throwing my tote on the bed, I halted. I swear I thought I'd caught a glimmer of moonlight on water— the Mighty Mississippi, wide as the sky, deep as the sea. A canyon stretching through the middle of the country, only you didn't think of it that way, due to the water filling it up.

I leaned close to the berth's large window. Stories I'd heard all my life swirled in my brain, tales of deadly currents that would confuse even the most seasoned pilot. Half-submerged trees that would rip a gash in the hull of your boat. Suicides jumping off the bridge at Vicksburg, not surfacing until New Orleans. Still, I loved the river, the same way I loved Pooh's homemade fig preserves. Pooh canned the preserves in a Mason jar with wax paper under the lid. Lemon crescents floated against the glass, the fat figs hidden in the depths of the jar. Smear the preserves on a hot butter biscuit and bite in. Sometimes you got a lemon peel stuck between your teeth.

Spit it out, you'd be fine.

*

I stayed up late watching the moonlit scenery roll by the window until I was sure Clyde would be snoring in bed; then, I called Mother, who was doing fine, but she sounded a little tired, which was to be expected. She wanted to explain the whole drug scandal to me again. She'd done the same thing after Daddy died, telling me over and over again about his last moments in the hospital room. "He called, 'Rita Rae!' I said to him, 'I'm right here, Bill Watkins.' But when I went to him, he was gone." Each time she returned to it, I bit my tongue—she had to describe Daddy's last moments for me because they had inexplicably chosen not to tell me he was so sick.

When Mother's retelling of the chicken scandal petered out, I asked, "So. Are you okay?"

She hesitated. "Everyone's being very cordial, not saying anything…to my face."

"I'm sorry, Mother." Folks being extra polite meant everyone was yakking nonstop behind her back.

"It's okay. Louisa Jennings pranced up, acting all concerned." Mother adopted a simpering sweet voice. "'I'm sure you'd always wondered how Bill could afford to buy that house for you.'"

"How dare she!" I exclaimed. The fairy-tale house had a front porch, bay windows, and a wooden staircase with a stained glass window at the top. In the mornings, colored light—scarlet and royal blue and lemon yellow—danced down the steps. Mother had pined after the house forever. Daddy bought it for her a couple of years before he died. "Louisa Jennings doesn't have the sense God gave a rock."

"I couldn't help myself. I snapped at her. I told her some things were none of her damn business. Peggy Margaret called"—Peggy Margaret being Mother's number-one friend and bridge buddy—"and said Louisa has been telling everyone in town how rude I was to her."

Pinching the bed sheets between my fingers—they were crisp, as if they'd been ironed and starched—I wondered if Mother had a smidgen of curiosity about the house. When Daddy died, we learned he'd left her the house free and clear, no mortgage. How had he been able to pay off the house that quickly?

I was glad I'd kept my mouth shut when Mother proceeded to say, "Bill Watkins worked hard his whole life to protect his good name. Minding his Ps and Qs, because he knew how small towns work. Once a rumor takes hold, it's impossible to dig it out. For Bennie Dayton to be sullying your dad's honor after he's dead and gone …. I'm glad he's not around to witness it.

"Anyway." She hesitated, and I recognized this particular pause. Mother had taken to injecting them into our conversations. They got on my nerves—she should go ahead and spit out whatever was bothering her.

"Mother, everything's okay with the money, isn't it?"

"What do you mean?"

If she hadn't heard about the cancellation of the CP contract, I wasn't going to mention it. "You'd tell me if something was wrong, right?"

As soon as I heard it coming out of my mouth, I wanted to take it back. Mother would think I was talking about Daddy dying. I longed to know why— why they had chosen not to tell me how sick he was. But on the phone on a train trip far from home was not the time to take that on.

She must have agreed because all she did was sigh. "If you get tired of being on that train, you can always come home. The Gun and Knife show's arriving in town tomorrow. We could run over."

"Do you want me to come home, Mother? I will if you want me to."

"No, no. I want you to go to Chicago and make Bennie Dayton do the right thing. I'm counting on you to clear up this mess."

I hung up. The Gun and Knife Show, my lord! That was Clyde's influence, that was. The man didn't work a lick, just lay on the sofa spouting opinions, his leathery face scrunched up, his white dentures shining. He was a pure product of Edison small-mindedness, and he'd lured Mother over to the dark side. Now, if it wasn't local, it didn't count. Say, for example, I won the Nobel Prize for nuclear physics and Mrs. Thurmond's daughter asphalted her driveway—little girl Thurmond would be the one exclaimed over. Making Bennie Dayton eat his words, though, that would impress Rita Rae.

When I was finally able to fall asleep, I dreamed. I was flying through the night air, my arms outstretched, my eyelashes sprinkled with stardust.

Waking suddenly, I was startled to realize the world had stopped. The train was idling. In the night sky, stars twinkled.

"I wish I may, I wish I might," I whispered, closing my eyes.

And what did I wish for? Something I knew could never be: I wished to turn back time. To return to the time Before—before Daddy had died, before I'd made a mess of the sacred institution of marriage, before Big Doodle Dayton had accused my daddy of stuffing illegal drugs into Jamaican goats and flooding the Southeast with weed.

What I longed for was the time of Still—when everything still seemed possible, when days were still happy, when growing up was a straight shooting arrow, uncrossed by death, disenchantment, and dead marriages.

When I opened my eyes, the stars twinkled.

Or maybe I was wrong.
Maybe they winked.

CHAPTER 6: A Scofflaw from Mississippi

When I woke the next morning, we were pulling into Chicago. A new day was splitting the horizon. Tall buildings stuttered past the window, bulky shadows in the dawn.

I jumped from bed into the shower—I did not intend to enter Chicago looking like a know-nothing skank from Mississippi.

The stainless steel shower stall reminded me of the spot on the starship where Captain Kirk says, "Beam me up, Scotty." It was narrow and cozy. But anyone who wasn't thin as an exclamation point would have trouble maneuvering in the space, twisting front to back, bending over to retrieve the soap. Those folks would probably go home with a very different view of the shower than me. I thought not for the first time that our view of the world was defined by where we stood in it.

It didn't take long to get ready. Nothing I could do about my hair. One side was half-trimmed by Ruth Anne, the other side uneven from where I'd snipped at it with the manicure scissors after the divorce. I'd been blind mad at the too-tiny scissors, furious at myself for believing Stirling wasn't the typical Edison dude who worshiped mama's fried potatoes. Oh, no, he was sophisticated—look at his leather tassels. He'd been in Europe, same as Daddy when he was in the Air Force. How was I to know Stirling was wearing the one suit he'd brought back from Europe to impress gullible chicks like me? I'd actually concocted a fantasy where Stirling and I bought my family's old ranch-style house—fluorescent lighting in the kitchen, walnut paneling in the den—and lived happily ever after. Instead, I'd wound up in the Kenny's basement with Jack-O snoring it off on the couch.

My cute pleather suit would make up for the awful hair. I topped it with a yellow wool swing coat with a fake fur collar and cuffs because, even though we only had a three or four block walk to the convention center, who knew what the temperature in Chicago in April was like. The coat was very Audrey Hepburn-ish in a *Breakfast at Tiffany's* way, a fabulous movie Erick had put me on to. Everyone loved the coat. I'd be walking down the streets of Jackson and someone would holler, "Love that coat!" The last time I'd worn it was to a wine tasting in a Jackson dive bar full of rednecks. I'd tried the bar after the divorce, telling myself I needed to get out more. The wine—*mer*-lot, they called it—came in burlap sleeves. The wine guy in charge had to whistle the rednecks away from the pool table to swish the *mer*-lot in their cheeks.

The coat was wasted on that crowd.

Chicago—now, that was worth it.

I buttoned the fur against my chin and put some pep in my walk so the swing would show off my legs.

I was thrilled when I stepped from the train and caught a glimpse of the Movie Star ahead of me in the crush of scurrying people.

And he got a glimpse of me. Then he was gone, but it was enough to lift my spirits. I shook off the rancid news from Edison like day-old garbage being tossed over the back fence. My heart soared.

Erick was flipping through a wad of tickets when I caught up with him. We were in the station, walking down a long corridor of blue carpet. The throngs had petered out, as if we were the only ones going our way. I mentioned the Bruised Magnolia had been looking for him the night before.

"After supper," I said when he asked what time I'd run into her.

"Where?"

"In the corridor, kind of wandering. She seemed sad, looking for you."

"And you didn't tell me?" He stopped walking. He was annoyed, which was unusual for Erick.

"Sorry. I didn't realize how important it was to you."

He glanced down the empty corridor. "Don't mind me. I'm worried I've made a terrible mistake."

"Entering the contest, you mean?"

He ran his fingers through his curls. "It's been so long since I did anything other than sling hash. What if I actually get on the show and make a fool of myself? What was I thinking?"

I clasped his forearm. "Look at me." I fixed him with my stare until he stared back.

"I don't know what your idea is or what you will do on the show, but whatever it is, you will be stunning. You're talented and gorgeous and smart as a whip. And so creative. You might've spent the last two years slinging hash, but you slung it with grace. Don't you worry one bit about the show. You'll wow them like nothing they've ever seen before."

He fingered the fake fur on my coat collar. "Thanks, babe. At least I have one fan. Big Doodle Dayton's not going to know what hit him."

It was early in the morning, not yet six o'clock, and our walk to the convention center took us through a city just waking up. One or two impatient people brushed past us, eager to get important things done, but mainly it was me and Erick, the buildings, and the morning light.

It was hard to imagine this tranquil, spring city in the blustery snow of winter. One of Mother's cousins had visited Chicago with her husband. He was interviewing for a job. It was December. The snow was falling so fast and the wind howling so hard, she'd had to pull herself along the sidewalk with a rope.

He didn't take the job.

That story was a staple in Mother's why-do-they-*live*-up-there repertoire.

Mother should have seen the city now. The light was so thin and orange you could lick it like a sucker. The earthy scent of the river rode the breeze. Trucks idled at curbs, store clerks straightened manikins. Men in uniforms skittered to and fro, all of it like a symphony tuning up. I would not be there to hear the song, but sometimes, the anticipation was the best part.

I was thinking of concrete—so much of it for a girl from Mississippi!—when we strolled past a department store window full of dolls. Big dolls, little dolls, blond-haired blue-eyed dolls, and a grownup lady doll with a trunkful of clothes on tiny coat hangers. While Erick walked ahead, I lingered, entranced by one particular doll.

The doll was big boned and long faced—who had thought to make such a doll? She stood head and shoulders over the other dolls, wearing a pinafore of washed-out blue and flat white shoes with bobby socks.

Stoic, I thought, accepting who she was, even surrounded by dainty, blue-eyed perfection. She was so ugly as to be exquisite, and if I could have justified buying her, I would have. I would take her home with me to remind myself to always love who I was. But I could not justify buying her, and I did not, so I walked on, hurrying to catch up with Erick.

At the convention center entrance, when I asked where Big Doodle might be, we were directed to a woman whose body was shaped like Natasha. You know, Boris's wife from the Rocky and Bullwinkle Show? Her thighs swelled and curved. Her skin was chalk white. Her jet black hair hung in a limp ponytail over her shoulder. The tip of the ponytail curled toward a teensy breast.

When I repeated my request to speak to Big Doodle, she minced her dainty pink lips. "Mr. Dayton is not here."

"Yes, he is. I saw him on TV. Less than twenty-four hours ago." I scanned the teeming convention hall. "The convention always lasts three days. Y'all are just getting started."

"Mr. Dayton departed for Chicken Headquarters last night on his Gulfstream G450 after the conclusion of the press conference to which you undoubtedly refer."

"I *told* him I was coming."

"He is, as I said, not here."

"I sent him a photograph!"

She paused. "You were the author of that prank? Then I am *positive* he would not want to see *you*."

Thumping her tongue against the back of her teeth, she slithered off, silent as a squid.

"Prank? Hey!" I yelled at her retreating back. "I have to talk to Big Doodle!"

She halted and slowly swiveled. "Mr. Dayton, as president of the world-famous Chicken Palace Emporium chain, is dealing with the treachery of a two-bit Mississippi scofflaw. Whatever your tiny little problem might be, Mr. Dayton will not be solving it for you."

I didn't know exactly what she'd said, but I was pretty sure she'd insulted both me and my dad.

"My daddy is one of the finest men who ever walked this earth!" I yelled. "It doesn't matter what you say, you overblown flunky. You can't hurt my daddy's feelings 'cause *he's already dead*!"

"Hey, hey." Erick gently turned me around. "It'll be okay."

"He knew I was coming, and he left, Erick."

"You don't know that."

"How am I going to talk to him now?" I pressed the heel of my hand against my eye. My mother was gonna kill me.

"Here." Erick pulled out his phone and punched in numbers. "We'll ask my pop. He knows how to catch skips. From his bonding work."

"Bonding?"

"He owns a bail bonding company."

"And he can help with Big Doodle?"

"He's a genius at finding skips. Making people show up at places where he can collar them." He paused then closed his phone. "Busy. But he'll help, I promise."

I stared at my feet. The world was the same as on my trip out, my mood forever altered. "Last thing my mother said to me was how she was counting on me to clear this up."

"We'll clear it up."

"The Watkins family is gonna wind up same as the Brandons whose daughter Melissa showed up at her husband's funeral and threw herself over the casket— with a two-karat engagement ring on her finger. Or the Yates, whose son Larry got caught peeping through mail slots, but just got transferred to sorting mail. We're going to wind up in the Edison Scandal Hall of Fame."

"Wait'll you meet my mom. She'll take your mind off all this."

A sudden breeze blew, and I tugged the fur collar around my neck. "She doesn't particularly care for people from Mississippi, does she?" Erick's mom had not been pleased when he settled in Edison.

"She'll adore you."

A man with a dog on a jangling leash walked by. The dog stopped at the fire hydrant, did a sniff and whiff, then lifted his leg.

I sighed. "At least this trip won't be a total waste— I'll be there for your audition. Have I asked you recently what your invention is?"

He studied the drifting clouds.

"Okay. I love surprises." I hugged him by the arm.

At the station, Erick settled into a chair to read, but I was too antsy, and I wandered.

I stumbled into a marble cave.

Down some steps and around a corner was a mammoth lobby with polished marble walls. A sign announced it as the Great Hall. The room radiated the hush of a church. Under the domed ceiling were oak benches lined up like pews. I thought about taking some photos, but I remembered my dad cautioning me against trying to snap a picture at the Cardinals game. "Flash won't reach that far," he'd warned. "You'll not catch one Redbird on film." I'd tried anyway, with the predictably-black results.

On one of the walls, as high as a man could reach, someone had hung a train ad: "Half Price for Half-Pints." More gracious was a brass plaque embedded below. The plaque boasted that seven hundred trains could whistle in and out of the station each day. During the heyday of the 1940s, over 100,000 passengers thronged its corridors daily.

Today, the Great Hall was quiet. The only footsteps echoing on the polished floor were my own.

As I circled the room, touching the smooth marble columns, I felt the men and women of the past shimmering through time and space—first a nylon leg, then a hand clutching a newspaper, then finally all of them. The ladies in their proper hats and the well-suited men with topcoats slung over their arms, hurrying. The men home from the war and everyone with so much to catch up on. Businesses to build, babies to birth. Typewriters to get clacking, papers to get stamped. All of them riding the amazing trains that would take them where they were glory bound to go.

Heavy footsteps reverberated off the walls.

If Lady Luck was with me, I'd whirl around in my swing coat, my palms skimming the air, and the Movie

Star would be sauntering up behind me, exuding that tough-guy sexiness and illegally smoking a cigarette.

I whirled around.

Luck was with me.

CHAPTER 7: Kissing the Future

The Movie Star nodded in my direction. "Nice coat."

"Thank you." I eased onto one of the benches, hoping he would follow. He did, settling his thighs on the wood, getting comfortable. He was dressed in black slacks with a houndstooth sports coat and a tie, as if he knew my fantasy always had him wearing something that could support a fedora.

When I was seated, the coat didn't work so well—it bunched up around my neck. I would have to take it off.

Unbuttoning, that would be the good part.

Slowly, I slipped the cloth-covered buttons through the buttonholes, smiling at Mr. Movie Star. "Isn't this gorgeous?"

"Could use a muff."

I was momentarily confused. Then I got it. "Not the coat." I waved dismissively, as if I hadn't been absorbed with the impression I was making. "The Great Hall." I finished unbuttoning. The coat hung open.

He leaned close to peer inside. "What you hiding in there?"

"Pleather." I mashed my fingers against my chest. "They call this a summer suit, because of the short sleeves, except it's in pleather."

"And what might pleather be?"

"Pleather is fake leather. It's better than leather because it bends easier. And it's kinder to animals." How lucky could I get? The man had zeroed in on one of my favorite subjects: my wardrobe. "It's vintage too."

75

"Let's see."

I shrugged out of the coat. The cute little suit emerged—short, brown pleather skirt, pleather jacket nipped at the waist with a matching belt and the essential short sleeves. I tugged down the skirt. It rode tight.

"I got it at a store where they take your check and turn it into an electronic transfer. They don't trust anyone to write a good check in that store." I was trying to make his eyes smile. All that blue, concentrating on me—it made me dizzy.

"Can't see it proper with you sitting down." He nodded across the hall toward the Half-Pint banner. "Take a turn."

Now, I believe I've made this clear, but in case I haven't, let me restate: I am not supermodel thin. I am bony. My hipbones stick out when I'm standing up. One time, when I was sitting naked in the sauna minding my own business, a woman next to me pointed to the knobs at the end of my wrists and shoulders and told me it was okay to eat a little something every once in a while. But I didn't want him to think I was all fidgety about my body.

I popped up from the bench.

I did my best imitation of a strut.

Making a turn at the end, I tucked my chin, giving him my sultriest look.

He laughed.

That's what I was talking about.

I twitched back in his direction, crisscrossing my legs. When I arrived, I spread my feet and lifted my chin. I planted my hands on my bony, bony hips. If you can't do anything about it, you might as well flaunt it.

He clapped. Slowly.

His eyes were smiling.

That's *really* what I was talking about.

I bent down, resting my palms on the bench. "If we were in an old black and white movie, say from the 1940s, right about now we'd be kissing."

"You thinking about Stella and Stanley?" His thumb stroked my knuckles.

"More like Bogart and Bacall. They never followed the rules."

Maybe it was the influence of the train, the temptation of transient, romantic sex. Or maybe it was my disappointment at not finding Big Doodle at the convention, adding yet one more failure to the never-ending line of failures in my life. Or maybe it was his blue eyes, flirting with me.

I slowly leaned toward him. He had to meet me halfway or else I was gonna feel mighty stupid.

He leaned toward me.

We kissed.

His lips were full and tight. The stubble of his beard scratched my cheek. Not a full beard, limiting in what was available to smooch on, but a beard from not shaving for a couple of days.

I palmed his chin so I could get a better angle on his mouth—also so I wouldn't fall over. His stubbly chin, his soft, compliant lips. Inadvertently, I moaned. Just a little.

But it was enough. He drew me onto the bench and wrapped his arms around me as if he didn't want to let me go.

The echo of a loudspeaker drifted in, and I flashed on the picture of us kissing on a pew in the cathedral of the Great Hall. I pulled back to take some air and plunged in again.

Burrowing my hand underneath the sports jacket, I found his lower back, the sweet spot they call the 'oyster' on a chicken, where the choicest meat hides. I stroked the curve of his lower back.

If this kept up, I'd be having sex on a pew in the Great Hall.

The loudspeaker blared again.

"Think that's our train?" I whispered, lost inside the extravagantly good kissing.

"Probably." His eyes were close to mine, his black pupils flicking back and forth.

I slipped my hand from the jacket and announced. "Rain delay."

He drew back to where he could study me. "You a baseball girl?"

I nodded.

"Ahhh. That makes you dangerous." He traced a line from my jaw into the dip of my throat, his fingers promising one thing and his words promising even more, but not in a way you could ever hold him responsible for.

Which made *him* dangerous.

*

Erick met us on the platform, concerned we were going to miss our three o'clock departure time. Handing me my Empire Builder ticket, he didn't raise an eyebrow at Augie's presence (that was the Movie Star's name, short for Francis Augustine Greene, from New

Orleans, named for both of his mother's favorite saints). I wanted to catch Erick up to speed, but when Augie suggested he and I meet in the club car after settling in, my polite friend slipped away. As soon as we sat down, Augie's phone rang.

The scenery flashing by didn't look any different from Mississippi. Same stinkweeds, same pine trees topping out. Same ditches beside the tracks. The passengers were new folks … almost all of them white. Even the Bruised Magnolia, trailing her long orange sweater coat, had departed. "I don't go north of Chicago, hon." Which made me wonder if New York was north of Chicago and, if so, whether she'd actually been on Broadway. People can tell you anything on a train and you can't confirm or deny it. For most folks, though, that only means they're free to tell the truth.

While Augie talked on the phone, I pulled out one of my garage sale paperbacks, a book on motorcycles, wondering if it could help my frustration over the drug scandal. The book was about karma and, in a way, so was the chicken scandal.

You see, in the olden days, people used to raise chickens in the backyard, wringing their necks once a month for Sunday dinner. Then chicken growers got to looking at the way Henry Ford did things, and chickens became widgets: raised in the smallest space possible then killed as cheap as possible. Dead chickens got shipped to China where they were cut up by overworked, underpaid Chinese chicken workers. The sliced and diced chicken parts were shipped back to the port of New Orleans.

Some creative person had gazed upon the smelly chicken parts and followed their travels to a chicken chain that sold Jamaica's national dish: curried goat. They combined that with the Jamaican pastime of smoking pot and came up with an inspired idea. The goats became mules, smuggling pot into the country, also through the port of New Orleans. Once the compliant—if dead—goats were relieved of their cargo, the drugs were trundled onto Chicken Palace Emporium trucks and stuffed between the cut-up chicken parts to fool drug-sniffing dogs. The pot was thus distributed to Chicken Palace Emporiums across the Southeast.

I wasn't saying Big Doodle Dayton brought this disaster on himself, but once he no longer insisted his operations be nice to chickens, how much of a leap was it for someone to start using the poor dead chickens to smuggle drugs? The author of the book I was so diligently holding in front of my nose might agree, but I wasn't sure.

The book was called *Zen and the Art of Motorcycle Maintenance*, about this guy who rides cross-country on a motorcycle, except in a Zen sort of way. His Zen approach causes him to realize that if a screw pops loose and the bike won't run, the motor might as well have dropped dead, the screw is as important as the engine itself. I had tried out the theory this morning when I was getting dressed and the back to my brown saucer earring rolled underneath the sink. Without the back, the earring was useless; without the earring, the outfit wasn't complete. It didn't make me feel Zen at all, just hopeless, so I stole a back from another earring and went about my business.

I was itching to change clothes. The train was hurtling toward Milwaukee. We would arrive in St. Paul mid-evening where we'd deboard. Augie needed to see another outfit—my time to impress him was short. Maybe my pastel pink faux rabbit jacket, which was not vintage but did come from the teen department at Target, so it was half the price and adorable. Pink fur would be good for ordering martinis from the club car, which was the next activity I had in mind—the train was hosting a "Ringing in the Dell" celebration in the sightseer car with party favors and fruity drinks.

Finally off the phone, Augie picked up a *Sports Illustrated*, flipping the pages. I was trying to concentrate on my book, but my mind wandered to the kiss in Union Station. It was magic when you first touched another person's skin. My very first kiss, when I was fourteen, my lips touched the boy's lips and I thought, *I am kissing the future.*

It was the eighth grade, a Friday night football game. We were seated on the concrete bleachers of the Scotty Bell Middle School stadium. The noise of shoulder pads knocked up from the field, and the boy offered me popcorn from his red-striped paper bag. When I declined, he said, "What about this instead?"

His lips were soft, like suede, but tight. My kiss roamed a little, and I found the down on his upper lip where he hadn't started shaving yet. His hand rested lightly on my shoulder as if to keep me in place for one more minute.

Of course, the boy was Stirling. I'd known Stirling since we'd made popsicle stick Noah's Arks in Vacation Bible School together. He'd always been cute, in a mop-headed sort of way. But when we kissed, the crisp night air, the stadium lights haloing above our heads—well, the smell of popcorn still makes me giddy.

Thank God, when Stirling and I broke up, Pammy had just fallen out with her boyfriend, a 350-pound tackle who didn't appreciate her nose ring. We hung out until I made it to community college where the dating pool was a little larger. I loved college, even if I did bounce around majors, from psychology (because the professor hypnotized me, I swear) to sociology (the course with the two-way mirror that so impressed Mother) and finally Administrative Support Technology-General Business (how to work in an office). Life was good …until the day I arrived at the hospital to find my daddy suddenly, terribly ill.

"Excuse me."

A woman stood beside Augie. She smiled nervously. The motion of the train swung her ponytail side to side.

"Would you mind?" She held out a napkin and a ballpoint pen. "My daughter would love your autograph."

"I'm not following." Augie closed his *Sports Illustrated*, and I wondered if my movie star first impression could have been correct.

"My daughter, she recognized you." The woman pointed down the aisle where a little girl with freckles grinned at us, showing Bugs Bunny teeth.

"No, Ma'am. I can't say that we've met." Augie shook his head.

The woman, who'd been wearing her happy face, faltered. "She said you were Pete somebody. In a movie about a runaway pig?"

"Sorry." Augie shrugged self-deprecatingly. "Never been in the movies."

"Oh." The woman glanced at her little girl, who had scooted to the edge of her chair. "Could sign it anyway? Something like, 'Love and kisses, Pete'? It would make her day." She re-offered the napkin and pen.

"I—" Augie's eyes flicked to the girl then back to her mom. "I'm afraid that doesn't feel right."

The woman flapped the napkin at him. "Come on, mister. Just sign it for her."

Augie took the napkin. Securing it on the arm of the chair with his thumb, he scrawled the pen across it. When he handed the napkin back to the woman, she swiveled it and read, "'Keeping it real, Augie Green.' Who the hell is Augie Green?"

"I am."

"My daughter doesn't give a fig about Augie Green."

Augie shrugged. "That's all I got."

"Jerk." She stomped off.

Augie's face was beet red.

"That was rude," I ventured.

"Put me on the spot," he mumbled, staring at his feet.

"Her mistake, and she took it out on you. But you did the right thing."

"You think so?" He rubbed his chin.

"Yeah. But, hey. No use crying over spilt milk. Or, as my mother's boyfriend would say, at least it ain't spilt liquor." I stood up. "Come on. Let's have some fun. That's what we're here for."

He stayed in his seat. "Sometimes life can get in the way of fun."

His seriousness made me suddenly shy. "Would you like to go down to the sightseer car and order martinis? I hear they're having a party."

"If they're throwing a party, *cher*, you count me in." He rose.

"You really are from New Orleans, aren't you?" I marveled.

"True dat. Paraded in my first Mardi Gras while I was still a babe in my mama's arms." He waited while I went down the aisle first. "You a fan of the Crescent City?"

"Never been there."

"You'd fit right in. They appreciate a woman who knows how to dress."

I glanced over my shoulder to see if he was making fun of me. "People in Edison think I dress crazy."

He shrugged. "You got style. People who ain't got style sometimes don't know what to do with the ones who've got it."

"That's sweet," I said, reassured. "I need to stop at my sleeper car first."

He was puzzled when I held him at the door of my berth and said, "Wait right here." I almost added, "While I slip into something more comfortable," but I wasn't that dorky.

Inside, I paired the faux rabbit jacket with silver lamé pants that fit tight as liquid bullets. I candied my lips with bubblegum pink lipstick and hung cascading silver earrings from my ears. I added a simple white cotton blouse and silver kitten heels. So the whole thing wouldn't look too contrived sexy, I plopped a Cardinals ball cap on my head, the one with the St. Louis slugger at bat.

Assessing the look in the mirror, I decided the silver and soft pink worked great, and the red ball cap added a pop of color. Beneath the brim of the cap, my eyes were batting even harder than the slugger.

If the man didn't know I'd stepped it up a notch, he wasn't worth the effort.

CHAPTER 8: People Hear What They Want to Hear

When I emerged from my berth, I got a surprise of my own.

Augie had hustled down to his room and returned in the same black trousers and white shirt, but he'd added a white dinner jacket to the ensemble.

A white dinner jacket? Could I have been so lucky as to meet the one man in today's world who owned, much less traveled with, a white dinner jacket? And, might I add, a man so unbelievably gorgeous that he did the dinner jacket proud?

I glanced over Augie's shoulder, certain the Devil would be dangling from the ceiling tiles. He twitched his spiked tail and leered. "You want this? Sell your soul and you can have it."

"You said you wanted to have some fun." He crooked his arm, extending the invitation.

Not the Devil. Augie.

Who may or may not have been the same person. How could a girl tell the difference when it was cloaked in such sexiness?

As we paraded to the sightseer car, the train lurched and stopped.

Augie did a two-step.

I held on tighter. We'd arrived in Milwaukee.

The party in the sightseer car was hopping. No one seemed to care that it was mid-afternoon and we were all day-drinking. We joined the throng, gliding into our seats. Augie ordered a gin martini, and—even though gin makes me crazy—I threw caution to the wind and ordered my own martini, straight up, extra olives.

After an interminable wait, our drinks arrived. We toasted our first sip, peering at each other over the sparkling rims. The train revved up, gliding away from Milwaukee, and deflated to a stop.

My martini sloshed. I gulped the spillage into my mouth.

We hadn't gone twenty yards.

A buzz ran through the car, everyone twisting and turning in their seats. "What's going on?" "Why'd we stop?"

"You spilled a drop." Augie waved at my jacket.

I glanced down. At the end of a strand of fake fur, a droplet wavered. I touched the ball with my finger. It grabbed hold of my pinky and melted into my skin. I stuck my finger in my mouth.

"Wonder what's going on?"

"Something on the tracks, maybe." He dipped his head and sipped from the martini glass. "One time I was on the train and a joker laid down on the tracks, drunk. Thought it was a good place to take a nap."

"Yikes!"

"The train stopped. Someone had called it in. The cops escorted him off the tracks. We went on our way. Easy fix. Sometimes there's a delay, and the train loses its place in line. You can sit for hours."

The ladies at the table beside us were murmuring: "That's right. They're giving me *all* my money back." "*All* of it."

I tilted my glass and took a dainty sip to make up for the prior sloppy one. "So, you know your trains?"

"Yeah, train's okay. Wouldn't matter if I hated it—it's the only thing the home office will pay for. Scouts are the bottom of the food chain. Nobody flies us around. Hell, they'd make us walk if they could." He hummed a few bars.

"'Walking to New Orleans?'" I guessed.

He grinned. "You got it, *cher*. Fats Domino."

"You're a talent scout?" I was still thinking movie star.

"Baseball scout."

"Baseball scout? Did you make that up?" He did, after all, know I was a baseball fan.

"Make what up?" Augie asked, startled.

"About being a baseball scout. Because you knew I was a fan and, you know, you said you loved it too so we'd get along better."

He pressed his palm against his heart. "I swear on my mama's gumbo: I have loved baseball all my life. I would not lie about being a fan."

"I believe you." I had to calm down—not every man I met was a lying Stirling Kenny.

"So." I raised my martini glass and examined Augie through the distorting liquid. "Who do you scout for? Do you go to the Grapefruit League?" My daddy had always wanted to go to the Grapefruit League—Florida in the springtime, all the players getting back in shape—but he'd never been able to, springtime being a very busy time in the chicken growing business.

"Yes, I do. I go to the Grapefruit League every spring. Grapefruit League's not glamorous. It's a roadside motel where the owner knows your name and the time for your wake-up call. I work for the Cubs, the Chicago Cubs."

"The Cubs!" I tilted my ball cap so he could see the St Louis slugger. "I'm a Cardinals fan."

"So I noticed. That makes us arch enemies."

"At least you're National League."

"Yep. No American League for me, *cher*. Designated hitter is for wimps."

I beamed. First, in the Great Hall, Augie and I had talked fashion—one of my favorite subjects—and now we were discussing National League baseball. Maybe the little fellow dangling from the ceiling tiles wasn't the Devil after all. Maybe he was my guardian angel who had a terrible sense of direction and only now had taken a right turn into my life.

Augie and I proceeded to discuss the Billy Goat Curse, how long it had been since the pitiful Cubs had won a Pennant much less the World Series, and how only the most loyal of fans could root for the Cubs. At least that was my take on the situation. At the end of the conversation, I was glowing from the unexpected gift of a true baseball fan ... or the martini.

"How did you get into...scouting?" I asked, even though that made it sound like merit badges and campfires.

"Gave up coaching at Tulane." He pronounced it *Too*-lane. "Green Wave baseball. My wife hated it when I got the scouting job."

"Your wife?"

He winced. "Ex-wife. She was my wife at the time. Then when I started scouting...."

I was silent, and he ran his finger along the rim of his martini glass, stalling it seemed to me.

"Coaching got old. Crazy parents of college-age kids interfering over who's warming the bench. It was time to make a change, and the scouting opportunity came along. It's less money. And I'm gone a lot. But that moment when you spy a new talent, a kid you can tell will really take off—it's worth it. I tried to get her to understand. Didn't work. All she wanted was to go back to the way things had been."

That made me a tad nervous, given my own tendency to hold on to the past. As soon as this thought flicked through my brain, I realized I was already evaluating how well Augie and I fit together. *Slow it down, girl*, I cautioned. *Don't let your miserable life transform this twinkling of fun into a supernova.*

"No kids?"

"Funny you should ask." Leaning, he retrieved his wallet from his back pocket. He flipped it open, unfolding a string of photos. "Twelve nieces and nephews. When I'm in the city, they keep me pretty busy what with soccer games and band recitals." He pointed at a boy with a cowlick. "That one's my namesake."

Several of the girls wore soccer uniforms. Augie's namesake peeped from behind a giant drum set. "They're cutie pies."

"Those little crawdads got my heart." He refolded the wallet and tucked it back in his pocket. "They're growing up too quick. Cliche, I know. Mama has us over by the house Sundays. Kids play in the yard, they hardly know I'm there, but I know I am."

"Sounds divine," I said with a twinge of jealousy. "You've got lots of brothers and sisters?"

"Four brothers. They all work with my dad at the Port Authority. I'm the black sheep of the family. I *had* to play ball. But they put up with me. Probably 'cause I make the best boudin you ever put in your mouth."

"I don't know what that is."

"You don't know boudin, *cher?*" he teased—his twinkling blue eyes, the man was absolutely the cutest thing.

"Boudin's easy. You take pork, rice. Season it up, fry it in an iron skillet. It's my mama's recipe. She's from Lafayette. Papa's from New Orleans. He makes the jambalaya."

"I've always wanted to go to New Orleans." I rested my chin on my fist. "Eat beignets at the Cafe du Monde. Watch the big boats ply the Mississippi, so romantic. *Laissez le bon temps rouler.*" I quoted the city's motto.

"True dat. Most folks come to the city, they think it means get drunk and throw up on the sidewalk. What the city wants is for you to 'roll with it.'" He made a waving motion with his palm. "Go with the flow."

"You're a laid-back kind of person?"

"I believe in that prayer about accepting what you can't change, changing what you can, and the smarts to know the difference."

"The Serenity Prayer. My grandmother's version is, 'Don't go banging your head against the wall.'"

"You really are from Mississippi, aren't you?" He parroted my question, his eyes sparkling.

"Yep." I nodded. "I am from Mississippi."

"Tell me about it." Augie stretched out his legs. "Tell me about that little town you're from."

"Edison." I considered my half-drunk drink, wondering if the alcohol was going to my head: had I told Augie I was from a hole in the road small town? "Why on earth would you want to know about that rat trap?"

"Then tell me how you got to liking baseball. Was it your dad?"

His question set off fireworks of emotions about the Chicken Palace scandal. I was trying to work my way back to a normal answer when I was saved by a chirping from my little green tote.

"Hold on."

Checking the number, I saw it was Mother. Oh, Lord—had her mother's intuition told her I'd dropped the ball with Big Doodle in Chicago? I was casting around for something to say that would distract her, but she got the jump on me.

"There's been a dustup at the McDonald's," she said, talking the way she did under the influence of the hayseed. She was referring to the new McDonald's on Highway 20. Everyone had been thrilled to get a McDonald's in town, but the service was slow as molasses. "Octavia Franks in the drive-thru. What?" she yelled.

"Wanda Franks!" I heard Clyde yell back.

"Wanda Franks refused to pull up," Mother said. "She declared, 'I'm going to sit my butt right here until you bring me my hamburger.'"

There was a scratching noise and Clyde was on the line.

"Her chocolate shake. It was five o'clock, rush hour traffic, and she wanted her shake. A line formed behind her damn near long as a Black mayor's funeral" —the line between Clyde and a racist was as fine as the hair on a toad frog.

"Let me—" I tried to say, but Clyde was on a roll.

"Everyone honking, and she won't pull up. 'Pull up,' they yelled, but she won't do it." He paused, breathing into the phone. "How's it going on the train?"

"They won't pull up."

"What?"

"We're stuck in Milwaukee."

"Oh."

Mother was back on the line, so I asked "Mother, did you call me to tell me about the McDonald's?"

"Men have been out to the house, Lucinda."

"Men?"

"Officials. FBI types."

"Asking about Daddy?"

Clyde snatched the phone from Mother. "Asking about *us*. They got their sights on your mama, girlie. We could be called to the grand jury."

Mother snatched the phone back. "They loitered in the front hall."

I did not know what to say to that.

Then Clyde breathed into the phone. "Sterling's getting married. To Kim Stratton. Has to."

"She's pregnant?" I was trying to imagine the ever-elegant Kim Stratton, who I'd so recently seen modeling clothes at the library, with a belly big as Texas.

"No. He's announced he's running for mayor. Gotta have a family-values platform for the campaign."

"Mayor?" I guffawed. "Like he's qualified for that."

"All you need is a strong jaw and a well-built wife," Clyde, the political analyst, opined.

"And what? He figures a new marriage will erase all of his horn-dogging from his last marriage? Everyone in town knows what a scumbag he is."

"People hear what they want to hear, dolly. Y'all in Chicago yet? You seen Big Doodle?"

I hesitated. I didn't know whether I should confess my failure or give Erick's dad a chance to fix it. "No, I mean yes. We've been to Chicago. Big Doodle wasn't there."

"Not there? You saying he's flown the coop?"

Clyde's joviality sent thoughts cascading through my brain that I didn't need to have. I wondered, not for the first time, if Clyde got on my nerves so badly because being back at home put me all up in his and Mother's business, a place a daughter shouldn't be. But whenever I saw Clyde bumping into the driveway in his 1999 puke-yellow Corolla, cheap black sunglasses perched on his nose, tree-shaped air freshener dangling from the rearview mirror, his elbow out the window, looking for all the world like a Cuban taxi driver, I thought I was being pretty rational.

"Did I hear Clyde say Bennie had flown the coop?" It was Mother, back on the phone.

"Yes," I reluctantly admitted. "But we have a plan B. Erick's pop knows how to track down folks, corporate espionage, that sort of thing."

"Corporate espionage, Lucinda?"

"Erick says his pop can make anybody do what he wants."

"It was like a scene from a bad movie, those men in my foyer, Lucinda Mae. They hardly moved their mouths when they talked."

"Do you want me to come home and take care of things with the FBI?"

She hesitated. "No, it's not a good idea for you to come home right now."

"Are you sure? I can do it."

"It would be too hard on you. With all the wedding planning. You'd be overwhelmed. The entire town is eaten up with the future mayor's nuptials."

"Okay then. I gotta run." I glanced at Augie, who'd been sitting patiently through all of this, and shrugged. He gave me a thumbs up sign.

"They're having Sammy Jones play the reception. They say Kim's gonna try to fit into her mother's wedding dress. But you know how tiny Mrs. Stratton is. Kim is a fine-bosomed woman, not like you."

"I'm hanging up now."

And I did, at which point Erick came strolling by our table and stopped. He leaned on the table, palms down. "They got some problem with the crew, gonna have to switch them all out for a new group. BTW, Pop is on the case. He's certain we can get Big Doodle to cooperate."

"Erick's boyfriend is in athletics too," I said to Augie.

Augie appraised Erick. "Oh, really?"

"J.J. He beats people up." I lapped up the last of my drink with my tongue.

"We're not leaving Milwaukee until they get a new crew. They say anyone who wants to stretch their legs can walk to the last car and get off. The cars at the end of the train are still at the station."

Erick was taking in Augie's dinner jacket, the heavy watch lolling on his wrist bone, memorizing the man's every last feature down to his elegant, white-mooned fingernails.

Or maybe that was me.

"Not much to see at the Milwaukee stop," Augie said.

"Not for you to worry. " Erick winked. "You carry your entertainment with you."

Then, having mortified me to death, he walked off.

"Did I hear you say you're going back home?" Augie asked.

"What? Oh, no. I was talking to my mom. Things are kind of wonked up at home."

"Oh yeah?"

Augie kept his eyes on me as he sipped his martini. My own glass was almost empty, but the crew didn't serve food or drinks when the train was in a station, so our delay probably meant I was out of luck.

"What's going on at home?" Augie asked.

"My dad has been named in a drug ring." I focused on the easier part of the tangled knot—a guy doesn't want to hear a girl bitch about her ex remarrying. "My mom is being questioned by federal agents. It's a real mess."

"Drug ring? That doesn't sound good. Was your dad...connected?"

"Connected? Connected how?"

He shrugged. "I don't know. Southern mafia or something?"

"Hellllll no!" I slapped my palms on the table, leaning in. "My dad wasn't in the mafia. He wasn't involved with the drug ring at all."

"Sorry. I must have misunderstood."

"You sure as hell did." I frowned at him, less than pleased.

"New Orleans, lots of folks you'd never suspect get caught on the wrong side of the line. I thought maybe your dad had."

"You want to know about my dad? Listen to this. He had this joke, except it's true. These old codgers are sitting on the front porch of the courthouse in Corinth. That's way up in the northern part of the state, nearly five hundred miles from the coast. Anyway, it's during the Cuban missile crisis. The old codgers are talking about the Cubans launching a missile at New Orleans, your city. They're worrying if they're in any danger. One of the codgers says, 'Hell, we could be next.'

"Another codger says, 'Corinth? You think?'

"'Well,' says the first guy. 'It *is* the county seat.'"

"Ha ha."

"The joke pokes fun at hicks from Mississippi, how ignorant we are. You know what my dad's favorite pastime was?"

"Telling jokes?"

"Sitting on the porch of our house on Main Street. Pure stereotype. The difference is, Daddy *knew* it was stereotype. But he loved it. He'd ease onto the porch rocker with his morning coffee, waiting for old Miss Casey to come by so they could talk about new books at the library. Or Mr. Levine, so Daddy could speak to his dog. 'Hello, Lucky,' Daddy would say. 'How's life treating the puppy today?' Daddy had everything he wanted right there on that front porch: his wife, his family, his neighbors, and his coffee. He would *never* sell drugs."

Augie shrugged. "Sometimes people find themselves in circumstances."

I nodded. "Yes, they do. And if my daddy found himself in trouble, he would never choose dealing drugs. Violence and guns and protect-your-turf macho bullshit?" I snorted. "Daddy wouldn't even hurt a *chicken.*"

"Not even a chicken." Augie joked, but I wasn't having it.

"I'm serious. If Daddy heard a group of chickens were in danger, then maybe—and I mean just maybe—I could see him doing something illegal to help them. But drug dealing? Here's what Daddy was doing: he was campaigning to get a local processor up and running again. The chickens he raised would've been grown humanely, killed humanely, then sold at the CP. He was proving it could be done commercially. And you've got people believing he'd turn the CP into a drug mill? It's insane."

"Gotcha. I didn't mean to imply anything."

I uncrossed my arms. "That's okay. The whole thing is getting on my last nerve."

Augie was asking me something else, but I was distracted by a woman navigating the aisle, her martini wobbling.

"Hey!" I exclaimed. "I can order another martini!"

Which is how we wound up in the treehouse.

CHAPTER 9: Trouble in the Treehouse

Augie and I were strolling in the gathering dusk, walking down a narrow Milwaukee street in a neighborhood of brick cottages. They'd let us leave the train because train regulations were complicated, and it took time to correct any screw-up. Apparently, a new crew would've been easier to get in Chicago, but it was a bitch to turn a train around.

We'd strolled no further than a block from the train station into a lovely neighborhood. Blue spruce swayed. Something tall and pink, like a gladiola, sprouted in the ditches. Yards twinkled with silver-leaved trees, and in one yard a woman snatched clothes from the line before darkness fell. The air was so fresh, you could understand why folks would hang their pillows on the line to dry, the wet cotton sucking in the last of the day's light then releasing it into the dreamer's dreams.

I tightened my jacket and tugged my ball cap low. The April warmth was following the setting sun out the door, night coming on. I didn't have high expectations for Milwaukee. An aunt of a school friend had jumped out of a hotel window in Milwaukee when I was a little girl. Still, everything around me was infused with the sparkle of a two-martini world. If I were back in the club car, I might have concluded I was buzzing along just fine and recklessly ordered another drink. Instead, I clutched Augie's arm, hugging him close.

"I'm in love."

He glanced up at me.

"With the train," I proceeded, smooth as sugar. "I feel guilty, abandoning her."

"She'll be there when we return."

"But isn't that abusing her love?"

"Who said she loved you back?"

He produced a leather flask from underneath his jacket and offered it to me.

Upending the flask, I swigged down a mouthful. The liquor—peppermint schnapps—exploded in my brain like the Fourth of July. Soon I'd be chirping and singing and telling *all* my secrets. Oh well. I was on vacation.

I threw back my head and laughed.

The stars had come out, pin dots in the sky. And the moon! A lopsided crescent, its grin shining down on us.

Augie sipped from the flask, and I leaned into him. He smelled like I imagined nights at the country club might smell: cigars and liquor and traces of expensive perfume left by fancy women.

"Hey. Did you know silver comes from the stars?"

"Is that so?" He slid his hand down the arm of my jacket, gently extricating himself. "Tell me something, *cher*."

"Like what?" I murmured, distracted by the stars, the moon, the entire romantic moment.

"Like who you are underneath all the fancy dress." He plucked at my fake fur jacket.

"I thought you liked the way I dressed?"

"I do like the way you dress. Now, tell me something deeper. Tell me what really matters to you. What'd you learn best from your mama, your papa?"

An owl hooted from a tree, a long, haunting sound, followed by two short *whoops!* I scanned the branches overhead to see if I could find the bird, but quickly straightened my neck—my head did not appreciate that tilting business.

"Can I have another shot?" I asked, doubling down.

The slug warmed me, smoother than before.

"Here's what I can tell you." I returned the flask. "My dad, he's deceased, in case I didn't make that clear. I've really missed him since he's been gone. My mom, she drives me crazy. With Daddy gone, she's taken up with a know-it-all redneck. I make stupid mistakes—I married my childhood sweetheart, only to divorce the horn dog six months later. But everything that's good about me—knowing right from wrong, any speck of courage I possess, whatever has kept me sane during the last two years, I owe it all to them. The bad things, I can't blame that on anybody but myself."

I glanced up for his reaction.

"I..." he faltered. "I didn't expect that...tribute."

"Me neither. Something about the night, I guess. Or the schnapps."

"Lucinda, you're a lovely woman."

"But?"

"No buts. You're a lovely woman, and I've enjoyed spending time with you."

"That's nice. Me too."

He gazed at me, and I tugged off my cap, stuffing it in his pocket—it's hard to kiss someone wearing a ball cap—which led him to give me a peck on the lips.

The peck gradually transformed into a slow, hot kiss, his fingertips stroking the back of my neck, my hand grasping his shoulder, our bodies pressing closer.

Mid-kiss, I opened my eyes to gaze at his face, and over his head, sticking up in someone's backyard, rose a treehouse.

I pulled back and pointed. "Look! A treehouse!" I'd had sex in a deer stand once, which is liable to happen if you grow up in rural Mississippi, but a treehouse? A swirl of excitement coursed through me. "Oh, come on!" I tugged him by the arm.

"Where?"

"There!"

The treehouse was in the middle of the backyard, a ladder propped against its trunk. Ladders were not made for skintight silver lamé pants—I could hardly bend my knees in these suckers. So—who knew schnapps would have such an effect?—I tiptoed to the base of the tree, kicked off my heels, and peeled off my pants, hopping on one foot then the other. Augie tried to steady me. "Where are we going with this?" he asked.

"Up there." I jerked my head toward the floor of the treehouse. Finally, the pants leg released its grip on my heel, and I was free.

"Ta da!" I flung out my arms. In a flash, I was up the ladder.

Safely in the treehouse, I stuck my head through the hole in the flooring.

"Come on up," I said in a stage whisper.

He climbed, fully clothed, my pants in his hand.

"Found these." He smiled, crinkling his eyes. "They belong to you?"

"Aren't you a marvel?" I whisked the pants from his grasp, giving him a sloppy kiss in the process.

Briefly, I tried to tug the britches back on, but it wasn't working.

"Oh, hell." I sat on the little bench seat, slapping the pants down beside me.

The tree house was a platform, no walls. I twisted to admire the view and—lo and behold!—behind us in the next yard, another treehouse. Popping up, I pointed across the yards.

"Someone went through here, selling tree houses. They do that with aboveground pools where I come from." I rose onto my tippy-toes, which made me wobble.

Augie caught my wrist. "Steady there."

I leaned my butt against the tree trunk, the man in front of me so gorgeous and the schnapps so warm I wasn't even worried about him seeing my hipbones.

"Come hold me up," I teased.

He hesitated.

I beckoned.

He gave in, pressing himself against me. I unbuttoned his shirt, slipped my hand inside. His skin was hot, the muscles hard. I wrapped my leg around his calf and shrugged off my jacket while he unbuttoned my blouse.

That's when the dog started barking. Barking, barking, barking. "Woof! Woof! Woof!"

"Dog. In a pen." I cut my eyes to the fenced-in area on the side of the house.

"We better leave." Augie scooped up my jacket.

Suddenly, the house's metal door banged open and a flashlight swept the backyard. A man hollered. "Stubby! Stubby!"

But Stubby boy kept right on barking. Got louder. Barked his fool head off.

I crouched behind the tree trunk but realized I'd be skinnier standing. I stood, plastering myself against the tree, which made the bark scrape the backs of my thighs, reminding me a man was waving a flashlight, trying to find me in his tree house, and I was without my britches.

Augie, ever thoughtful, retrieved my pants from the bench, and I aimed my foot into the skinny leg, trying to stay hidden by the tree trunk. I could have done it too. A small turn sideways and I would've been slender as a knife. But the hopping and squirming with the pants was messing things up.

"Your shoulder." Augie pointed to my bony shoulder protruding around the tree.

I zipped my pants and squeezed the shoulder out of view, which perked my chartreuse bra into view. Augie fixed that by covering my breast with his hand. "Here, let me help."

"Shhhh!" I swatted his hand away and buttoned my shirt as best I could.

"He's gonna see your ass." Augie squeezed my behind, strumming his thumb across my silver pants.

"Stubby! What is it?"

The man swept the light across the grass as if we were a possum or something. Surely it wouldn't be long before he thought to look up, and the light would ricochet off my pants sharp as the sun off tinfoil.

I rolled from around the tree. I could see Stubby, running circles in his pen. Augie stepped into view beside me. "Hide yourself," I whispered. He hesitated. I stomped my foot.

He stepped back behind the tree trunk.

"Hey, Mr. Stevenson! It's me. Mandy Johnson."

I eased down the ladder, jumping the last rung and shoving my feet into my shoes. When the flashlight swept toward me, I waved like crazy. "Mama said it would be okay to come over. To collect bugs."

"Who is that?" the man growled.

I stopped, my voice taking on a puzzled tone. "Is that you, Mr. Stevenson?"

By now I was almost to the porch. The old coot was leaning as if in a great wind, holding on to the doorknob. A yeasty belch filled the air. The man wiped his mouth, his hand missing the mark by a mile.

He was drunk as a skunk.

"The beer that made Milwaukee famous!" I clapped my hands. "I have a joke, a baseball joke."

"The beer that made Milt Famee walk us," he muttered, unimpressed.

"You've heard it." I pouted.

"Old as the hills." He screwed up his face. "What did you say about bugs in my tree house?"

I swiveled and pointed to the tree house in the next yard. "My mistake. Wrong tree house." I offered him my sweetest smile.

He kept leaning on the doorknob, squinting at me. "You don't sound like you're from around here."

"I'm adopted."

That did the trick. He released the handle and let the door slam behind him.

I exited the yard, glancing over my shoulder to make sure Augie was following.

In the moonlight, I could see the backside of my new friend as he descended the tree house ladder. His dinner jacket was hiked up over his hips, his square butt stretching the fabric on his trousers. My fur jacket dangled from his hand. He was throwing his weight at odd angles, clumping down the ladder.

Suddenly I knew.

The man was maneuvering as best as he could with a boner.

*

Back on the asphalt, me leaning into Augie's shoulder, he said, "That's not something I saw happening when I woke up this morning."

I laughed. "He kept yelling, 'Stubby! Stubby!'"

"You hopped right out of that treehouse, taking charge. That man didn't stand a chance."

I glanced up at him. "You get yourself into trouble, it's best to get your own little self out."

"That's a good philosophy, *cher*." Halting, he pointed at the moon, a white sliver. The clouds surrounding it rippled like sand at the beach when the waves have receded. He crooned a snippet of a song, his voice low and smooth as velvet.

"'Moon River'!" I exclaimed. "I love *Breakfast at Tiffany's*."

He stepped back, taking my fingertips and extending his arms. "You going my way?"

I twirled under his arm and sang, my voice thin and warbly in the night.

We came together, our palms touching, then Augie lifted his arms and we both spun, back to back, the hem of his jacket flapping. We finished face to face, our arms stretched taut, and I let my arms rise, slowly parting. "Spin again," I directed. "Just you."

Which he did, adding a little two-step into the bargain.

I clapped, and he bowed, and I bowed, and he retook my hand as we continued on our way. "You're kind of like Holly Golightly yourself."

"My friend Erick says that." I swung my arm. "I thought, yeah, she started off as a hick too."

"I'm sure that's not what he meant."

"I love it when she's in the rain yelling for her cat, and her hair is dripping wet. You don't see Audrey Hepburn a mess very often."

"That movie's a charmer. And so are you."

I glanced up at him. Moonlight shadowed the planes of his face. This time I heard no *but* at the end of the sentence.

The evening did not progress to sex. We didn't even kiss again. I could've been upset about that, but I wasn't. It felt right, and, thinking about it, I couldn't remember if Holly Golightly had sex with her man at the end of the movie either. What I remembered was the two of them in the rain, coming together in that moment, laughing in recognition of who they were, of what they were feeling.

Our footsteps echoed on the asphalt. I snuggled into Augie's chest, my hand clasping the lapel of his dinner jacket. I softly hummed the song, unsure of the exact words. Something about breaking a heart. The elusive owl hooted.

CHAPTER 10: An Acceptance, of Sorts

Back on the train, waiting.

Augie and I had hotfooted it to the station where they'd herded us on board, then nothing.

We hadn't moved a lick.

Except backward. And forward. And backward to our starting place. Something about waiting our turn in line, which left us hovering, sliding up and down the tracks without proper direction.

Nine o'clock at night, and I was in a post-alcohol fugue. I was all by my lonesome. As soon as I'd plopped into a club chair, Augie's phone had beeped and he'd excused himself—the man was very popular. He hadn't returned, and I was beginning to wonder if the tree house incident had gotten to him. Maybe in the saner confines of the train, my behavior struck him as a tad exuberant.

My cell phone rang. I checked the number.

"Mother."

"Lucinda! Are you okay?"

"Okay?" I refused to rise to the bait and scream, OF COURSE, I'M NOT OKAY!!!! If I did, she'd grill me, I'd get snippy, and she would object to my tone. I'd resolve it by hanging up, which resolved nothing. Instead, I studied my fingernails and remembered Augie's polished half-moons. Could I get comfortable with a man who had prettier nails than I did?

"Pammy said you weren't okay. She said nothing could keep you safe if those people started acting up."

Pammy, who'd had the unfortunate run-in with the Polish Women's Association. On top of everything else, Mother was now hyper about Erick's oompah family.

"Lucinda, I worry about you."

It was Mother's standard line whenever she was hell-bent on questioning what I was doing: "But I *worry* about you!"

There was a pause while I didn't respond then, "You meet anyone?"

"What is it, Mother?" In a flash of brilliance, I added, "Is it Clyde?"

That led to a resounding silence.

"Mother, why did you call?"

"I wasn't completely honest with you earlier. The Feds didn't just loiter in the hallway. They're being punitive."

"What does 'being punitive' mean?"

"They're going after everything we own. Peggy Margaret says they can take my fur coat. 'Ill-gotten gains' they call it."

Mother's fur coat was a full-length squirrel monstrosity she paraded around town in whenever the temperature dropped below fifty degrees.

"Give it up," I said. "Hand it over. Get a receipt."

"Thank God *you're* not my lawyer."

From the way she said it, I could tell that she actually had a lawyer. I was afraid to ask which Edison bozo attorney she'd put on the payroll.

"Skippy Van Zant is helping me," she offered anyway.

That was unsettling. Skippy Van Zant only took high-profile cases that would either make him a lot of money or give him camera time. Either way, it didn't look good for the home team.

"Why'd you get a lawyer, Mother?"

"The money's dried up. The Feds slapped a lien on the Chicken Palace money. Until they decide otherwise, we have no income coming in."

"You mean the money you get from Daddy's investment? Not the note from Sonny Floyd?" I hadn't even known to worry about the CP money.

"I mean the money I *used to get* from Bill's investment. And there is no more money from Floyd."

So she'd heard the bad news. "I'm sorry, Mother, about the CP no longer buying their chicken from Sonny."

"Oh, yes. That. Your father is rolling over in his grave, the CP selling chemically-induced, antibiotic-tainted chickens. Bennie's running away from the CP as fast as his short legs can carry him."

"And you don't have any savings?" Mother was not a particularly extravagant person, unless you counted the new Cadillac she bought every two years, but that's because she dinged them up so bad, running into curbs and fenceposts—Mother was very near-sighted but too proud to wear glasses.

"Why do you think I've been so worried about the scandal? Do you think I'd send you all the way up to Chicago to talk to Big Doodle for nothing?"

I wasn't going to answer that question—*because you obsess about everything*—and was formulating a new inquiry when she added, "They've taken my car."

"Your car?" I pictured Mother's latest pride and joy: a navy blue Cadillac sedan with white wall tires and built-in GPS … in case Mother got lost in Edison.

"Came by the house this afternoon. They claimed Big Blue was used in the perpetration of criminal drug activity. Confiscation, they called it. Big Blue is at the impound lot in Jackson. Skippy says it's all perfectly legal. Punitive, strong-arm tactics, but legal."

I was about to ask how she was getting around but immediately envisioned her riding in the puke-yellow Cuban taxi, the tree-shaped air freshener swinging from the rearview mirror.

"Oh, Mother. I'm so sorry." So much for my suspicion that Mother might be exaggerating the situation. "They actually took your car?"

"We have Clyde's car. It's just..."

"There's something else?" I offered a silent apology to the Universe for doubting my mama.

"The Feds are making noises about the house."

"The house?" The early morning rainbow from the landing's stained glass window danced in front of my eyes.

"They're saying Bill worked his illegal operation out of his home office. And he bought the house with drug money."

"Good Lord."

"Good Lord is right."

We both sat in silence while the seriousness of what was happening sunk in. This wasn't a typical Edison, Mississippi, disaster. Federal agents were involved, and if they were slapping on liens and seizing property, they meant business. Unbidden, Louisa Jennings' cat-that-ate-the-canary question about how Daddy had been able to afford the house seeped into my mind. Was it possible folks in Edison knew something Mother and I didn't?

"That's nothing but coincidence, Mother, Daddy buying the house when he did." I didn't know if I was addressing Mother's fears or my own. "Can't Skippy convince them Daddy wasn't involved? What on earth makes them think otherwise? Some lame comments by Big Doodle? Who listens to unnamed 'inside sources'?"

"They won't say…except…"

"Except what?"

"The secret password to get the drugs implicates your daddy."

"The secret password?"

"Walk up to the counter, say 'I'll have the Chicken Bwwwatkins! But make mine with goat.' They'd take you to the back, unload the drugs."

The Chicken Bwwwatkins! was named for my daddy. Chicken salad with green olives and pineapple, Daddy's favorite.

"I didn't think they served Chicken Bwwwatkins at any Chicken Palace Emporium except Edison." That's because most people can't abide a green olive in their chicken salad.

"They don't. That's the point. You walk up to the counter, ask for a dish they don't serve then mention the goat. It was the code. The Feds are acting very sure of themselves. Skippy says they keep hinting they have documents, records, evidence of money changing hands. He says the drug laws are all in their favor. They can do whatever they want."

"But why are they picking on you, Mother?" My mother's worst known crime was rolling Big Blue through a stop sign.

"They think I have information."

"What kind of information?" Truth tell, I wasn't sure I wanted to know. If Mother gave me one more bizarre answer, my head might explode.

"They want me to ID his successor, the new guy in charge."

We were both silent. I was waiting for the *whoosh!* of my brains shooting through my nose. Mother was probably waiting for me to say something that would return our world to normal, but I had nothing.

In a moment, Mother said, "So, anyway. I thought you might want to know the whole story. In the past .... I might have made a mistake in not sharing as much information with you as I should have about your dad's illness."

"That's okay, Mother." I was too undone by what she'd described to get into that difficult area now.

"I do need to talk to you about your father, Lucinda." She added more starch to her tone. "But I don't intend to do that on the phone."

"Talk about what?"

"What did I just say?"

"Okay. I'll see y'all soon."

I hung up, thoroughly thrown off by the phone call. That happened sometimes, right in the middle of the game. A heavy hitter smacked a pitch, the baseball soared into the blue sky, higher and higher. The outfielder was running, his head thrown back when— high sky, and he lost the ball. All that blueness, so glorious a minute before, and he flubbed the easy out.

The train gave another massive, unproductive lurch, and I trudged off to bed.

*

At 3:00 a.m., I bolted wide-awake.

How could I have gone to bed?

My mother was on the way to the poorhouse. Pooh would never survive the shame of her daughter becoming homeless. Then Ikie would be out on the street too. That little dog was a scrapper, but he'd never make it in the wild. Soon, all the Watkins would be singing for their supper.

Frantic, I groped around in the dark, hunting for the cell phone to call Chicken Palace Emporium Headquarters. When I finally found it, I had no bars. Throwing off the covers, I studied my Speed Racer pajama pants and my orange striped Denise LaSalle t-shirt. It could pass as appropriate train wear. Anyway, it was worth the risk. I'd noticed the cell phone reception was best in the lounge car. As Daddy always said, even the worst mistakes could be righted with a little initiative.

A train felt like a pretty contained space until you started tromping around in the dark. I was feeling my way down the aisle, creeping in the direction I remembered the lounge car lying.

Everything was quiet—and dark as sin, relieved only by a thin stream of light from the safety bulbs on the floorboards.

Until I got to the club car.

The chalky moonlight cast everything and everyone into the stark relief of some half-forgotten movie. The Bad Guys were played by the train staff. The Loner, played by the new lounge car attendant, sat on the edge of the group, coolly smoking a cigarette. The Victim was played by the mice, scurrying out from beneath the club tables. The Bad Guy's weapon of choice was

114

something resembling an oversized battery. The missile *thunked!* whenever it hit a Victim.

"Bull's eye!" the Bad Guys cried.

The Loner squinted, lost in his own thoughts.

The Victim squeaked and expired.

"That's disgusting!" I said.

The Loner gave me a pensive look. "You want mice in your club car?"

Another Victim scurried out.

"He's yours, Alfredo."

A flabby white boy, who looked like the pasta sauce itself, chunked a battery at the mouse. *Thunk!* The mouse was flattened, all except for his twitching leg.

I didn't need to see that.

"Torpedoing mice." I was disgusted at the casual cruelty.

The Loner shrugged. "Price you pay for being a mouse."

"You better hope there's nothing to this karma business," I warned. "Or else you're all coming back as lab rats."

Afraid of what I'd find next, I returned to my berth and crawled back in bed.

*

Early in the morning, long before the sun opened her sleepy eyes, I awoke to a tapping at my door. Sometime during the night, the train had restarted, and I thought the noise might be the berth door knocking against the lock. But when the tap repeated, I cautiously opened the door.

It was Augie, catching me in my pajama pants and billowing t-shirt with my raccoon eyes from not washing my face before I fell into bed. I suspected I resembled Mary Martin playing Peter Pan: only the smallest of hints gave away the fact she was actually a girl.

"We'll arrive at the station soon. Thought you might want to get a cup of coffee." He cocked his head. "So this is who you really are?"

I flapped my arms at my side. "This is it."

He was wearing those thin gray gym shorts that cut a man no slack. He didn't need any slack. His thighs were thick and muscular. At the top of his shorts, where his t-shirt rode up, you could see the rope of muscles dipping to his groin, like Michelangelo's *David*. He was beautiful, and I was woeful.

I hung my head, afraid my loneliness and disappointment at the ragged edges of what was supposed to be my fun train trip might seep out in a tear.

"You cute, *boo*, for sure." When I glanced up, he was smiling.

The smile—so unexpected, so genuine—broke across me like sunshine on a cloudy day. "Life's been unraveling since I last saw you."

"Life unravels, time to stitch it back together. That's what my mama always says." He leaned against the doorjamb, crossing his arms.

"I like your mama."

"My mama would like you." He motioned to my shirt. "She's a LaSalle fan."

I tucked my chin, glancing at my shirt. "My mama wouldn't know Denise LaSalle from Donna Summers."

"You grow up in New Orleans, you know your food *and* your music. Else you wind up eating your horns and dancing to your red beans and rice."

"You're funny."

"You're nice to laugh at my stupid jokes."

"I didn't think I would be laughing this morning."

"Life's too short not to laugh, *cher*."

His eyes danced, and my heart skipped a beat. The man was so kind, so gentle.

"We like each other," I said.

"We do," he agreed.

I was on him in a heartbeat.

He resisted, as any honorable man would. "I'm not sure this is a good idea," he mumbled as best he could with my lips locked on his. "We're just getting to know each other."

I gave him a small nip, which shut him up.

We had sex once, fast and hot, then lay in the crumpled sheets. Me, flat on my back, him propped on his elbow, and we explored.

Oh my God—his touch. Not a grasping, taking touch, but a giving one, his fingertips skimming down my legs, across my stomach, the pad of his thumb tracing my hipbones. When he commented on how tiny I was, he said it with wonder. Even though I'd tried to make peace with how very different my body was in the land of the "pleasantly plump," Augie's pride in my tininess was as soothing as cool buttermilk on a painful sunburn.

Augie was caressing my skin and suddenly he was hard again. I was pushing with my hips to get more of him inside of me, deeper and deeper, the tension building until it broke free, as hard and pure as water rushing after a summer storm, and everything in my world was turned inside out, fresh and new, panting and sweating and FUN.

I burst out laughing.

"Can we do it again?" I covered his face in kisses. "Please?"

His chest was heaving. He puffed up his cheeks and exhaled a burst of air.

"Give me five minutes."

Five minutes.

Can I pick 'em or what?

*

Augie had nodded off, and I gazed at his face as he dozed. Napping, waking, his look was the same: serene, but happy, as if he was ready for the next good thing to come along.

I'd seen the same look on the face of a friend of mine in community college when he'd realized his days playing JuCo ball were it—not a stepping-stone into the SEC, not a chance at the majors, not even a uniform with his name on the back. The end. Good as it gets. And he loved it.

I'd seen the look on the face of the manager at my bank, whose little boy had wandered from the backyard, crossed the ditch, and weaved into the oncoming traffic. Hit, the boy lay in the ditch for three hours before a driver spotted him. For two days he fluttered in and out of consciousness then woke up, eager to go home and zoooom! his red truck across the carpet again. Now, when I deposited my paycheck, I saw that look on the bank manager's face.

Most important, I'd seen the look on the face of my daddy while he joshed with my mom in his hospital room. He'd joked about men who might be a good match for her after he was gone. I was perched on the edge of the bed, Mother in the steel-framed chair, not amused. I still thought Daddy had a bad case of diverticulitis, nothing more. The AC huffed on and off, confused by the spring weather, while the hospital intercom squawked in the hallway. "Wert Farnley!" Mother exclaimed, indignant at the mule breeder Daddy named as his favorite suitor. Daddy's eyes twinkled, and I giggled. Three weeks later, my Daddy would be dead and yet, at that moment, in that drab hospital room, his face carried the look of peaceful acceptance.

The look could arrive at any time. After Life had thrown everything it had to throw at you, and you'd survived. Or after the Universe had given you your heart's desire, and you'd survived. The change that occurred happened underground, like when the plates of the earth shift and fit together differently, never quite the same. It was the acceptance that follows accepting. A calming down, a stilling. Something I'd been searching for every way to Sunday. And now in my bed was a man who carried that look in spades.

*

When Augie opened one eye, then the other, I told him all about it.

I told him about Daddy dying and Mother taking up with a man who renovated our garage so he could leave his tanning bed up all day—never took the bed down, never even unplug it. I told him about my disastrous marriage and Stirling's quick proposal to a woman who had so much more *polish* than I did—a wedding in a

119

church, mind you, when Stirling had dragged me to a justice of the peace, I thought because he couldn't wait to get married but, as it turns out, the lazy turd hadn't been running for mayor and didn't need a big ass church wedding *that* time around.

It was a long, rambling telling to which he listened quietly. By the time I was finished, the morning sun was filling the berth with glowing red light.

But I didn't feel refreshed.

I felt retreaded, like when you don't bother to buy a new tire but just slap a new tread on the worn-out tire. I was walking the same old steps, which wasn't going to get it for me. "I want what you have."

He stroked my hand where it lay on the covers. "What do I got that you want, *cher*?"

"That...serenity. An acceptance of life that makes you truly happy." I flashed back to the sense of exuberance the French guy's book had given me after Daddy died. "I almost had it one time, close as my fingertips, but...."

"Don't put too much faith in strangers, Lucinda." He sat upright in the bed.

"You're not a stranger." I trailed my hand down his bare chest. "At least not a total stranger. I know you're kind. And fun. And you won't fool a child into believing you're a movie star when you're not. What else is there I need to know?"

"I got more bad habits than strip clubs on Bourbon." He ran his fingers through his hair. "If you knew 'em, you mightn't think so much of me."

"What? Do you pick your toes in bed? Or put ketchup on your black-eyed peas?" I persisted.

"Naw, I would never put ketchup on my peas. Eat 'em with a little okra, yeah."

"We put okra in our peas in Mississippi." I tapped him on his hard chest. "That's not a bad thing."

He clasped my hand in his. "You gotta trust me on this one."

"But not too bad, right?"

"I can only hope not."

Then he drew my hand to his lips and kissed my fingers, and pretty soon I'd forgotten all about the heavy stuff.

CHAPTER 11: Can't Run Away from Leopard

We were about to arrive in St. Paul, so I groaned out of bed and began dressing. As I picked through my suitcase searching for something memorable, Augie talked.

"When I was a boy, my papa had his heart set on building his dream house on a big vacant lot on Jefferson Avenue. Papa hated the side-by-side we grew up in. The kitchen filled with smoke whenever my mama fried fish in the skillet. Anyways, Papa got fixated on an old home site in Uptown. Live oaks, half a block deep—it was a beaut. A house had been there once, but it was gone. Daffodil bulbs bloomed in the spring."

I smoothed the front of my white turtleneck. Somewhere I had white stretch jeans too. A dazzling angel, I would burn my brightness into Augie's brain. Tugging the turtleneck over my head, I listened to Augie tell his story.

"Finally, my pop bought the lot—got it for a song—and built his dream house. My mama got her big kitchen, everything was great."

"Life came through for you?" I offered, even though I knew the story wasn't finished.

"Come springtime, first hard rain, the yard started leaking. I mean, the rain would fall and the ground would bubble. You stepped, and the grass squished. They never figured out what caused it. A high spot in the water table, maybe."

I sat down on the bed, jeans and turtleneck on, white cowboy boots flopped to the side.

"My old man, he tried to take the seller to court, but New Orleans judges can't abide whiners. We had to move to an apartment with roaches big as airplanes."

"How old were you?"

"Sixteen, and full of piss." He sat down beside me, doodled his fingers on my jeans. "Kudzu vines took over our house. If I drove by today, I bet it wouldn't even be there. Just daffodils blooming in the spring."

"Things aren't always what they seem?" I guessed at the point of his story, returning to his earlier comments about trusting strangers.

"The world is full of things you can't control. You've gotta hold on to what's important and roll with the rest of it."

"*Laissez le bon temps rouler,*" I repeated.

"Couple years later, my papa got a promotion. We moved to a great old house in Mid-City. Papa never thought about that defective lot again."

"The house where your nieces and nephews play in the front yard?"

"Exactly."

"Are you saying that's the answer to happiness?" I struggled with the cowboy boots, which always felt two sizes too small until they finally slid on and fit perfectly.

"You asked me about my take on life. I wanted to finish the conversation before I left."

"I'll see you in a couple of days." We would both be in St. Paul for five days, me with Erick and his oompah family, Augie at a sports convention and banquet (which included an Academy Awards spoof, hence the white dinner jacket—I knew it was too good to be true). After Mr. Gminsky had helped me put the squeeze on Big Doodle and Erick had won the million dollars, Augie and I would reconnect on the train ride home.

"True dat, but we might have to start all over again, who knows. I wanted to tell you now, while it's still easy between us."

I quit fighting my boots. Whatever was bothering him, he wasn't going to let it go, and he wasn't gonna tell me what it was. Which left me in the peculiar position of having to trust him when he said I shouldn't put my trust in him.

"Take off that boot, bet your sock's all wadded up inside."

I tugged off the boot. My sock was crumpled in on itself like a ball of snakes.

"How'd you know that?"

"I watched you do it. You work a boot side to side that way, the sock is gonna slide down your heel, wind up in a ball."

I fixed the sock. The boot slid home.

We were ready to go.

Which wasn't what I wanted. I wanted his arms back around me. Or even his fingers grasping mine. *Please,* I pled with Life, *a few more minutes.* "I wanted to tell you about Pooh."

Standing up, Augie gave me a quizzical look. "I know plenty about poo."

"I mean my grandmother, Pooh. And her husband, my Poppa Dean. Poppa Dean had a pet chicken named Hunt."

"Was this your dad's father?" Augie asked. "I ask because of the chicken."

"No, that was Mother's dad, but Daddy gave Hunt to Poppa Dean the same time he gave me Peck. They were very attached, Poppa Dean and Hunt. When Poppa Dean died, Hunt grieved himself to death. We had taken him—Hunt the chicken, I mean—to the funeral home to show him Poppa Dean's body. But it didn't help. It's supposed to help, for a pet to see the dead body. Then they know what happened, that they weren't left. But it didn't help. I was eighteen when he died. Poppa Dean, I mean. Not Hunt."

Augie gave me a strange look.

"You said you wanted to know about Edison and my family."

He nodded slowly. "Yes, I did."

The train whistle blew. We were entering St. Paul.

"Do you think—" I wanted to ask if he thought we'd done the right thing, having sex so soon after we'd met.

The train whistle blew again.

"We have to go," Augie said.

"That's what always happens." I glanced out the window so I wouldn't have to look at his set face. "It's always time to go."

*

When we ran into Erick getting off the train, I burst into a grin.

Sidling up to me, he said, "You about to pop, Ms. Williams?"

He was right. I was dying to tell him everything that had happened with Augie, but it's hard to start jabbering about someone when that someone is standing right behind you. It would have to wait until the cab ride to his house.

Turning to say good-bye, I was surprised to see Augie holding out a piece of paper.

"My phone number. Maybe I could get yours too?"

As I tore the paper in half and jotted down my number, he said, "I was thinking about dinner while we're here. Write down Erick's address. I'll make reservations near his house."

"It'll be fun. Thank you." I returned the paper to him.

He fingered the paper and stuffed it in his pocket. "I enjoyed it, Lucinda. I hope it works that we .... I guess I'll see you soon."

Then he offered his hand for a soft squeeze and gave me a soft kiss and softly we parted.

*

Settling into the cab with Erick, I swiveled in my seat, tucking my leg beneath me.

"So, how are you?" The cab ride to the Gminski's house would be short, and after we waded into Erick's family life, who knew when we would have another opportunity to share?

"Okay. Too much listening to J.J. gripe." He rubbed his forehead, smoothing out the furrows. "When you separate that man from his pecs, all you've got is a whiner. What about you? If I understood the note passing correctly, you've got a dinner date."

"I do, but it's a little odd." I told him about Augie's warning about not trusting strangers.

"That *is* odd. Usually, when a guy is playing you, he doesn't announce it."

"I know, right? What do you think it means?"

He gazed out the window, watching the buildings zip past. "I have no idea. I guess you'll find out sooner or later."

He was right. And while I couldn't put my finger on it, something told me it would be sooner rather than later.

*

I swear to God, Erick might have been adopted. He was so incredibly different from the rest of his family. Of course, my first impression of them might have been influenced by the fact we'd arrived in the middle of a practice session.

The living room was dark (low ceiling, shag carpet) and packed with a leftover funky smell that I could almost put my finger on. The family was planted in the middle of the room: a mom, a pop, and identical twins, making a shit-load of noise. Erick's dad wore green suede lederhosen, which I later learned he wore to weddings and other special events even if the band wasn't performing. He was grinning from ear to ear, churning away at the accordion.

"Right on time!" he roared and stomped his foot to the beat. "Robert Gminksi! Come on in!"

This was the espionage expert on whom I'd pinned all my hopes. Then I told myself to take heart: Mr. Robert Gminksi was obviously a master of deception.

Erick's twin sisters wore Heidi braids and dresses with that flat breast piece and crinoline skirt. Their heads were round as sweet peas. One was playing a foot pedal tambourine and tapping a wooden spoon against something that made a *clock! clock! clock!* sound. The other girl worked the slide of a trombone.

The mother was dressed similar to the girls, except her chest wasn't flat. The tops of her breasts rounded from the dress with the exuberance of two snuggling whales. Her hair was done up Princess Leia style, and she was puffing on a baby tuba. Every time she huffed on the tuba, a bird in a metal cage flapped its wings and squawked, "Jimmy! Jimmy!"

They were wailing away at some hauntingly familiar song. Erick leaned over and whispered, "Whiter Shade of Pale."

We were eye to eye, almost nose to nose. I was trying not to get tickled, and Erick was being dead serious right back at me, his eyes growing round as saucers with the effort. "Their specialty is drug music from the seventies."

I whispered, "And your instrument was?"

He made an *eek!* mouth. "The recorder."

The group foot-stomped into a Led Zeppelin medley—"Stairway to Heaven," "You Shook Me," and "Kashmir"—while the bird, whose name was Dr. Detroit, croaked out the name each new song. "Stairway to Heaven, braaaack."

When the group segued out of the Zeppelin medley, hitting the opening notes of "Come Together," the twins' heads bopping, the parents' faces glistening with sweat, Dr. Detroit hopping in a frenzy, I almost lost it.

But I didn't. Because the twins kept darting glances at me, shy, as if wanting to see if I approved. Lord help me if I was gonna be responsible for embarrassing two young girls who still thought their family was the most wonderful thing God put on this earth and not God's own demented *Saturday Night Live* skit.

"Now look at that." I pointed to one of the tiny trophies displayed on the end table. "A miniature tuba."

More trophies were stacked on the mantle in a pyramid. A cutie-pie silver-pleated accordion topped several. I fingered one with braids that could have been modeled on the twins.

"Best costume!" Erick's mother shouted over the accordion. "Girls won three years running!"

The girls beamed. I gave them a thumbs-up.

Erick plopped down on a leopard printed sofa. I wedged in beside him and patted the upholstery. "My aunt Stacy had a leopard love seat exactly like this."

"I could have predicted."

"You can't run away from leopard."

He smiled. "No, you sure can't. You cannot run away from leopard."

*

I arrived at supper eager to find out what Mr. Gminski could do to help find Big Doodle. The family was still in costume, gobbling down their meal before tearing off to a competition.

Turns out, oompah band competitions are very similar to barbecue contests. You enter every little hole-in-the-wall contest until you start winning. Then, when you've amassed a reputation and a pile of trophies, you get invited to what they imaginatively call Invitationals. BBQ contests had their categories—shoulder or pulled pork or even baked beans. Oompah competitions encouraged the same type of specialization—hence the Gminskis' focus on druggie music. The circuit was small, and families wound up in heated rivalries. Unlike some of the barbecue contests I'd known, no one had been killed…that Erick's family knew of.

"My mother's boyfriend, Clyde?" I offered while we ate. "He had a half-brother from his father's illegitimate family in Jackson who got shot during a family board game."

Robert, Erick's dad, twirled his pinky through a highball glass, bobbing the maraschino cherry, while I explained about the board game. I understood from Erick that the alcohol wouldn't really start to flow until Saturday when the aunts and uncles and cousins would arrive to celebrate Erick's visit.

"That game where you draw pictures on a pad?" Robert stuck his wet pinkie in his mouth, sucked on it. He had Santa Claus cheeks: round, hard balls with a rosy flush. Karen, Erick's mom, called him Bob. Bob and Karen Gminski. "Hard to see where that could lead to a killing."

I scooped mashed potatoes from a bowl, the spoon clinking against the china. "The half-brother told his cousin, who was winning the game, that his cat's pointed ears looked like birthday hats."

What the man had actually said was, "Why you always putting fucking birthday hats on your fucking cats? Fucking dogs too. Every fucking animal you draw's wearing a fucking birthday hat."

But it was best to start stories off slow with people you didn't know.

Erick was in close conversation with one of the twins, Ingrid maybe. Her face was tight with excitement. As she talked, her hands crawled through the air. Erick nodded, intent. I'm sure he was interested in whatever his sister was saying, but he was hiding too. People did that—ran to the kids in the family so they wouldn't have to deal with the grownups and their questions. Even though I hadn't noticed Erick's family peppering him with difficult questions, an outsider couldn't really judge that type of thing.

"And he got shot for that? Playing a board game?" Erick's mom was looking at me, startled.

She'd already asked me some pointed questions about Mississippi, as if she were storing up ammunition to use against Erick later, trying to get him to move back home. It made me defensive, wanting to stick up for my regional tribe.

"He cursed at him. That was what did it. We don't take to rudeness in the South."

Karen whipped around to her son. "That judge was rude to you, the remark he made about your dancing. In *Mississippi,*" she fairly spit out. "Which, last time I looked, was in the South."

Erick feigned exasperation. "Ma, he was a French judge. From the *French* delegation."

"In the state of Mississippi." She folded her arms across her chest.

"The competition was held in Mississippi." Erick rolled his eyes my way. "You can't blame them."

"Well, I do." She glowered at me.

That was as unfair as blaming the city of Memphis for Dr. Martin Luther King's death because some cracker knuckled over from Georgia and shot him on the balcony of the Lorraine Motel, I wanted to say, but I didn't. I was a guest in Mrs. Gminski's house, and my momma had taught me better than that.

"What I want to know—" Mrs. Gminski began, but Erick interrupted her.

"It's been two years, Ma. Give it a rest."

"That judge threw your whole life off kilter. A brilliant dancer like you." She shook her head. "What he said. Now you're down in Mississippi, God knows why."

To change the subject, I asked Mr. Gminsky if he thought he could help me contact Big Doodle. I was explaining to the rest of them about the drug scandal when Mrs. Gminski interrupted me.

"Oh, we know about that. It's been all over the news."

"I wasn't sure." On the train, you might as well be in a news blackout. The train ran through dead zones, and the connection to the outside world ceased. You wound up getting news with all the reliability of pigeon droppings. "Did they maybe say anything about my daddy?"

"Yeah, we were sorry to hear about your pop being mixed up in it." Mr. Gminski helped himself to more cabbage, which I'm pretty sure accounted for the funky smell in the living room. "I understand an inside source tipped off the Feds about his involvement."

"Actually, Big Doodle Dayton mistakenly identified the local investors as the cause of the scandal." I hiked a spoonful of potatoes into my mouth. I'd been afraid we'd have beets—I hate the vinegary things—but the mashed potatoes were homemade (you could tell by the lumps) and delicious. "That's why I need to contact him. To make him recant."

"That's not what *USA Today* said," Mrs. Gminski corrected me. "They said an insider called the tip line and named your dad."

"Not the tip line," said Mr. Gminski. "The Investor Relations department."

I nearly spewed potatoes all over the Gminski's tablecloth.

"Investor Relations?" That might have been the department I landed in when I called Chicken Palace Headquarters to express my condolences.

Mr. Gminksi nodded, his mouth full of roast beef. "The authorities believe the tipster was probably trying to protect her investment."

"Her?"

"A woman. She said your whole family regretted the public had found out about your dad's involvement in the scandal."

What I'd actually said was the Watkins family wished to go on record expressing its regret at the sordid circumstances unfolding at the Edison Chicken Palace Emporium, it being the family's sincere wish that the public would focus on the role Bill Watkins played in the formation of the Chicken Palace rather than this potential stain on his legacy.

That's what I got for cobbling together my Associate Sciences Technology-General Business learning with snippets from the sympathy cards we'd received at Daddy's death.

CHAPTER 12: Off on a Quest

Lying awake in the Gminski's guest bedroom, I tried to convince myself my phone call had not lit the fuse that had blown up my daddy's good name. But the facts kept lining up against me. A woman (that would be me) had called Investor Relations (the department I'd stumbled into) and left a message that sounded suspiciously similar to my (somewhat garbled) condolence call. This "tip" had led Big Doodle to identify the "local investors" as the wrongful party, which caused the Feds to begin investigating Daddy, where they found a link between his favorite dish and the code to "order" pot, along with the suspicious timing of the house purchase and other supposed hard evidence of money changing hands, etc.

Once I concluded I had probably played a part in the fiasco (okay, hell—I *had* played a role in it), my first step in accepting responsibility was to stick my head under the pillow.

When that got emotionally and physically uncomfortable, I sat up and started pounding myself over the head with all the other mistakes I'd made in my life. Stirling, for God's sake. Why had I believed a man who had ruined our first relationship by cheating on me was writing a book about sex addicts, yet wasn't the main character? And what about this very trip—was I really a good daughter trying to save my daddy's reputation? Or had I jumped at the chance to run away from my problems, again?

That was what the last two years of my life struck me as: running away. I'd run away from my grief over Dad's death into the la-la land of happily-ever-after with Stirling. I'd run away from Edison when the chicken scandal became one too many things for me to handle. I'd run away from talking to my mother about the last weeks of my dad's life. All this running away and the only concrete thing I'd accomplished was to sling mud on Daddy's good name, which he valued more than anything.

Enough was enough.

No more running away.

From now on, I was running full-tilt into the future.

*

I awoke the next morning to a clarified world.

Rising, I gathered my clothes from where I'd strewn them the night before and stuffed them in my suitcase. Tapping once on Erick's door, I slowly tiptoed toward his bed and knelt, shaking him gently by the shoulder.

His eyes flew open. I put my finger to my lips.

"I'm going," I said, talking low so as not to disturb my decision.

Erick raised himself onto one elbow and rubbed his eye with his fist. "It's too early, Ms. Williams. Go back to bed."

"I can't. I must leave right away or it will be too late. Any delay and all could be lost."

"Why are you talking like *Beowulf?*"

"I'm off on a quest. I'm going to Chicken Headquarters to confront Big Doodle Dayton." I raised my eyebrows in anticipation.

It took him a second because it was five o'clock in the morning, so his brain hadn't clicked into gear yet. "I thought my pop was gonna help you? Figure out a way to get Big Doodle on the phone."

Mention of the phone made me wince. "I need to take care of this myself. I might have created a confusion, and I have to clear it up so Big Doodle can clear up Daddy's name. I am going to restore the Watkins' family honor."

Erick sat up in bed. "Want me to come with?"

I threw my arms around his neck and squeezed. He opened his palms for balance, but let me have my moment before drawing away. In that brief second, I smelled his sleepiness, a scent that reveals our true selves. Erick's was as clean and fresh as cut hay.

"You're a sweetheart, but you have to stay here and win the million dollar prize for your world-saving idea and appear on national TV. Me, I've got to make Big Doodle Dayton tell everyone my daddy had nothing to do with stuffing illicit drugs in raw chicken parts and trucking them across the Southeast."

Erick scrunched up his beautiful face. "You're not going off half-*cocked*, are you? It sounds like a mighty *fowl* undertaking." His smile turned down at the corners in apology. "Sorry, it's early. But you'll be back in time for the show, right? In case I make the cut?"

"Yes, you'll make the cut, and, yes, I will be back."

"I want you to see my idea."

"I want to see your idea."

"You'll be surprised."

"I can't wait." I tucked my hand in his. "I'll take care of things then I'll come back and we'll celebrate your amazing, unbelievable success."

"Are you sure you don't want me to go with you? You don't do alone very well."

Erick was adorable in his Elvis t-shirt, and I was tempted to accept his offer. But this was my own responsibility. I would be tested—quests always tested you—but I'd emerge on the other side victorious. "It's the right time, Erick. A Goldilocks moment."

"Okay." He squeezed my hand. "At least tell me your plan."

"The train will take me almost to Big Doodle's front step." I pictured myself at San Francisco's Chicken Palace corporate headquarters. The office building probably had white columns—anyone from Mississippi gets enough money, sooner or later, they're building their very own Tara. "I'll talk to him real sensible, remind him how he and Daddy go way back."

My words were to reassure myself as well as Erick. Even if my memory of Big Doodle as a delightful co-conspirator was only that—a child's hazy memories— surely he still held some fondness for Daddy.

"There's been a total misunderstanding, blown out of proportion. We'll get it settled. Then I'll hop on the train and tear back here, so I can see you on TV and fire up the flame with Augie. Train, chicken headquarters, train, here. How much trouble can I get into?"

"Don't ask that question." Erick threw off the covers, revealing undershorts of a startling pink. "You call me and let me know what's going on. I don't want to have to tell your mama I lost you. 'Oh, she's somewhere between the Midwest and the West Coast, Rita Rae.'"

He was standing, looking around—for his pants maybe.

"What are you doing?"

"Giving you a ride to the train station. Or did you forget that part?"

Men.

They think logistics rule the world.

*

I walked through the coach car where puffy-eyed people hugged pillows. Tomorrow morning, I would be one of them. No more lovely sleeping berths for me. I was out in the open with the seething masses.

As I passed on the way to my seat, a little boy chirped, "Bye bye!" I waved at him with my pinkie. His mother twisted to see who her son was talking to. Not recognizing me, she frowned.

I took a seat. The familiar roll of the train started up.

Plastic water bottles rattled beneath my seat. The chairs in my row rocked, empty. From the outside, I could be chugging along, headed into the Great Plains, off on a Grand Adventure.

On the inside, I was on a train, all by myself.

No Erick. No Sampson. No Bruised Magnolia. Not even the girl with the tramp stamp who bent over too much or Alfredo who killed baby mice while the rest of the train slept.

Most of all, no Augie Green. I hadn't anticipated how much the train would remind me of Augie. I wanted him with me so we could continue our conversation. But who ever heard of a heroine going on a quest with her new love interest? Quests had to be undertaken alone or else they didn't count. When I returned, flush with success, I'd have plenty of time to resume with Augie.

In a minute, I had Pammy on the phone.

"Do you know what time it is?" Her voice was gruff. Pammy was tiny, barely over five feet, but she was a pistol.

"No. I don't even know what time zone I'm in." I glanced out the window where the rising sun streaked the sky. "I thought you'd be wide-awake by now, you know, getting ready for work."

"I work at night, remember? Glamor Galore's Number One Spa Lady?"

"Ug. I wasn't thinking." We were hurtling between towns. The train shuddered across overlapping tracks, lurched, and recovered. "Hey, I need you to do something for me."

"A train spa? I don't know, the logistics of that sound difficult. Do they even have plug-ins for the pedi-pool?"

"No, no—not that. But, yes, they do have plug-ins. I'm not riding the stagecoach."

"What is it, then? Advice on dealing with the Polish ladies?"

"No."

"I can't go back to the Museum, girl. Cecil Everette is *kin-ky*."

"I want you to offer my mother a spa."

"Mother's Day gift?"

"Today if possible. As an excuse to get in the house and find dirt on Big Doodle Dayton without my mother knowing what you're up to."

"Spying, you say?" Her interest was rising.

"Exactly."

"I heard the Feds took your mama's car."

"They're trying to strong-arm her, and they know what they're doing—everyone in that house is living off chicken money."

"I didn't know your family had an actual financial interest in the Chicken Palace. Bragging rights, maybe."

"Daddy held forty percent of the original Palace. We hardly made any money off it 'til several years ago when the CP started throwing off more money than a prostitute at an aluminum siding convention. I always thought it was because of the ecoli scare at Fred's Burgers."

"Might've been the weed."

"Exactly. And the Feds are using that to squeeze Mother into giving up information on Daddy's involvement in the drug ring, but that information doesn't exist because he wasn't involved in the drug ring. It's a real conundrum."

"A Catch 22."

"Or something. The point is, I need to get the Feds off Mother's back. I'm on my way to see Big Doodle at Chicken Palace Emporium headquarters to fix everything."

"No shit? Chicken Palace headquarters? Where's that?"

"San Francisco."

"California." She whistled low. "Girl, that sounds like us back in high school, dreaming about getting out of Edison. Any chance you might stay?"

"Leaving Edison was your dream, Pammy." This was true. Pammy was always more adventuresome than me—I'd never even begun exploring Jackson until after Daddy died. "I only wanted life in Edison to get better."

"That's happened for me, hasn't it?" she mused."I found my niche with the spa ladies." Leaving the rest unsaid—*what happened to you?*

"Anyway, if you could find something that would make Big Doodle officially take back what he said about Daddy, that would be great."

"Do you think Big Doodle knows he's leaving your dad swinging in the wind? My mom says he was always a little flaky."

"I don't know." I wasn't willing to tell Pammy about the "anonymous tip" that might have caused the confusion. "But Big Doodle already caved to business pressures and abandoned Daddy's 'be nice to chickens' philosophy. Why not throw Daddy under the bus over the drug scandal too? After all, Daddy's dead."

"That's cold. What do you think I'll find on him in your house?"

"I'm not sure. But Daddy kept files on everything. The file cabinets are in his office in the upstairs spare bedroom." When Mother and I had been settling the estate, we had shut the door to the bedroom, leaving for another day the job of sorting the files. "If there's anything there, I guarantee you it'll be in a file labeled 'Dirt on Bennie Dayton.'"

"Big Doodle's first name is Bennie? That's lame."

"Are you up for it?"

The sound of flipping pages filled the line. "It's your lucky day, sweetheart. I haven't got anything until 6:30 tonight. I'll call your mom, tell her it's urgent she have a Glamour Galore spa now. We'll fill a living room with gals for a late afternoon spa. I can snoop while the ladies sit luxuriating under the GG Gel Eye Mask. No one will know I'm gone. Sometimes the ladies fall asleep— the GG Gel Eye Mask is quite soothing."

We said goodbye, and I hung up, confident Pammy could talk Mother into accepting my "gift." My work done, all I had to do was settle back and wait for San Francisco to arrive.

*

A little over four hours later, we crossed the North Dakota line and rolled into a station where the rail cars swirled with fat-lettered graffiti. As the brakes screeched, a surfer dude who'd been hitting on a young woman diagonally across from me stood and escorted the chick from the train car. Someone said, "Shoooot," long and slow, and shuffled a deck of cards.

Before we started up again, the conductor hollered, "All aboard!" The walkie-talkie in his back pocket squawked. He checked the newcomers' tickets, asking each one to verify their destination.

A man with a ponytail and an earring entered behind the conductor. He bent low to clear the doorframe. He was wearing mirrored sunglasses. I thought he might sit in the empty seat beside me, but he continued to the seat the surfer dude had vacated. He didn't remove his dark glasses.

The train whistle shouted.

I glanced out the window where fields of waving sunflowers passed. Here and there oil wells shaped like grasshoppers munched the earth. I didn't see a single fence line, only fields spreading for miles. My daddy always said the Mississippi cotton fields had no fences because no one would go into a cotton field if they could help it, and the poor folk couldn't leave if they wanted to. My daddy had been eleven years old and working the fields when his daddy died. The call came from the cotton gin. There'd been an explosion. Mr. Watkins was dead, and someone needed to come get the body. Daddy walked to the gin and brought his daddy home.

Imagine my surprise one day when Daddy stopped his truck and put me out in a cotton field.

We'd been driving a country road, the truck windows rolled down to let in the breeze. Field after planted field whizzed by, the cotton exploding white on brown, clattering stalks. Daddy slowed the truck and pulled onto the shoulder, crunching gravel as he braked. He shoved the long gear stick into neutral and turned to me.

"You go on out there." Reaching, he opened my door. "You can't be from Mississippi and never have picked cotton." Daddy talking as though we had been discussing this the whole time. He tapped my knee and pointed to the door, telling me to get a move on.

I exited the truck one-legged, stretching until my toe hit grass. Daddy was watching me.

"Go on now," he said.

I released the door handle, on my own.

The shoulder sloped into a ditch, the cotton on the other side. I tiptoed down the ditch, avoiding the tough stalks of dried weeds. The bottom of the ditch sagged with marshy water. My tennis shoes sank and I scrambled up the other side. I'd heard enough about picking cotton to know to be careful. I gently pried open the mouth of the cotton boll, wary of the brown husk, until the boll parted like a blooming flower.

Choosing a petal, I peeled the cotton away from the husk and snatched that sucker to victory.

I raised my wad of cotton in triumph.

Daddy held up two fingers.

He wanted another.

I repeated the process, nicking my finger against the petal when I wasn't looking and pricking my thumb so that I had to stick it in my mouth and suck for a second to stop the pain but coming up with the prize.

Daddy held up three fingers.

When I tried to tug loose the cotton from the third petal, the husk snapped and the cotton got tangled so that I had to work to separate the strands, yanking when it didn't want to let go, biting the inside of my cheek while I struggled to pick all the cotton free.

I was afraid to hold up my third cotton. I just looked at Daddy in the truck. Four fingers.

My cotton boll was ragged. Wisps of cotton clung to the petals, the white flecked with blood. I tackled the last petal, stripping the cotton away but leaving a big chunk behind.

Daddy wouldn't know. He was in the truck.

I raised my arm. It sagged in a white flag of surrender.

Daddy nodded.

I wadded the hateful cotton in my fist and threw it on the ground. Head down, tears hot, I stumbled back to the truck.

"I can't say what your truth is, Lucinda Mae." Daddy stared at the road before cranking the engine. "But a long time ago I swore I'd never be part of a business that treated a man's death as an inconvenience handled by a phone call to his eleven-year-old son. I'm not saying I've been perfect, but I've tried to keep that in front of me. It's the only way. Decide what's important to you and hold it close. Otherwise, the world will roll over you."

Inside the train, something had gone flooey with the HVAC. It was so cold I retrieved my jeans from my knapsack and tugged them on over the foolish pair of shorts I'd chosen in the morning's confusion. Our new conductor, a man named Hadley, watched my gyrations and said, "The temperature can drop forty degrees quick as that"—he snapped his fingers—"in the North Dakota spring."

Great.

Outside, houses popped up, shacks actually, one with a bicycle lying in the dirt driveway, the wheel spinning. Dust turned the windows of the shack golden in the slanting sun. White butterflies swirled for miles.

"Welcome to the geographical center of North America," a sign announced in Rugby, North Dakota. "Right," I grumbled to myself. "If you include the Arctic Circle."

I was wondering what the hell I had been thinking when the phone rang. Erick. His invention had made the cut! He was so excited. He told me all about the woman in charge, a battle ax who barked orders at the participants, hardly giving each person a chance to describe his or her idea before lowering the boom. *Bam!* You got on the taped auditions. No, you didn't make it.

Erick had made it.

"The woman in front of me was so nervous she was wiping her armpits with a tissue. She didn't make it."

He was thrilled, and it made me want to hug him through the phone. "I'm so proud of your invention."

"It's not an invention. It's an idea."

"Huh."

"Some of the recent winners were t-shirt ideas."

"T-shirts? So it can be anything?"

"Not anything. It has to be a new idea on how we can save our world from destruction and chaos."

"Are there any ideas big enough to do that?"

"Maybe mine is. They're going to tape the next round. That's where you explain your idea. The presentations will be on TV. You can be in the audience, Lucinda, maybe get on TV yourself."

I so wished I could. I'd never been on TV, except one time in Girl Scouts when we went on a field trip to WLBT, Channel 3 in Jackson, where the camera panned the group and we saw ourselves on a studio screen. Seeing ourselves on TV like that, it was as if we'd stepped outside of who we'd always been into a fun, new place. Surely national TV would expand that experience to the nth degree.

"I can't. My obligation is here."

"I figured, but I thought it was worth a shot. If I make the finals, you'll be back in time for that."

"I will, don't worry."

"I'm not worried. You'll make it in time. Have you called Big Doodle?"

"For what?"

"To let him know you're coming."

"I've tried calling him several times, but the phone system is a bitch. Besides, what if he doesn't want to see me? He might have known I was coming to

Chicago and skedaddled. I may be better off surprising him."

"You might be better off not traveling for days only to arrive and find him missing."

"That's the question, isn't it? I'll figure something out. Love your heart."

"Love your heart too. Whatever happens, remember that."

He sounded so serious, I called into the phone, "Erick!" but it was too late. He'd hung up.

Making my way to the lounge car, I struck up a conversation with an elderly man who exclaimed when I told him I was from Mississippi—"Edison? My granddaddy had a place outside of Bolton." The man let me talk about how smart baby chickens were then he reminisced about his grandaddy's cucumbers that grew twelve inches over*night* and how as a child he had to pick them every blessed *day.*

Strangers did that on the train, shared. The man knew I wouldn't ask if he loved or resented his grandaddy for the cucumber chores. On trains, our lives unfolded in silo stories, each one standing straight and tall, none of the tellings breaking free and cavorting in the barnyard, kicking up their heels, smashing fences and breaking hearts. People were warm too, interested in what you had to say, "uh-huh–ing" and following right along with your tale.

"Excuse me," I said to the old man when the phone rang. It was Augie.

"Hey!" I made no attempt to hide my delight at hearing his voice. After all, the man had called me.

"Hey, yourself."

"I've been missing you." I didn't mention the train had triggered my loneliness. Scampering across country to take on the head of a major corporation—to someone who didn't know you very well, it might appear a little … demented. Better to recount my success when I returned.

"Just checking on you. Wouldn't want you running away when I wasn't looking."

I cut my eyes at the phone. Did the man have a sixth sense?

"Guess what Erick just told me?" I dodged. "He made the next cut in the contest. He's very excited."

"That's great. But you're doing okay?"

"Doing fine."

"Okay. Keep me in the loop." And he said goodbye.

Just like a man, so functional, no time to chat.

I settled back into my chair, the afternoon almost gone.

After a bit, the train halted at another North Dakota station. A horse stood on an island in an adjacent pond, swishing its tail. On the pond's far edge, the water reflected the sky. The horse dipped its head. Drank. The reflection rippled. Overhead, the fading sun burnt a hole in a cloud, a matchstick held to film, burning away the past, searing into the future.

Back in Edison, they were enjoying the lavender spills of wisteria vines and the scarlet, balled azaleas. Dogwoods, pink and white, lined the narrow streets back in Edison. At Mother's house, Pooh was gliding under the pecan tree, eating cold fried chicken with a green olive sandwich on white bread, the pecan tree's new leaves fluttering over her head. At Pooh's feet, Ikie sniffed daffodils then lifted a leg to pee. Upstairs,

Mother was tugging open the sticking windows to let in the fresh air. At the edge of town, the fields were blooming in yellow alfalfa. Back in Edison, the sweeping ligustrum wept. Back in Edison …

I hugged myself, warding off the freezing cold. Why, I wondered, did absence make something nestle so deeply in the heart?

The phone rang again—I was the belle of the ball today. This time it was Pammy.

"Spa went great," she said. "Sold seven GG Gel Masks. Those babies have the highest markup of any of our products. Plus, one of the ladies offered to set up a spa at her husband's bank. I'm developing a real specialty in bank spas. I've had two at the Edison Savings and Loan already. I'm gonna see if Mary Martha will set up a spa at Sinclair's Temps."

"What about Daddy's office? Did you find anything useful on Big Doodle?"

"Oh. That didn't go so well."

"How do you mean?" I asked a suddenly quiet Pammy. "You didn't find anything?"

"The problem is what I did find, girl."

CHAPTER 13: In the Thick of Things

"I went for the money files first," Pammy said of her sleuthing during the spa for Mother.

"That's smart." I nodded to myself on the rocking train. "Follow the money."

"You see, our group was small. I don't want to jump to conclusions, but I'm afraid your mama had trouble getting people to come. All the buzz about the drug bust, it should've drawn ladies to the spa like flies to a dead possum—everybody wants to brag on how they know more about a scandal than anyone else. But when it's really bad, people don't want to get too near, afraid the stink will rub off on them."

I said nothing. Interrupting Pammy would only make it take longer.

"I knew my time would be short. I set the ladies up under the GG Gel Masks and turned on soothing music, to drown out any noise I might make. Lord, Lucinda, your mama could use some work on her stair treads. Anyway, you were right about your dad keeping everything neat and organized. In the front of the first drawer was a file: 'Tax Returns, 5 Years.'"

"Okay."

"Follow me on this, Lucinda."

"I am."

"In 2007, your dad listed income of $89,000."

"Okay."

"The next year—"

"2008. The year he died."

"The return listed about $40,000 in income, give or take."

"That makes sense. Daddy died in April, so he would've had about half a year's worth of income."

"Right. But that year included a charitable deduction."

"So?"

"A charitable deduction of $500,000."

"That's not possible."

"I saw it, Lucinda."

"No way, Pammy. My mother said they didn't even have any savings. Where would Daddy get that kind of money to give away?"

"Cash income he didn't want to report?" Pammy guessed. "Gambling, that sort of thing?"

"You mean drugs?"

The question hung in the air.

"Okay. Let's back up. Maybe he got an inheritance? Or sold some property?"

"No, Mother would have told me if they'd come into that kind of money."

Then I remembered walking into the hospital room, three weeks after my previous, laughing visit, only to find my dad hooked up to machines, the beep, swish, and gurgle making clear what my mother hadn't.

"Did the tax return say who he'd given the money to?"

"Etcetera."

"You mean, all the rest?"

"As in 'ETC' followed by 'See Attachment.' He must not have wanted to list it all on the skinny line they give you. I was flipping to the back of the return for the attachment when your mother's boyfriend came clomping up the stairs, singing some old country song about a dude shooting Billy."

Clyde, interfering as usual.

"Sorry, girl. I know you wanted me to find something on Big Doodle, not on your dad."

I ran my finger in the groove along the train's window. I didn't know how much I could ask of Pammy. We were still friends but based mostly on old high school ties. Oh, what the hell—Pammy would let me know if I overstepped.

"Could you use your bank connections to find out what other income Daddy might have had. You know, where the money came from?"

"I love you, babe, but I'm not going to jail for you."

"Yeah, there is that," I agreed. Probably not smart for Pammy to do something sketchy, given the brushes she'd had with the law. None of them were her fault—only senile old Mrs. Thompson would schedule a spa, forget she'd done it, and call the police on Pammy when she found her jimmying the lock to let herself and the spa women inside.

"You okay?" Pammy asked, concerned.

"I don't know." Hadn't Mother said the Feds had hinted at "money changing hands"? If the drug laws were as strong as Skippy Van Zant said, the Feds had probably already pulled Daddy's tax returns. In this new light, my idea that Daddy's problems were the result of my stupid condolence message seemed terribly naïve. And here I was hurtling on the train to confront Big Doodle. "I might've made a bad decision."

"You've been that way ever since your dad died. It's like you've got decision making dyslexia. If the smart thing lies in one direction, you take off in the exact opposite direction. I wouldn't mention it, but you brought it up," she hastened to add.

"Thanks anyway, Pam."

"Glad to help." After assuring me she was there if I needed her, she hung up.

What I needed was beyond anyone's help.

Could the Chicken Palace have legitimately earned Daddy half a million dollars? Or was the "chicken money" the same as the "chicken medicine" my Poppa Dean used to keep in his garage. "Chicken medicine," he had told me when I asked what was in the Mason jars. But when I asked my daddy why Poppa Dean's chickens were so sick that they had to take medicine, Daddy guffawed. "Chickens don't drink that 'medicine.' Your Poppa Dean does. That's his moonshine."

I watched as a woman in the next row tucked a Chihuahua-shaped pillow under her neck. The man with the mirrored sunglasses glanced at her, too, then turned back around. If Daddy actually had been a drug dealer, surely he only did it for a good reason, maybe expenses for his illness—maybe when he first started having nagging back pain, he'd known something terrible was wrong, and he'd begun planning for the end. Or maybe the Feds were right, and he took the money to buy the fairy-tale house. Or maybe his "natural" chicken methods weren't taking off, and the business was short on cash. Or, worse, maybe he did it because he wanted to make sure Mother and I were taken care of after he was gone. After all, Wert the mule breeder couldn't have much money. What if Daddy turned his back on his principles so Mother and I could be happy?

My mind kept hopping around worse than a squirrel treed by a hunting dog. One minute I told myself I was jumping to conclusions. The money, the insistent Feds, the purchase of a house we never could have afforded—it proved nothing. The next minute I felt even more naïve for making up a myth of an altruistic, drug-dealing Daddy.

Surely Mother would know where the money came from, but did I have the guts to ask her? We'd been totally off kilter since Daddy had died, as if we didn't know who to be without him balancing us out. We were too much the same, her and me. My scrawny legs to her scrawny legs, my scrambled decision-making to her scrambled decision-making. My snippiness to hers. My Lucinda Mae to her Rita Rae. Hesitant to talk to each other about the things that mattered, Mother even afraid to say *I love you.*

When the conductor called out, "Williston!" I yanked my backpack from beneath my seat. It snagged on the footrest, breaking the strap.

"Great." I bundled the bag into my arms and joined the exiting line. With my sight thus impaired, I tried to navigate the narrow opening into the stairwell. I miscalculated and banged into the corner, bouncing into the woman behind me—we were a tight-packed line with everyone getting off at Williston for a three-hour layover. The woman had her own burdens—including a rolling cooler—which I tripped over, landing on my ass.

Righting myself, I tromped down the stairwell and emerged onto the platform where I kicked the yellow stool that was supposed to help, not hinder, your de-boarding. The plastic stool skittered down the concrete.

"Life goes that way sometimes." The woman with the cooler stopped to watch the tumbling stool. "Don't you worry about it."

I smiled weakly, shivering in the darkening cold. The train station resembled something from an old Western movie, standing all alone in the empty landscape. The man with the ponytail and mirror sunglasses leaned against a post, taking advantage of the break to smoke a cigarette. Where the platform met the grass, ice nestled. The wind blew grit in my eye, and I winced.

I was in a snowstorm of white people. Every person around me—family, friends, and neighbors collecting homecoming passengers—was white. It had been getting whiter and whiter since we left Chicago, but now I was in a veritable whiteout. I couldn't help it; it made me nervous. Being from Mississippi, whenever you walked into an all-white room or an all-white country club—or the state of North Dakota—you had to think: Who's keeping all the Black folk out?

The only African American in sight was the kind woman beside me, rocking on her heels. She was a large woman, her curves packed tight inside her skin. "Sorry about this cooler tripping you up. I told Darius it was gonna cause trouble."

I must have looked as off-kilter as I felt, because when the woman's ride pulled up, she asked, "Are you gonna be all right?"

Her voice was buttery smooth, like Pooh's cream cheese pound cake, warm and soothing.

I could take my ex-husband re-entering marital life with a girl who was much more sophisticated than me. I could take the possibility I'd screwed up by leaving St.

Paul and would never, ever get to know Augie Green any better. I could even take the possibility I had inadvertently sic'ed the Feds on my mom. What I couldn't take—not when I'd learned the daddy I was traveling cross-country to defend had a hidden stash of money that no one had ever mentioned—was someone being kind to me. Tears sprang to my eyes.

"What is it?"

"My daddy died." I reverted to the bedrock problem.

"That'll do it to you every time." She shook her head. "Makes you flounder around like a drowning person, grabbing ahold of anything that floats by. You're apt to take everyone down with you. You're lucky I'm a member of the Heavenly Christ Holy Temple of God, where we consider ourselves God's angels on earth. I'm going to take a chance on you." She nodded at the idling car. "That's my brother Darius picking me up. You need a ride somewhere?"

"I need to go home."

"I didn't sign up for that, not as far down South as you come from."

"I'll wait for the next train."

"If you're talking about heading back to Chicago, there isn't a 'next train,' not until the train comes back through here."

Wiping the tears from my cheeks, I set my knapsack on the platform.

"Listen." The woman rearranged her luggage, getting a better grip. "You don't need to sit there. You come with me. We're about to have a celebration. It'll wipe that frown from your face."

"I made this decision. It was sort of sudden, and I thought it was brilliant. You know, I wanted to try a new approach to life. Yeah, it sounds like typical Lucinda"—I wagged my head back and forth—"changing my mind again, but new information keeps popping up and biting me on the butt, things I don't want to know. Lord!" The idea of my daddy being a millionaire drug lord landed on me like a ton of bricks, and I plopped down on the knapsack. Maybe I could live with Daddy doing something criminal, but I simply could not stand it if he'd gone against everything he believed in because he was worried about Mother and me. "I need to quit this foolishness and go home."

"No one's trying to talk you out of going home. All I'm saying is, in the meantime, no point in sitting here by yourself, stewing in your own juices. It'll be night soon. Come with us."

She smiled so encouragingly I couldn't say no.

*

In my short time on Earth, I've sung "Kumbaya" at Baptist summer camp. I've danced in the moonlight around a tiny Stonehenge I built in my family's backyard. In fifth grade, I dipped a splinter into a glass of water to see if the cutest boy in class loved me back. In eleventh grade, I packed peanut butter and jelly sandwiches and went on a walkabout around Johnson Lake. In my cinderblock dorm room, I ate mushrooms and traveled with Carlos Castaneda and the faithful Don Juan, paperback style. After Daddy died, I ignored Mother's claim that the summer solstice wasn't Christian and went with Erick to a concert where the jagged music made me weep. I've celebrated the Day of the Dead (with Pammy); I've been to a foot washing (with Pooh). I believe the little Slavic children when they say they've seen Mother Mary. I've had a Greek god or two (call it a weakness), and Erick and I laid on top of the Choctaw Indian mound on the Natchez Trace in the nighttime where we counted the silver stars. I've seen the Father/Mother God behind the sun and Jesus Christ over my daddy's ever-loving grave. But I'd never had a religious experience like the one I had at the Heavenly Christ Holy Temple of God.

*

There was not a cross in sight. Not on the altar because there wasn't any altar. Not in the stained glass windows because there weren't any stained glass windows.

What there was, was a choir. "We've got new robes," Coletta bragged.

And fine robes they were, blue with lightning bolts zinging down the front. The choir stood on risers, three high. The risers spread the width of the stage. In the center, the soloist blazed in a red embroidered coat, red silk pants, and a red and gold fez. A man at the corner of the stage sat poised over an electric organ. All the guys on the back row of the choir were bald.

Coletta and I settled ourselves on a pew down front. As the congregation filtered in, their perfume arrived too, reminding me of Pooh's country Methodist church where the women wore rose-scented talcum powder and rose-scented toilet water and rose-scented hand lotion, until roses filled the church and the pink light streaming through the rose-colored windows deepened to blood red.

I was squenched into the pew.

We were going to have a good crowd this evening.

I wasn't the only white person in the group, but I was definitely the exception. I would not have been surprised if every Heavenly Christ Holy Angel in a five-state area had gravitated to that box of a church. My guess was that we were honoring the late Dr. Martin Luther King, Jr., who'd been shot so many years ago that day. Later in the service, when the pastor began recognizing people from Sturgis, South Dakota, and Billings, Montana, welcoming them to the "I Have a Dream" celebration, I realized I was right on all accounts.

"Little brother looks nervous." Coletta pointed to Darius, who had picked us up at the station. He was front and center in the back row—bald.

"Does he live in North Dakota?"

"Yep. Little brother had to be different."

The man at the organ dropped his arms, and Darius's voice rang out. "Sanctify us, Lord." Several women on the front riser softly tingled tambourines. "And glorify Your name," they trilled.

The women in the middle row were slowly clapping their hands, setting the beat. When the soloist wailed into "John the Revelator," the women raised their fists into the air. Then the soloist did a throat holler in the tradition of the great Mahalia Jackson, and we were off.

I'd been on stage once with the Mississippi Mass Choir in front of two thousand swaying festival fans. A friend of Pammy's had gotten me the tickets. The Mass Choir was heaven itself, me wrapped inside, the Holy Spirit zipping through the air. But that didn't hold a candle to the Heavenly Christ Holy Temple of God choir.

Coletta whooped, and the woman next to me jangled—her clunky jewelry was so big I could've taken the coin earrings and the medallion necklace and worn them as a bikini. Her long jacket swirled with the colors of the rainbow, shot through with a golden thread. She spread her feet, improving her stance. In front of us, an old man in a black suit stood stiff as a funeral board.

I'd removed my Cardinals ball cap and rested it on my lap. I was hoping my blue jeans were camouflaged by my baby-doll top with violets and puckered smocking. It didn't matter. No one seemed to care what I had on.

The choir was swaying, the bottom row swaying to the left, the middle row swaying to the right, alternating, breaking apart and snapping back together like magnets. When the singing entered the Valley of the Shadow, the women crouched low. "Don't look back," the soloist exhorted. But maybe she was singing about Peter walking on the water with Jesus and was saying, "Don't look down." I don't know. To me it sounded like "Don't look back," but we each hear God with our own peculiar ears.

"Yeah, yeah, yeah, yeah," the women's high voices rang.

"All right, all right, all right," the men's low voices conceded to the power.

The electric organ slid in between the cracks of the singing and the whole tapestry of shaking, thrumming praise held until the air itself vibrated. Darius threw back his head and shouted, "My God! My God!" and the divider between choir and congregation melted away.

We were on our feet, swaying and dancing, shoulders colliding, hips bumping. The woman beside me clanked, her joy—and her jewelry—unleashed. When her elbow hit mine, she grabbed my wrist, shaking my arm to the heavens, our hands reaching for the Almighty, higher and higher. "King of kings!" The soloist hollered, and the congregation exploded: "Lord of lords!" We shouted and released our tears from their three-day prison, joy flowing onto our trembling cheeks.

The everlasting "Glory, Amen! Glory, Amen!" echoed through the sanctuary when the choir began peeling off the risers. They were stripping off their blue robes as they split and descended the steps into the aisles. Their white cotton gowns shone like sanctified nighties. "He's the One." The breath of the congregation swelled with the marching, invading choir. "No one. No one." Hands fluttering, tambourines shaking, the choir's throbbing voices washed into us, their heads held high, confident in the glory of their Lord. As they mingled into our midst and surged forward, the congregation waded from the pews and joined the procession.

The woman next to me barged forth like a bull, her hand still clamped onto my wrist, and suddenly I was swimming in the choir. Nothing could have prevented it. We were a flood of human bodies flowing with the Spirit, going where God led us.

Seems He was leading us outside.

An old man held the door, his turkey head bobbing. We shuffled past, the choir and me and the woman, squinting at the sparkling stars.

We were making a beeline to a cow pond.

Through the rough grass we processed, the choir leading the group, clapping and singing, the congregation wadded up like spent tissue behind us. Darius shouted, "Come on, Jesus!" and headed toward the scooped-out pond.

That water had to be cold as shit.

When the first of the choir waded in, rippling waves in the moonlight, I knew it was come-to-Jesus time.

What was I doing here? Taking advantage, dipping my toe into the hospitality of the holy, scamming someone else's salvation, skating on the feel-good gush of God? Had I meant it when I vowed to quit running away and instead run full-tilt toward the future? Or was I going to let the first setback on my quest throw me off track? Now was my chance to prove I was willing to plunge in. Take on the bracing cold of unexpected revelations, risk the unpleasant squish of a muddy bottom.

The man behind me nudged my shoulder. "Go on, girl. Step on out."

It was time to follow my heart into whatever new place it might lead, even if that new place was a cow pond in Williston, North Dakota, still rimmed with gleaming cracks of ice.

It was cold as shit.

My baby-doll top stuck to me like plastic wrap.

My jeans sagged down my tailbone.

Everyone was shouting "Alleluia! Alleluia!" as Darius cradled the baptismal candidate in his arms.

Everyone but me.

I was counting, "One Mississippi, two Mississippi, three Mississippi," trying to distract myself from the numbing cold. When I breathed out, "Oh, Sweet Jesus," I meant it.

Then the candidate was gone, her head and body and riotous soul lost inside the dark water. Darius lifted his eyes to heaven, crying, "Praise be to God!" and He redeemed her into the nighttime air.

Everyone clapped and hugged, and we sloshed our soggy bodies out of that frigging pond.

Back on land, the congregation produced towels and wrapped us in the warmth. Obviously, they'd done this before. From somewhere a coyote howled.

My teeth were chattering, but I was ecstatic. I felt it deep in my bones: I was doing the right thing. I was going to find Big Doodle and confront him. It was all going to work out fine—for me, for him, for my daddy's memory.

Coletta appeared and slipped a cup of coffee into my hands. She could have been an angel in her fluffy sweats. I threw a big old hug around her neck before I remembered I was dripping wet.

"Now, now." She backed away but kept a firm hold on my fingertips. "You a small town gal who needed a dunking to make your soul feel better."

"How'd you know I was small town?" A water drop fell from my nose, but I didn't want to release her hand to wipe it away.

She jiggled my fingers. "Don't you worry about where you come from. You're in the thick of things now."

She didn't know the half of it.

CHAPTER 14: Legal Bull Hockey

My experience in the pond hadn't exactly worked a conversion, but it had convinced me I should stay the course. I might not be able to fix everything, but I could fix my own mistakes, clear up the confusion over my message, and hope the rest of it had its own solution. I changed from my wet clothes and wadded them into a plastic bag. Coletta dropped me back at the night-darkened station. The train was still there on layover. I'd be able to make it to San Francisco and back in time for Erick's show.

*

I hadn't been back on the train five minutes when my phone rang. I was surprised—pleasantly—to hear Augie's voice.

"Hey, *cher*. Where y'at?"

"What?" I thought he'd asked me where I was, which was a question I didn't intend to answer.

"Sorry. New Orleans talk. What are you doing?"

"Nothing," I answered because I couldn't think of an honest answer that didn't include, *Oh, I just participated in a baptism in North Dakota.*

"I was making dinner reservations. How does tomorrow evening sound?"

"Tomorrow? Mrs. Gminski has something special planned for tomorrow, honoring Erick, you know. What about Friday night?" I crossed my fingers—if I remembered correctly, that was the night of Augie's sports banquet.

"Naw. That night I'll be eating rubber chicken and listening to athletes say, 'Uh, I couldn't uh done it witout my man Jimmy.'"

"I guess it'll have to be Saturday after Erick's show." I pushed it to our last night in St. Paul.

"Okay. Seven o'clock?"

"Make it eight. I don't know what time Erick's show airs, but that should give us plenty of leeway."

"Do you have any special requests? Italian or Chinese, maybe? Pretty sure we can't find any etouffee up this way."

"I'm sure whatever you pick will be perfect." I sounded as robotic as a Stepford Wife, but it was dang hard to talk to someone when you couldn't mention any of the important things happening in your life.

"You still want to go to dinner, right? You don't have other plans?"

"Heavens, no. I mean heavens, yes. I do want to go to dinner, and I don't have other plans. I can't wait to see you again. I'm hoping I'll have good news to share," I added, because it was almost genetically impossible for me to keep a secret.

"Good news? You want to tell me now?"

"Nope. It can wait."

"Yeah, you right. Good news can always wait. So, how are you entertaining yourself while Erick's becoming a star?"

"Oh, you know. Listening to gospel music. The great Mahalia Jackson. The famous Coletta and Darius."

I needed to stop talking.

"Okay," he said. "I'll make the reservations. See you soon."

"I'm really looking forward to it," I gushed, grateful to tell the truth about something.

The phone call reminded me that I'd never decided if I should call Big Doodle and tell him I was on my way to Chicken Headquarters. The truth was, if I couldn't trust that Big Doodle wanted to see me, all was lost anyway. So I called, working my way through several options (Network Administration and National Sales) and left a message with Customer Service, wondering if anyone had ever had such an intimate relationship with a phone system.

Later, I was trying to calm myself into sleep mode when Hadley, the conductor, stopped by to tell me Olaf and Sven jokes. I didn't know if Olaf and Sven jokes were polite or not because I was in foreign territory, but I listened attentively. Hadley delivered the punch line— "It did last year!"—and glanced at my noggin. "Nice hairdo," he said and walked off.

With no time to shampoo, I'd braided my bangs on each side, but because my hair was short, they didn't lie flat but kind of stuck out, off-kilter from the interrupted hair trimming—better to look crazy than nasty. My mother, of course, would've been mortified if she could see me now. "Lucinda!" she'd say. "What if you see someone you know? What will they think?"

I picked up the fan Coletta had given me—a hand fan emblazoned "Heavenly Christ Holy Temple of God" with a giant "Key to Salvation" printed on the back because the fans were sponsored by a locksmith. I lazily fanned the air. The fan reminded me of when I was a little girl at my first formal piano recital. Mother

166

had left Daddy in charge of getting me ready. She'd laid out my recital dress, showed him how to tie the bow. He couldn't mess it up. Mother was in the audience fanning away the heat when I emerged from behind the curtain. Wearing my taffeta dress, and my cowboy boots.

I wore my cowboy boots all the time, which is what I told my mortified Mother afterwards. "But not for the recital," she wailed, her eyes glued on the other little girls, serenely sipping punch in their starchy ribbons and patent leather Mary Janes.

Daddy winked. "You knocked 'em dead, sport."

That's the way we'd been before Daddy died. Mother trying to pat me into the shape of a proper Southern lady, which was annoying, but tolerable, because Daddy was on the other side, winking at me. Without Daddy, Mother and I had wound up lopsided. We needed to find a new way.

Maybe I would take the fan back home to Mother. She'd like the fan. She would enjoy the story of my baptism in the North Dakota pond. She might act scandalized, but she'd laugh later, telling Pooh about it. Maybe if I could sort out this chicken mess, I could sort out things with Mother too.

*

I woke shortly before Seattle when Hadley the conductor paraded down the aisle, informing us it was breakfast time in the buffet. Feeling as scuzzy as the inside of a drain, I decamped and spread the train schedules onto a buffet table, trying to connect the dots. A woman with a blabbering baby sat at the table next to me. The woman was stuffing pureed green mess into the baby's mouth. She and the baby smelled of milk and yeast and closeness. While the baby burbled and the mother cooed, I studied the train routes.

I was focusing on my primary question: how do you get to there from here?

The first folder showed the route I was traveling across the top of the United States, ending in Seattle. There, I'd switch trains and board the *Coast Starlight* to Emeryville, which was actually San Francisco, but for some reason they called the stop Emeryville.

At Emeryville/San Francisco, I had several options to get back to Minnesota. I could retrace my exact route, or, after my meeting with Big Doodle, I could stay on the *Coast Starlight* to Los Angeles then take the *Sunset Limited* to San Antonio and on to New Orleans. The *City of New Orleans* would carry me back to Chicago and on to Erick in Minnesota, same route I'd already taken. That was a terrible route.

On the other hand, I could get off in San Francisco, meet with Big Doodle, then board the *California Zephyr* to Chicago. The *Zephyr*'s thick red line zippered right through the middle of the United States, tracing its route across America: from California to Nevada to Colorado; then on to Nebraska, Iowa, and Illinois. It was the quickest route possible, assuring I would get back in time for Erick's show.

I sighed, stretched, and checked my watch. I had approximately twenty-two hours to San Francisco. In between, I had the glorious scenery of the Pacific Coast. Or maybe I'd take a nap.

The phone rang.

I let it ring a couple of times because I knew it was my mother, and I was deciding whether to be straight with her about what I was up to. Sometimes being straight with Rita Rae crooked things up even more.

"Hi, Mother. I'm in Washington."

"Washington, DC? St. Paul is in Minnesota."

"And I am in the state of Washington." I peered out the window. "I think, anyway. It's hard to tell with the West."

"Lucinda, what are you doing?"

"You don't have to worry, Mother. I'm going to clear all this up."

"Clear what up?"

"I'm going to talk to Big Doodle."

"Do you think I haven't tried calling Bennie Dayton? It's impossible to get through to him."

"Tell me about it. That's why I'm headed out there."

Silence. "You're what?"

"I'm going to see Big Doodle at his office in San Francisco to get him to clear Daddy's name."

"Lucinda, I don't want you to do that."

"You're the one who told me to come find him. I thought you'd be glad!"

"I've changed my mind."

"I can handle it," I said with more conviction than I felt.

"Deep down, Bennie's heart is good, but he can be slippery."

"I will be fine. I'm on a quest."

"You're on a misguided mission, and you don't know what you're getting yourself into. I *worry* about you, Lucinda."

There it was again. Mother's standard line for whenever I wanted to do something exciting and she was losing the argument. At her wit's end, she would exclaim, "I'm worried about you!" That was what she'd shouted when I'd first wanted to try the rope swing over Bear Creek. Daddy held me aloft. Mother waited on the bank, covering her eyes when she couldn't stand it any longer. I gripped the coarse, knotted rope, about to launch into the wild blue yonder, when Daddy asked, "Cindy Lou, are your eyes closed? Open your eyes, Punkin. There's no point if your eyes are closed."

"Lucinda?" my mother said into the phone, and I opened my eyes.

"Mother, I'm worried about *you*."

Silence. "How so?"

"Did Daddy come into extra money before he died? Or did y'all have money I didn't know about?"

She was quiet. "You need to quit this foolishness and come home."

"Tell me what's going on."

"I was worried about the money, and I sent you off on a wild goose chase. But it's gotten totally out of hand, that's what's going on."

"What is etcetera?"

"Etcetera? It's an abbreviation that means 'and other similar things.'"

"What is the etcetera on Daddy's income tax return?"

"Come back to Edison. We can talk then."

"That's not an option."

"Lucinda."

"Mother."

A standoff.

I checked my watch. In less than twenty-four hours, I'd be in San Francisco. Two hours later, Chicken Headquarters opened. Give or take an hour with Big Doodle, plus a cushion. "I'll be done in thirty-six hours. I'll head home then."

"I'll give you thirty-six hours." Rita Rae sniffed. "Then I'm coming after you."

When she hung up, I immediately did an internet search. My request for info on "etcetera charity" gave me bizarre results (including a fundraiser for the movie "The King and I.") But then it occurred to me the charity might actually be "etc," and Pammy only read it as etcetera. That search was a bust too ... until I added "chicken" to it.

ETC was a charity for the Ethical Treatment of Chickens. The internet had little information on the charity other than a handful of homemade videos of kids pretending to be chicken terrorists. A random reference to "Mississippi" led me to believe ETC might have something to do with my home state. I kept clicking and discovered the Ethical Treatment of Chickens was a Mississippi corporation. A business info site showed its basic facts.

Registered agent: Skippy Van Zant.

Registered address: our house on Main Street.

Okay. That was weird, but not that surprising. I could definitely see my daddy founding a charity to protect chickens ... then donating a half a million dollars to his own charity. Money I'd had no idea he had.

I punched off the website. I knew nothing about criminal activity, and as far as I was concerned "money laundering" was only a term for mob movies. But if someone wanted to launder funds, say from an illegal drug operation, what better way to do it than hide the money in your own chicken charity?

*

I was in the scenic car with its glass bubble top. The bubble top was designed so you could gaze at the lovely, craggy scenery. I was scarfing potato chips, sizing up my fellow passengers. How many people on board this very train were secret criminals engaged in nefarious activity? The woman in the caftan, for sure. She couldn't quit cracking her joints. She popped each knuckle twice then slipped off her mules and cracked her toes. If she unhooked her bra and cracked her ribs, I was gonna run screaming from the train.

I checked my watch: 8:30 p.m. My latest paperback lay ignored by my elbow. Darkened fields flew past the window, then random houses, then another open stretch. During that cycle, a lifetime of thoughts had clacked through my brain—was my dad a secret chicken terrorist financing guerrilla chicken warfare? Was he producing underground chicken videos using fake chicken blood? Hadn't I said something similar to Augie—the only illegal thing I could ever see my dad doing was protecting helpless chickens?

Chomping a potato chip, I rechecked my watch. 8:33 p.m. In those three minutes, I'd aged a hundred years. By the time we arrived in San Francisco, I would be old as Methuselah. Or stark raving mad. Or both.

Thank God Rahtz lumbered aboard the train.

CHAPTER 15: "Lif Wif Abandon"

When Rahtz first walked into the club car, I was reminded that your nose keeps growing your whole life. Rahtz's eyes were slightly crossed, as though the heavy nose had cratered them. And it didn't take much effort to see where the doctor's forceps had yanked him kicking and screaming into the world. His long head was indented in the middle like a peanut.

The head pinching had taken place a while back, at least fifty years. His hair had receded to its new-baby phase, a fuzzy tuft front and center. His gait was rolling, like was favoring a hip. I think it was the roll that gave the impression of lumbering. It wasn't his size. Rahtz was no bigger than Thumbelina.

He paused at my side. He stared at my head.

I'd forgotten it was done up in braids.

"Aren't you just the queen bee?"

His greeting was actually more "Ahnt thew chust the queen bee?" A mush-mouth kind of talking but cute. He hiked his satchel in the air for emphasis, reminding me in his baggy suit of an old-fashioned company man traveling on the train.

I swept the empty potato chip bags from the seat beside me.

He arranged himself onto the cushion, laying his satchel on the tiddlywink table. His feet swung two inches off the floor.

He turned to me. "Haight Ashbury your destination? Or perhaps the Mission District?"

"I'm not sure." Who knew if downtown San Francisco was anything other than 'downtown'?

"The train is a miracle, is it not? My maternal grandparents rode the train to see Niagara Falls in 1934. It was frozen solid."

I was tongue-tied, trying to think of something witty to say.

He waited. And waited. And rose to leave. "You know what they say: there are two hundred ninety-three ways to change a dollar."

I blurted out the first thing that came to mind. "Did you know a fluke is a worm? And ringworm isn't a worm at all. It's a fungus?"

This made him pause mid-gathering.

"I'm reading this book, see." I brandished my paperback. "All my life, I've been saying 'It's a fluke.' Or 'My life is lousy.' Then I read a book about a Civil War soldier trying to make it home, and I find out we say lousy because once upon a time soldiers were crawling in lice and the singular of lice is louse. A garage sale paperback knows more than I do. That makes me feel ignorant. It makes me feel *lousy*."

I thumped the book onto the table.

Rahtz settled back down. "One does live and learn, doesn't one?"

"I'm tired of learning. This trip has flat worn me out with new information."

His crossed eyes blinked, his long mouth opened. A string of saliva stretched from his upper lip to his bottom tooth. The spit glistened silvery in the cave of his mouth. I waited, transfixed. What wisdom was this oracle about to offer?

"Life is a lengthy trip of solving for *x*."

"What?"

"Each one of us has a goal in life. Let's call it h for happiness. We have certain factors that can help us achieve our goal, our knowns. Call them ys. The problem is, life is constantly throwing new things at us, little xs. The secret is to discard all the xs that do not help us achieve our happiness goal. Will this new piece of information, when added to our current y, equal h? For example, am I any happier saying louse than I am saying lices? If not." He tossed his hand. "Out the window with it. I suspect you are a woman who can readily make such a distinction."

After that, Rahtz and I were fast friends.

*

Rahtz was an aeronautical engineer. He taught aeronautical engineering to college kids. He was working on a Masters in Space Operations at the Aeronautical Engineering School in Colorado Springs. Four times a year he had to actually show up on campus. This, he said, was not an imposition, riding over the Rockies on his way to conquering space.

He told me his name, Lazarus Rahtz Templeton, which "lead to the neighborhood sobriquet 'Dead Rat.'" I told him I was Lucinda Mae Watkins, and a JuCo football player with a body like a sandbag once flipped back the covers and growled, "If I'd wanted to see a skeleton, I could've exhumed something." I also told him how my marriage had cratered after six months and how Clyde quizzed Mother at the supper table, testing her on the habits of animals living on the Serengeti, then clicked his cheek and said "Gotcha!" when she missed. I did not tell him how I'd met Augie or how Coletta had taken me under her wing because, so far, we were only bonding over bad things.

175

It was late afternoon, and I opened another bag of potato chips. Rahtz underlined something important in his book with a squeaky yellow highlighter. I sat back, trying to add up how much money I had spent on train tickets, performing the calculations in my head because I was afraid to see them on paper.

In the middle of the club car was an ATM. The entire trip, when I'd needed cash, I'd been tapping into these ATMs. Soon, I was going to have to transfer money from my savings account, where Sonny Floyd's monthly payments were deposited, into my checking account or else the ATM would be scolding, "Insufficient funds for the desired transaction."

The bank officer at the Edison Savings and Loan who handled my account, a man named Gunther Armstrong, probably would make the transfer for me, but you never could tell. Gunther wasn't more than three years older than I was, but he acted like a clucking old maid when it came to the account. I swear, he thought I was going to haul off and loot the account first chance I got. He mailed me complicated bank statements each month which, given my current confusion over my family's finances, I probably should've read.

"No use living with regret." I crumpled the empty chip bag and looked around for a trash can. It was over by the ATM.

"Lif wif abandon," Rahtz said, by which he meant, live with abandon.

He squeaked his highlighter across the page.

As I walked to the trash can, the train swayed, lurched, and recovered. Much to my surprise, I didn't miss a beat.

I had developed train legs.

I dropped the crumpled chip bag into the trash. It joined about a hundred other crumpled chip bags, only half of them mine. On my way back to the seat, a woman glanced up and smiled. Everyone on the train was so pleasant. Maybe if we shoved all the people in the world on a train together, all the crazy stuff would stop happening, like wars and famine and people putting sugar on their grits.

Back at my seat, I didn't want to sit down again. "Are you interested in taking a walk around the train?"

Rahtz slid sideways from his chair. "Like old-timey people strolling on gravel paths in the park." He looked left, right. His gaze lit on the staircase to the lower level. "Downstairs. Let's see what lies below."

I didn't tell him the lower level was the source of my chip supply. Who was to say he wouldn't find something interesting down there that I'd missed?

Ever the gentleman, Rahtz descended first. The stairs were metal, the walls high and close. We could have been in a submarine from an old World War II movie, where the hero has claustrophobia but he can't tell anyone or they'll kick him out of the service and the service is his life because he wants to prove he's a real man and being a submariner is the only way he knew to do that.

Halfway down, the staircase turned at a small wedge-shaped landing. When I arrived there, a man's head popped from the bottom of the staircase. His noggin was big as a cauliflower, his nose long as a carrot. Just as I decided we had a vegetable salad as a traveling companion, a heavy boot hit the top stair behind us.

"We're about to be the ham in the sandwich." I envisioned tiny Rahtz and me smushed between our fellow passengers.

"No, it's fine. We are in a logjam!" Rahtz called over his shoulder. "You can continue down and no one will be able to move. You must halt. You." He spoke to the salad man. "If you come up, we will all four be in the narrow staircase together and nobody will go anywhere. You must give way."

"'Lo?" the vegetable salad said, dense as the cabbage he looked like.

The man descending the steps stopped. He grabbed the sides of the staircase and bent, staring at us.

It was the man in the mirrored sunglasses. A black mustache curved toward his chin. His arms draped like a vulture. "What y'all up to?"

I wanted to ask him what type of man wore his sunglasses in a staircase on the train. But maybe he was blind, so I said, "Not much. You?"

"Hunting a hot dog is all." He stared at Rahtz then slid his gaze to me. "With chips."

I poked Rahtz. "Let's get going."

"We are descending!" Rahtz called down the stairs. "Make way!"

The vegetable salad retreated, disappearing around the corner. The man in the sunglasses emerged into the small, low-ceilinged canteen behind us, his steel-toed boots leading the way.

"Y'all making me work for my hot dog." He smiled, but there was no warmth in it.

"Let me." Rahtz retrieved his wallet from his back pocket and addressed the clerk. "May I have your finest hot dog?"

"We only got one kind of dog," the clerk replied.

"I'll take that." Rahtz accepted the sleeved dog. "Relish on the dog and a side of chips."

"You dress your own dog." The clerk added a packet of relish and bag of chips to Rahtz's bundle.

"For you," Rahtz handed the dog and chips to the man in sunglasses whose smile was frozen in place.

"That dog for me?"

"And the chips. If you want."

"I do want." The man accepted the offering, and nodding at me, he disappeared back up the stairs.

"That was strange."

"It's my experience that when someone has ticked you off, you should force yourself to do something kind for them. It relieves the anger and opens the way for them to be nice to you in return."

"I mean he was strange. I've seen him on the train before."

"Obviously on his way to the same place you are."

"I don't trust him."

"Excellent. The only people who can hurt you are the ones you trust."

That wasn't a particularly comforting thought, given my current situation with Augie. "What if someone basically said, trust me—there's something about myself you probably won't like?"

"Do you mind if we sit? The incident on the stairs has squelched my desire to explore." Rahtz slipped into one of the two booths in front of the canteen. "What exact situation have you got in mind?"

I told him about Augie.

"So a stranger on a train told you he was keeping important information from you and yet you still trusted him?"

"You could say he was a stranger on a train but Augie was—"

"Different?"

"We just—"

"Clicked?"

I shot him an annoyed look, and he settled back, resuming a demeanor suited to the logician he was.

"We'd only started to get to know each other...before I left."

"Set that aside for a minute, we'll get back to it," he said, and I could almost see him standing at a chalkboard drawing parentheses around it. "Let's examine why you are, some would say, irrationally, trusting this man. Was he good-looking?"

"Drop dead gorgeous. A little girl on the train mistook him for a movie star." I cut my description short, afraid my gushing might make Rahtz feel bad since he was not exactly movie-star material.

But he straightened in his seat, the tiny professor.

"And ... how should I put this?" He covered his mouth with his palm.

"Did we have sex?"

"Exactly." He held up a policeman's palm. "Don't get too graphic."

"We did have sex."

"My inquiry being, is it possible the sex impacted your view of the man?"

Did it ever. His hard chest, his ropy arm muscles taut as he arched above me, his blue eyes locked onto mine.

"And that is when you fell for him?"

I considered. "No. Earlier. When he asked me about my mom and dad. Then we danced in the moonlight." On the Milwaukee streets, when Augie had sung "Moon River" and two-stepped across the asphalt, the hem of his white dinner jacket flapping.

"Sounds fun. Or at least seductive."

I chewed my lip. Could I have fallen in love with Augie's white dinner jacket, the same way I fell for Stirling's Italian loafers? Surely not. Augie was honest—he wouldn't even sign the little girl's autograph request. And his touch was so giving. And he had a cute accent when he chuckled, "Life's too short not to laugh, *cher*."

Maybe I had jumped into things a little quickly with Augie because Life had been so shitty lately, but Rahtz's analysis didn't feel right. I tried out one of the word games Erick's sisters had played at the dinner table. "Your prescription is invalid for this invalid. Erick's twin sisters taught me that. They're smart as whips."

"That's on the internet. 'This number is making me number.' Kids in class say it all the time."

Well. Maybe the twins weren't smart as whips. Which made me wonder if I had a lick of sense.

When I was quiet too long, Rahtz said, "You mentioned a lousy ex-husband. Did sex cloud your first impression of him too?"

"I was in the eighth grade," I objected. "All we did was kiss."

"A kiss is a kiss."

"It wasn't the kiss. It was ... the time of the kiss."

"Ahh. You want to add time to the equation?"

"We kissed when I was happy, a kid. My whole future was in front of me. Then my daddy died, and I ran into Stirling again. I think I was hoping he could take me back to that happy time."

Rahtz shook his head. "Substitution never works. People are not factors. X or y, one or the other, doesn't matter, just placeholders. People, on the other hand, are not fungible. We still try, of course. We lose a loved one, and we search around for a replacement, when what we need is to realize our loved one is no longer."

"That's no fun."

"No. We tend to run away from the difficulty of it."

"I'm not running away. I admit it, I've been prone to run away in the past. But I'm on a quest. A really, really important quest." I raised my eyebrows. "A super secret quest."

"Out with it, Mae."

And, quick as a wink, I had a new nickname.

CHAPTER 16: The Famous Golden Gate

I told Rahtz of my trip to see Big Doodle. Also, that Big Doodle didn't actually know to expect me. "I'm not sure how he might react to my request. Or even my presence. There's a chance"—I held up my fingers to show how eensy the chance was—"he left Chicago because he knew I was coming."

"So you are hoping to meet with him. On what are you pinning such hopes?"

While I explained the family relationship with Big Doodle, Rahtz absentmindedly tapped the tabletop. "It sounds illogical, but I think as soon as I see him, I'll know where he stands," I said.

"It's not illogical. Even math, with all its emphasis on logical progression, contains an element of intuitive understanding, a flashpoint when you look at the chalkboard and know the answer to the equation. Not because you've worked from A to B, but because you see the logic of the whole thing."

"That's wonderful. What if we could look back at the equation of our lives, strung out behind us in chalked letters, and suddenly see the logic of it all?"

"Not a chalkboard big enough."

Which made me imagine something entirely different: Rahtz at a regular-sized chalkboard, hopping on one foot to reach the upper stratosphere of the board.

"I use a stool," he said when I couldn't help but ask. "Nonetheless, you cannot rely on the supposed affection of Big Doodle to carry the day. The human heart is the most unpredictable factor in the universe. The best way to get Big Doodle to admit he was wrong about your father is to *prove* your father is innocent. Find out who was actually running the drug ring."

I remembered the looping images of the pimply chicken clerks ducking into the cop cars. "The clerks who were slinging weed at the CP are in jail. Maybe they would sing."

"Excellent. How will you get them to 'sing'?"

"I have Pammy. She's my friend in Edison who's helping me sleuth."

"An aider and abettor. Again: excellent. Ask her to investigate for you. But first call Big Doodle and tell him you are on your way."

"Gotcha."

Of all things, a live person answered! The woman claimed to be Big Doodle's executive assistant. She informed me he was in a meeting. I explained that my call was quite important, but she refused to put him on the line. I was forced to leave a message about me ("Lucinda Mae Watkins") and my business ("chicken business") to which she replied, "That don't narrow it down much, honey."

Nonetheless, I hung up with a punch of triumph. No stupid phone system was gonna get the best of Lucinda Mae Watkins.

"I sense it went well?"

Standing, I tugged Rahtz up by the arm. "I feel my luck is about to change." I paraded him to the stairs, wishing I had on something more stunning than jeans and my appliquéd cardigan. Oh, well. I held my head high...with its wacky braids.

When we arrived upstairs to the club car, the man in mirrored sunglasses was moseying past our seats.

Pausing, he ran his gaze across Rahtz's stuff. He sauntered on.

"That jerk from the stairwell!" I pointed. "He's nosing around your stuff."

"A Nosey Parker, you say?"

"More than that. He was targeting you. Did you see where he went?"

"I did not even see *him*."

As I trotted to the seat, my cell phone tingled inside my green tote. I checked the number making me number: Pammy.

"Excuse me." I stepped aside so as not to bother Rahtz who was settling back in with his highlighter. "Pammy! I was fixing to call you."

"I said I wouldn't go to jail for you, girl, but I did!" Pammy crowed.

"What?"

"I went to the jail in Jackson. You talk into a telephone just like on TV, but you don't actually see the person. They're on a video screen. Like jail video chat."

She had done what I was going to ask her to do, but it was a little unsettling she'd hauled off and done it on her own. "Who was on the video screen, Pammy? Did you talk to one of the CP clerks?"

"Naw, girl. Went straight to the top. I interrogated Little Davey." She was referring to J.J.'s on-again-off-again boyfriend who managed the Chicken Palace.

"Little Davey's in jail?"

"Yep, the Feds nabbed him."

"Are you saying the drug ring actually was run out of Edison?" I couldn't believe this—surely it made more sense for the operation to be based in, say, New Orleans where the importing took place?

"Feds think so."

I rolled my braids between my thumb and forefinger. Little Davey was a weasel from way back. Coaxing the truth out of him would be harder than forcing a politician to take a stand during election year: impossible. "Did he say anything helpful?"

"Well...."

"What?"

"Oh, you know Little Davey. He said your dad was the Boss Man who turned to a life of crime because his stupid life in Edison was so boring."

"Pammy, tell me you're not seriously believing anything Little Davey says? He's an idiot."

"I know, I know. But you know how true-shit boring Edison is. And he gave me some pretty convincing details on the chicken distribution system."

"That's the way idiots work," I argued, as much for my own benefit as Pammy's. "They stick close to the truth so they won't get tangled up in lies."

"He said the Feds are giving him immunity, his intel on your dad is so awesome."

"He's making that shit up. There is no immunity, and if there is, it's because a really bad dude is in charge of the drug ring, and Little Davey's afraid the really bad dude will order him shanked in prison if he snitches, but Little Davey desperately wants out of jail, so he's fingering Daddy."

"Okay. That makes sense. But listen to this. Right before I left, he said, 'That trip Lucinda's on? She better be careful. The drug ring's watching her every move.'"

"How did Little Davey know I was on a trip?"

"What did I just say? They have a man on you."

"What kind of man?"

"You know Little Davey. He drops a bombshell then clams up like, whoa, I've said too much already. He actually pled the Fourth."

"The Fifth."

"I know that. You know that. Little Davey doesn't know that."

I thought about the guy cornering me in the stairwell. "There may be someone following me."

"Listen, you be careful, girl. And hang tough with Big Doodle. You don't want to be a temp all your life. Play your cards right, and you could be in management."

"Management?

"Manage the Chicken Palace Emporium. Little Davey's going up river. They'll be hiring new personnel."

"Pammy, the Chicken Palace manager wears a paper hat. He squawks when you walk in the door, 'Welcome to the Chicken Emporium, *brawk!*' You want me to be like Little Davey?"

"All I'm saying—"

"I'm doing something important here, trying my best to sort out this mess and restore my daddy's rightful place in the history of fried chicken lore, and you're telling me the Chicken Palace would be a smart *career move?*"

"You said you wanted a niche same as me."

187

"*You* said that, Pammy." Another thing about Pammy: she tended to project. "My future does not include cleaning out the grease fryers at the CP."

"Don't be snooty," she said distractedly. "BTW, I might have said something to your mother I shouldn't have."

I'd been studying the scenery out the window—the Pacific coast was a tad rocky—but Pammy's confession snapped my attention back to the phone. "You did what?"

"I took her the GG Gel mask hostess gift from the spa. She was quite grateful, thanking me for the spa and talking about your trip. I asked her a few questions about your family's finances."

"You did? What did she tell you?"

"She didn't *tell* me anything. She asked me how much you knew."

*

"Dang!"

I plopped down at Rahtz's table in the dining car. Five-thirty in the afternoon, and he'd already ordered supper. Eating like an old person. The train would do that to you.

"You have spoken with your sleuth, and it is not good?" He gnawed off a piece of stubborn corned beef from his sandwich. Sauerkraut spilled out with the beef.

"Everyone in Edison has drunk the crazy juice."

Swallowing, Rahtz wiped the lid of his canned drink with a napkin then popped in a straw. The man was fastidious. "Order something. You don't want to arrive at your assignation with Big Doodle tomorrow looking wan."

I glanced at the menu sheet. "My sleuther wants me to be the manager of the local Chicken Palace."

"That doesn't seem a good fit for you, Mae."

Taking his hand, I silently mouthed, *Thank you.*

The menu offerings weren't exciting, and another long night of sleeping in my seat stretched in front of me. "Tell me about San Francisco. We'll have almost two hours to kill before I wow Big Doodle."

"Not kill. Enjoy. And you want me to come along?" He sucked on his straw.

"Please. I don't know anything about the city. It's my friend Erick's favorite city. He always wanted to move there and dance for their ballet. He says it's too expensive for a short-order cook's salary."

"The city is full of delights, but it does think highly of itself."

"My mother's cousin visited years ago and went to a sex emporium. Of course, when folks in Edison heard 'emporium,' they didn't think sex toy megastore. They thought chicken emporium. The woman kept having to say, 'No, we didn't go all the way to San Francisco to see chickens having sex.'"

"We will be in San Francisco. We will not be visiting a sex emporium."

"What then?"

Rahtz crumpled his napkin on his plate. "We shall do the bridge."

*

The next morning, Rahtz and I were standing not two hundred feet into the Golden Gate Bridge. In front of us, an official sign provided the phone number of the Suicide Prevention Hotline.

"If you're calling for assistance this early in your trek, you aren't very committed." I remembered my own decision to turn back in North Dakota.

"You are, in point of fact, still over dry land," my observant friend pointed out.

I leaned over the railing. Rahtz was right. Muddy, slurpy-looking land, but land nonetheless.

The seagulls were swaying over the water, blue skies were beckoning, and a ways past the sign, everyone on the bridge was hanging over the railing, looking down. As if someone *had* jumped.

Rahtz and I joined the group.

No jumper. A pickup truck, stuck in the mud.

"People are crazy! Everything in the world to enjoy on a walk across the most famous bridge in the world, and a stuck-in-the-mud truck grabs everyone's attention."

I flung my arms at the scene unfolding below. When I did, a man in the group glanced my way, his long hair whipping in the breeze. How anyone on the San Francisco Bridge could look familiar to me, I don't know, but he did.

"Do you see that man?" I pointed to the tall guy, but he'd melted back into the group.

"Who?"

"Nothing, I guess. I thought he was the man from the stairwell. I'm getting paranoid." I hooked my arm in Rahtz's, and we strolled.

The breeze whipped my dress, an orange pique A-line. I'd added psychedelic daisy bobby socks to my white patent leather Mary Janes. Going all out to impress Big Doodle, I'd finished with a pink straw pocketbook and plastic polka dot earrings. "Lovely earrings," Rahtz had said when I emerged from the train's public toilet—leave it to Rahtz to identify the essential touch. He wore a soft denim suit. "Chambray," he said.

The famous Golden Gate was surprisingly short. The sweeping tallness made you think "big," but it was mostly grandeur. We were on the other side in no time. Then there was nothing to do but turn around and tromp back. Midway across, we halted.

The bay was choppy, peaked in white caps. The breeze felt wonderful after the closed confines of the train—two nights of sleeping in the coach car had not been a joyful experience. In the distance, the island of Alcatraz rose from the sea. I'd always thought San Francisco was shrouded in fog, but the bay and the little town across the water were crisp with sunlight.

We leaned on the concrete barrier, taking it all in. Rahtz was about chin level with the top of the barrier, his fingers crimped around the cold concrete.

"It would be fun to see all the lovely cities in the world," I said.

"Ummm," he said, absorbed in the gorgeous scenery.

I swatted him on the arm. "I could go see all the places Clyde watches on the Travel Channel."

"You'd get tired of it, Mae." He'd stuck with the Mae in my name. Same as Erick's Ms. Williams and Daddy calling me Cindy Lou—men, thinking they were the original Adam, making up their own names for the world.

I squinted at him. In profile, Rahtz's nose curved slightly, sharp as a knife. "You think? What's to get tired of?"

Across the bay, a jerky sailboat hugged the shore.

"Always skimming the surface, never lighting anywhere. That's not you."

I wasn't so sure—it sounded exactly like me, never wanting to dip my toe very far into the *why* of what I was doing, a mosquito skimming on the lake of life, never committing.

I kicked the concrete barrier then stopped, afraid I would scuff the Mary Janes. "I wish my dad could've seen this. Erick loves the song about leaving your heart in San Francisco. My daddy always sang the one about when you go to San Francisco, wear flowers in your hair."

"Maybe he's watching us." Rahtz clomped his chin against the concrete. "From above."

"I'm not sure he'd be too happy with what he'd see: the mess I made with Stirling, Mother shacked up with Clyde, his name being dragged through the mud."

Rahtz stared out to sea. No response to the truth, I guess.

"I miss my daddy. He was always there for me, encouraging me. What if...."

I stopped, unable to voice my fear: What if the allegations were true? What would I do? The man who had raised me and guided me and loved me more than Christmas would never be involved in the drug business. If it turned out the drug ring was in fact run by the "local investors," I would lose my daddy all over again, and I wasn't sure I could bear such a heartbreak a second time.

Rahtz's gaze followed the gulls dipping and swirling over the bay. "What he'd die of?"

"Pancreatic cancer. Six weeks from diagnosis to death."

"That's tough."

"I didn't know he was so sick. We were in the hospital, joking about who Mother should hitch up with after he was gone." I rubbed my calf, sore from the Mary Janes and the walking. "I was about to graduate community college. That's what I thought was important."

"He picked someone out for her, a replacement?"

"Yeah. He was laughing about Mother needing someone to take care of her if he wasn't around. I didn't know he was dying."

A man and woman in matching Oakland Raiders sweatshirts strolled by, holding hands. Behind us, on the other side of the protective wall forming our walkway, traffic zipped across the bridge surprisingly close. I rocked back on my heels, my face to the sun.

"One of the guys Daddy picked out was the mortuary owner who'd sponsored my church softball team when I was a little girl, the Burners."

"The…Burners?" Rahtz swallowed. "Sponsored by…a mortuary?"

"The Burners. I was so happy to be on the team. I played catcher. What does a nine-year-old know from a mortuary? We wore black shorts and black t-shirts."

"Black?"

"Black…with an orange flame."

Rahtz tried to fix his face, but couldn't. He giggled, a little boy's sniggly giggle. "A flame?"

"On the front. The back said: 'Burn 'em, baby.'"

"This…." Rahtz's watery eyes were jumping, a balloon about to bust. "This is who your dad picked out…for your *mom*?"

"It was either him or Mr. Franley." I pictured skinny Mr. Franley, Daddy's second choice, and I couldn't stand it. I burst out laughing. "An eighty-year-old…."

"Eighty years old?"

Rahtz was sputtering, I was grabbing his arm, and we were both going down on the walkway.

"A mule breeder." I held tight to Rahtz's arm, the concrete cold against my buckled legs, Rahtz's legs splayed like a rag doll's.

"Mule…breeder?"

"Named Wert! Wert Franley!"

Rahtz's rubbery face stretched, his watery eyes agog with surprise. "I have a cousin…named *Wert*!"

We coughed and rolled on the concrete and shouted "Wert!" while feet hurried past until gradually we came back to ourselves, untangling from our laughter, hiccuping an occasional "Wert," and coasted back to the world of sane adults.

Rahtz twisted his face in the breeze. "Fresh air feels nice after the train, doesn't it?"

"Clean. No people smells."

He patted my hand. "Remember, Mae, sometimes when we lose a loved one, it sends us off in a mad dash of activity, when what we should do is sit quietly, letting our hearts heal."

I saw my daddy's death as a big red button that had punched me into "go" mode, searching for my "lost" dad. How odd that the ever-moving train had slowed me down. I stroked Rahtz's arm. The downy hair on his wrist tickled my skin. "How do you know so much?"

Rahtz struggled to his feet, holding out a hand to help me up. "That, my gull, is a question for another day."

His arm around my waist, he steered us back to shore.

Which is when the earthquake hit.

CHAPTER 17: YOU'VE GOT MY ATTENTION!

The Golden Gate Bridge shook as if a giant from some cosmic dance club had discoed up and bumped his hip against the pylons.

"What the hell!" The sidewalk rolled under my feet.

"Sit!" Rahtz commanded but too late.

Gentle as a swell on the water, rising and converging, the bridge billowed like a freshly laundered sheet snapped in the wind.

The rocking entered the soles of my shoes, passed through my thighs, knocked my chin up a notch, and was gone.

"A tremor," Rahtz said from his spot on the walkway.

"Tremor?" I asked, incredulous. "A tremor is when Pooh's hand shakes, and she spills iced tea on the lace tablecloth, and Ikie and I look at each other and shrug"—I shrugged—"because it isn't the end of the world, no big deal, just a trem-*or*!"

I paused to check for bodily damage, running my tongue across the edge of my teeth. "I may have chipped a tooth." But I didn't feel anything; then I studied my Mary Janes to see if they'd scuffed. They hadn't. Unbelievably, everyone around us appeared to be okay too. Most had known to sit and were nonchalantly standing up, unperturbed.

"Safest place is on the bridge." Rahtz rose. "Made to absorb the motion, release it back into the atmosphere."

"What are you talking about? We were in an earthquake!" I clapped Rahtz by the shoulders.

"An earthquake, probably not. As I said, a tremor."
His almost-crossed eyes were thoughtful, studying to
see if I was okay. The tips of his chambray jacket
caught the breeze, twirled in the wind. "You've never
felt it before. Must be quite a new experience."

"New? This is nothing new for me. Earthquake!
Pfffft." I held on to Rahtz's shoulders too tightly, but I
couldn't relax my grip. "This is my life. You're
laughing; you're having a fun time. For once, you're
not fretting about your dead daddy or your no-count ex-
husband or your difficult mother. You're enjoying your
new friend, giggling, for God's sake. And Life comes
along and grabs you by the shoulders"—I squeezed
Rahtz tighter—"and shakes the ever-living crap out of
you until your eyeballs pop, your teeth rattle, and your
neck snaps. Then, when you're lying on the ground
unconscious, Life says, 'Oh, sorry. I wanted to make
sure I had your attention.'"

"You weren't unconscious, only teetering on the
sidewalk."

"Can't a girl exaggerate?" I twisted my head
heavenward because I knew what was coming next and
I didn't want to holler in my friend's face, but holler I
did: "OKAY! YOU'VE GOT MY ATTENTION!"

My feet were glued to the walkway; my palms were
glued to Rahtz's shoulders. I wanted to sit down, but
the walkway reminded me of the earthquake, and I
didn't want to sit on it. I saw my straw pocketbook on
the concrete, where I must have dropped it in all the
confusion.

"Rahtz, will you pick up my pocketbook for me?" I
envisioned us two-stepping over to the spot, him
bending and retrieving.

He eyed the straw as if it was the intertwining strands of a chalkboard equation he'd been puzzling over for a while.

"You get it, Mae." The wind was making his eyes water and he blinked. "You've become attached to me because we share a similar sensibility. It's been delightful, and we probably would have gotten along anyway, but your quick attachment speaks more to your emotional state than it does to me, probably due to unattended grief over your father."

"What?"

"Get your pocketbook yourself."

I could not let go of his shoulders, but neither could I let go of my pocketbook—not when it matched the A-line dress so well, the dress's orange exactly the right color for the pink straw, because my earrings…I touched my earlobe with my hunched shoulder to make sure the earrings were still there—had pink *and* orange polka dots.

I released my grip on Rahtz's shoulders.

For a minute, I felt as if I were going to float and lift to the cloudless sky, a balloon let loose on a windy day, my wavering body thinning as it rose, weightless, until all you could see were the soles of my Mary Janes like pin dots of blackness, then gone.

But I didn't.

I retrieved my pocketbook, brushed it off, edged my feet an inch or two apart to make sure I had the best stance, and threw the pocketbook over the railing into the glistening bay.

"Interesting," Rahtz lisped.

"It was empty. I carry it for show." I patted the slit pockets of my A-line dress, where my driver's license, train ticket, and lipstick hid. "The big city, you know. Can't make yourself a target."

"The grand gesture?"

"I was tired of holding on. It was nice, laughing with a new friend about my dad for a change instead of all that…sadness." I cringed, scrunching my shoulders, half expecting another quake to slap me upside the head.

"Scared?"

"Yes, I'm scared." Even now, I felt wobbly on the bridge, as if I didn't have enough support, but I made it to the railing so I could see the pocketbook floating in the choppy water.

Nothing, not so much as a ripple.

"It's gone," Rahtz said.

"Gone," I repeated.

"Sunk."

"Sunk." I was repeating everything Rahtz said, leaning on him to solve my problems, which is why he had made me retrieve the damn pocketbook myself. He was leaving soon, and after that, he would not be around to retrieve pocketbooks for me. I had to learn to stand on my own two feet.

But when I tried to come up with my own thing to say, I floundered. The same way I'd floundered after Daddy died. Dating Stirling, sniffing around the ranch house—did I even chop off my hair because I'd worn it short in the eighth grade?

"Trying to be in control," I said.

"How's that?"

"I was trying to be in charge, prove death couldn't overtake my life, even though it had."

"You okay?"

"Completely okay. I'm going to do this thing."

"Excellent." He squinted. The wind whisked his hair this way and that. "I'm your new friend?"

"You are absolutely my new friend."

In a hauntingly familiar gesture, he held out his arm, inviting me to take it—exactly as Augie had done when he said good-bye at the train station.

Friend, friend.

Augie, Rahtz.

Lover, friend. Stranger, friend. Stranger yet.

No stranger than you, Lucinda Mae. Standing on a bridge in San Francisco in the middle of an earthquake with your hair done up in braids while you're learning to cope with your daddy's death and staring into the heavily crossed eyes of a tiny aeronautical engineer.

I took Rahtz's offered arm. Then I spun us around, making my A-line billow.

"To Chicken Headquarters," I declared.

*

When we arrived at the Chicken Palace Emporium Corporate Headquarters, I bid Rahtz a momentary goodbye.

"Proud of you, Mae." He settled into the backseat of the taxi, his little legs sticking out from the seat. "We'll be right here."

But Big Doodle Dayton wasn't in the office. He wasn't even in the city.

"At his house in the Rockies," the oh-so-helpful executive assistant informed me. Her desk was decorated with Stuckey's finest. A fake license plate proclaimed "Georgina's Desk," and a clutch of Nut

Bars stood in a "See Rock City" coffee cup. Give her an apron and a flyswatter, and she could have been a Stuckey's waitress herself, what with her beehive hairdo and bright red lipstick.

"Georgina, it would have helped if you'd told me that over the phone."

"I could have." She was probably mid-sixties, her beehive a jet black that could have only come from a bottle. "But Big Doodle pays me to do only what is best for Big Doodle, not what is best for pesky strangers."

"I went to Chicago. He wasn't there. I come out here. You tell me he's in Colorado."

She narrowed her eyes. "Are you stalking him?"

"Did you give him my message?"

"I did. And he's not here, is he?"

I didn't appreciate her insinuation. "He didn't know how important it was. I've gone to a lot of trouble, and I'm missing my best friend's audition. It's a matter of…parental importance."

"Parental importance?" She pursed her lips. "Parental, as in paternity?"

"Yes." I improvised, clamping my hands onto my hips, and offered up a bald-faced lie: "Big Doodle might be my daddy."

She eyed me. "I don't believe you. You too skinny."

"Big Doodle was skinny as a beanpole in high school!" Photos of the young Big Doodle were plastered all over the Chicken Museum: Big Doodle in skinny gym shorts; Big Doodle in a skinny wrestling uniform, Big Doodle in a skinny tuxedo in front of a big red heart. "Big Doodle was *skinny*."

She cocked her head at me.

"Lynn, Glen, Wren!" I called out the names of Big Doodle's siblings, a list that always made me want to shout at the end, "And Flynn!"

The phone rang. "Yes, Mr. Big Doodle?" the traitor cooed into the receiver.

"Let me talk to him!" I reached for the phone.

She dodged, so I shouted, "Lucinda Mae Watkins from Edison, Mississippi! Bill Watkins's little girl!"

Through the phone line, I could hear Big Doodle squawking, "Bill Watkins's little girl, do you say?"

"I need to talk to you, Big Doodle," I shouted across the desk.

"I'm in the Rockies, honey."

"I'm coming to the Rockies!"

"You come on out to the house, girl. Miss Sissy and I will be waiting for you."

"Tell me where you are, Big Doodle!" Given half a chance, Georgina would cut me off at the pass.

"Georgina? Are you still there, Georgina? You tell Bill Watkins's girl how to get out to the house."

"Now," I said to Georgina, who wasn't happy with Big Doodle instructing her to do exactly what she'd been desperately trying not to do. "While Big Doodle is on the line."

So she uh-huh-ed with Big Doodle and wrote out directions, along with a phone number and fax number and cell phone number. I guess Big Doodle had gotten her attention.

When she tore off the note and passed it to me, I read it and casually said, "They won't let you dye baby chicks anymore. They say the dye makes the baby chicken's brains wonky. The same dye they use in bad hair jobs." I stared at her do. "I'm just saying."

Which was kind of unfair, because she was still on the line with Big Doodle, so all she could do was stick out her tongue at me.

*

When Rahtz and I were settled on the *California Zephyr* train—me in my new sleeping berth thanks to Rahtz's Travel-with-A-Friend card—my phone burped, showing the worse caller imaginable: Erick.

When I left St. Paul, I had plenty of time to get to San Francisco and back before Erick's show. According to my math, I still had time to get off the train in Denver, see Big Doodle, re-board the train, and make it back to St. Paul, but not by much. If any more surprises popped up, I'd roll into town Sunday morning like a slutty game show walk-of-shame.

WHERE R U?

Thank goodness it was texting—easier to fudge.

I tapped in: HI!

WHERE R U?

We were back at the beginning.

SAN FRANCISCO.

There was a long pause, probably while Erick digested the fact I was in his dream city while he was at home in Minnesota with his oompah family where I was supposed to be, except I was in his dream city. Which I hadn't mentioned during my early morning departure—that Big Doodle's corporate headquarters were in San Francisco.

GOOD?

WALKED AX BRIDGE W/RAHTZ. I was tapping, but something must have gone wrong, because Erick typed back, RATS NOT GOOD. CM BACK.

I was trying to type in my next destination but it came out: OFF TO THE ROCK.

SWEET, Erick responded.

This set me back. I had no idea where the conversation might stand.

WAITING 4 U, came next. CM HOME FOR SHOW.

MORE LATER, I typed in, which was how Pammy signed off when she was tired of talking to you but didn't want to appear rude. It seemed the only thing to do to a hopelessly corrupted messaging that wouldn't be improved by the truth: I might miss his big event.

I must have screwed up again because LATE? 4 WHAT? blinked back at me. NOT FOR TV SHOW?!? I NEED U HERE!!

LUV UR HEART, I was typing but the screen flashed to black.

We had entered a tunnel.

After we emerged on the other side of the long tunnel, I waited for a while, staring at the tiny screen, but no more messages materialized. While I was on the phone, I gave Augie a call. He'd called me twice—I probably should've returned his call before now. But the recording answered: "Augie Green. You know what to do."

I almost thanked the message for its vote of confidence but instead told him to call when he could.

When we were approaching Reno (the Biggest Little City in the World), I changed for supper and vacated my berth to find Rahtz. The train was rocking as it forded the Truckee River, touted by the railroad literature as a "scenic highlight." Leaning over an empty seat, I laid my palm against the glass. The river was as impressive as a dribble of spit, but then I hailed from the land of the Mighty Mississippi. Surely, the Continental Divide would be more memorable. After we crossed the Divide, we would arrive in Winter Park where Rahtz would de-board.

I spied Rahtz in a swivel chair in the coach car. He looked dear with his neck bent, studying his gigantic textbook. Tears inexplicably started in my eyes, and I quickly wiped them away, telling myself to get a grip.

Sitting beside him, I smoothed my skirt and adjusted my pearl necklace, a three-strand choker from the vintage jewelry store. One of the pearls had lost its thin skin of pearl essence, but you had to look closely to see it. My appliquéd cardigan was lavender, with flitting, glittery butterflies. Rahtz was intent on his studying.

"How can you read with this rocking motion? I'd make me car sick and I'd wanna puke. Train sick, I guess."

"Time and motion are merely dancers upon the stage of space," Rahtz opined, not looking up from his book.

"You wanna see the list I made?"

"I do." He closed his book, holding his place with his finger.

I passed him the "Big Doodle To Do" list I'd spent the afternoon creating.

"Cock-a-doodle-doo." He grinned showing his fang teeth. He read out loud. "'Issue Press Release—local investors aren't involved in drug scandal. Call Authorities—Daddy had nothing to do with the drug ring. Reinstate contract with Sonny Floyd—start buying his chickens again. Fix Daddy's Legacy—make Big Doodle be kind to his chickens.'"

He handed it back to me. "The last one is particularly nice."

"Yeah. I asked myself, if I could accomplish only one thing on this quest, what would it be? I realized my daddy would care more about the future of the chickens than he would about his good name."

"It's a fine list, Mae." His watch dinged, an alarm. Maybe to remind him to get ready to deboard.

"I'm gonna miss you when you go off to college." That's what Mary Martha said when her cats were about to die, to keep herself from getting too maudlin: they were going off to college. I'd started thinking of Rahtz that way, but he didn't need to know I was comparing him to a dead cat.

"Don't be sad. You must persevere in your quest."

"I've missed Erick's interview and the taping. One more hiccup and I could miss the whole show." I fingered my braids. I'd tried to spiff them up to better match my lovely outfit, but after the windy walk on the bridge, they were getting ratty.

"Come here. Give me your head."

When I leaned over, he began undoing my braids. "You can't try to sweet-talk Big Doodle looking a mess. I'll redo them."

"You know how to do braids?" I was highly skeptical.

"It's a pattern, not dissimilar to a mathematical equation. I'll pay attention as I undo, then redo in reverse." He peered around and smiled his fanged smile again. "I'll redo your do."

"You're making me miss you more."

He yanked, and I squawked.

"Sorry," he said, but he didn't mean it.

I tilted my head. "Maybe someone new will come on board so there won't be any lonesome dead spot after you leave."

"Perhaps. Be careful what you wish for."

No sooner were the words out of his mouth—his hands grappling with my braids, my head tilted at an angle—than my mother walked into the lounge car, Clyde by her side.

CHAPTER 18: Is Everything Lovely with You?

Rahtz was the epitome of a gentleman, hopping off his chair to shake hands with Clyde.

Clyde was Clyde, shaking Rahtz's hand but asking, "You mighty short. You fully grown?"

"I am."

Mother waited until the size question was settled before grabbing me to her chest.

"Oh, my baby!"

"Mother, I'm perfectly okay."

Typical Mother: in a panic because I'd been riding the train with who knows who, going who knows where while being subjected to who knew what opinions of the greater, wide world.

Clyde was circling the lounge car, jangling the change in his pocket and sucking on his cheeks.

"But Pammy told Mary Martha you weren't coming home....Your hair!"

Her hand faltered mid-air, unable to touch my hair, which undoubtedly stood straight up, half braided, half unbraided.

Clyde, who'd made a full circle by now, threw himself into a chair. He splayed out like an octopus. "What a dump! Something smells bad." He glanced around, his eyes lighting on an old woman wearing a baggy green-and-white checked shirt and opening a jar of pickles. "It's the women."

"Mother, I told you to give me time."

"You said thirty-six hours." She flicked her wrist to squint at her watch. "It's been thirty-seven. Pammy said you were in trouble."

"Pammy?"

"Your mama made me hop on the plane right away," Clyde groused. "I talked her into hitting Reno. Always wanted to see the lighted arch that leads you into downtown. Kind of a disappointment, though, smallish." He stared significantly at Rahtz then grimaced, cracking lines into his leathery skin. His unbuttoned collar showed off his farmer's tan: Clyde wore an undershirt in the tanning bed.

Don't ask me how I knew this.

"Mother, Pammy told me about y'all's conversation. I know she asked you about Daddy's finances."

Mother deflated quicker than the train hitting its brakes, but then she rallied. "It's a mother's duty to look after her child."

Clyde was examining his seat, checking right and left. "They don't have seat belts on this train, Roscoe?"

At first, I thought Clyde had misremembered Rahtz's name, but he was staring at me. Clyde was calling me Roscoe, like a redneck cop arresting a drunk.

How, in only four days, had Clyde acquired a brand-new, annoying habit?

"No trains have seat belts," Rahtz told him.

Clyde gave Rahtz the evil eye as if he was the mastermind behind a seat-belt conspiracy of massive proportions, and I could tell we were about to receive some Learning Channel wisdom. "In one year alone, over twelve people in the US are killed flat out when a train up and jumps the tracks."

He squeaked his seat with the motion of the train.

"This train rattles so." Mother laid a faint hand on her tummy. A butterfly pin rode the lapel of her jacket, a loud lime-green-and-black plaid. "How do you keep down your dinner?"

"That's my Southern gal." Clyde beamed. "Thin blood, delicate constitution. But you're a handful." He reached around and whacked Rita Rae on the fanny.

"You sit down, Mother." I led her into a chair. She brushed a crumb from the table before sitting. "The motion is easier to take sitting down. I'll get you a soft drink, soothe your tummy. There, now."

When she was settled, I jerked my head at Rahtz to follow me to the counter.

"I can't believe it!" I smacked down my change, asked for a soda in a plastic cup, lots of ice. My mother, the Southerner, wouldn't think she'd gotten her money's worth unless there was lots of ice. I'd learned Northerners didn't like too much ice. "Ya cheating me?" a guy outside of Chicago had growled. My mother was not a Northerner.

"This is the worst," I said.

"Unexpected, but not the worst." Rahtz self-consciously combed his hair with his fingers, patting it into place.

"Did Clyde say something mean about your hair?"

"You're overreacting."

"He said you weren't fully grown! He's awful."

"He asked if I might be not be fully grown."

"You wait. It'll get worse."

"Remember what I said about substitution not working with people? It doesn't work with anger either. Anger is always a secondary emotion. I expect in your case it's secondary to sorrow over your dad. Something lies between you and your mother, and you're taking it out on Clyde."

"I can't believe she showed up when I told her I would handle this."

"She was worried." Rahtz, ever the pragmatist.

"Pammy said something that lit a fire under her." I gazed at Rita Rae, who was yakking with some woman. "Or maybe she wants to talk. She's been saying that. Hand it to Rita Rae to ruin my trip over something she could've done anytime at home."

"If she wants to talk, you probably should talk to her."

Mother and Clyde were sliding their gaze all over the buffet, disdaining everything they spied. "I'm not going to let them tromp after me when I talk to Big Doodle. I won't have it," I hissed as Rahtz walked away.

I accepted Mother's drink from the clerk and followed Rahtz to the table where he addressed Mother: "Might Mae and I join you?"

"Mae?" Mother looked from me to Rahtz to Clyde. Her look would come back to me, going around the horn like the baseball players throwing the baseball from first base to second base to third base after an easy out. Whenever my mother's look went around the horn, it always came back to me.

But Rahtz intercepted it. "Mrs. Watkins, you are as lovely as your daughter. The two of you are spring butterflies. Your pin matches Mae's sweater."

Mathes her swetha, Clyde mouthed to Mother, as if Rahtz and I couldn't see him.

Rahtz laid a calming hand on my wrist.

"Something going on between you two?" Clyde stuck his leg into the aisle. A passenger demurred, stepping around his protruding boot.

"Yes, there is." At Mother's stricken look, I added, "Lazarus is the best train companion one could ever ask for." I switched to Rahtz's first name for fear of giving Clyde the advantage of "Rahtz."

Mother smiled weakly at Lazarus.

"Hard to pay attention for all the babies crying," Clyde said. But he grinned, having a good ol' time.

Smiling sweetly, I asked the table, "How *are* things in Edison?"

"Your family is the number-one topic of conversation. If it's not the drug scandal, it's your ex remarrying." Clyde glanced at Mother. "Sorry. I wasn't supposed to mention that."

"Everyone in Edison has the attention span of a gnat."

Saying it made me pause. Could be the public gawking over my family's role in the drug scandal might die a quick, natural death. That is, if Mother didn't wind up living on the streets.

"Active thyroids," Mother announced. "That's how they stay warm in all that cold."

Pleased as punch, she folded her hands on the table.

Her nails were painted Peppermint Pink.

Turns out, in the short time I'd been getting Mother's drink, she'd met a real live North Dakotan, or whatever they called themselves. "Mrs. Aurick, that was the woman's name, she said 'above,' like 'eighty above' when she was talking about the weather."

Mother lifted her palms in a 'who knew?' gesture. "They only have three trees in all of North Dakota."

I was trying to remember if I'd seen more than three trees, when she started in about the oil camps in the 1950s and burning garbage with leftover gas from the oil wells. "The fires burned all day and all night."

Since when had Rita Rae thought garbage was an appropriate topic for the table? But Clyde was exclaiming over her, and Mother was smiling, so proud, and it made me wonder: did Rita Rae need to get away from Mississippi for a while too?

"What are y'all's plans?" I casually asked whoever wanted to answer.

"We'll travel to St. Paul with you." Mother fiddled with her silverware, surreptitiously inspecting it for dirt. "I want to be there, Lucinda, in case you discover this Augie fella isn't all you've made him into. You'll need your family."

I stared at her. How on earth did she know about Augie?

"I'm not going to St. Paul," I lied. "I'm going to D.C. and then to Boston."

"Your ballerina friend thinks you're going to St. Paul." Clyde hijacked Mother's drink and swished a mouthful.

"Erick?"

"Ballet dancer," he said from the side of his mouth. "Got a dancing invention."

"You know what Erick's invention is?"

"He told us all about it. Said not to cheep a word of it to you."

I turned to Rita Rae. "Did Erick tell you about Augie?"

"He said your phone wasn't working right." Mother set the silverware aside, fixing me with her full attention, eyes bright. "He said he was talking to you about coming back to St. Paul to see him on TV when your phone died. He wanted us to make sure you returned in time. He is quite concerned about his performance. Something about proving a Frenchman wrong?"

"The judge who knocked him out of the ballet competition," Rahtz repeated what I'd told him.

I sat silent, feeling guilty. Erick had been my rock for the last two years. It was my turn to be there for him, and I was clear across country on a train.

"I'm getting back to him as fast as I can," I said. "As long as nothing else comes up along the way to screw things up."

"Language, Lucinda." Mother shook her head.

"They're having a throw down at his house," Clyde said. "During the TV show."

"They're having a party? And Mrs. Gminski invited y'all? She knew you were my family from Mississippi, right?"

"She did. We're looking forward to meeting Erick's family. After," Mother added pointedly, "your meeting with Big Doodle."

Well. She knew about that too.

"Mother, can we talk in private for a minute?"

Clyde was saying, "No secrets between us," as Mother was saying, "Of course."

Clyde looked like a wasp had stung him on the nose.

Mother patted his hand. "Give us a moment, dear."

Rahtz rose from his seat. "Allow me to show you the dome car. It is quite lovely."

As they walked away, I heard Clyde say, "Is everything 'lovely' with you?"

Mother trained her gaze out the window as a man sauntered to the counter. He ordered a single-serving box of cereal as if it were breakfast rather than quickly approaching night. The attendant handed it to him, no questions asked.

"Mother, why are you here?" I addressed her profile, reflected in the almost-darkened window. "Does this have to do with the conversation you wanted to have with me about Daddy but wouldn't talk about over the phone? We aren't on the phone anymore."

"Bennie Dayton has not treated your father well."

This was hardly breaking news. "Yep. I'd say accusing Daddy of masterminding a drug ring is not treating him well."

"No, Lucinda." She turned toward me. "I mean when Bennie took your daddy's money to expand the Chicken Palace. He formed a new corporation for the chain but didn't give Bill an interest in that company. Instead, he left Bill with the Edison CP, cutting your daddy out of all the chain's profits."

"Oh. I didn't know it was so...deliberate."

"Bennie undoubtedly told himself he was being magnanimous in 'giving' Bill almost a half interest in the CP. In reality, he kept the best part for himself. Even a smidgen of ownership in the Chicken Palace Emporium would've set Bill up for life."

"Is that why he let the Edison CP go to rack and ruin? Because he shared it with Daddy?"

"I don't know, Lucinda. It's probably more typical Bennie, blowing hot and cold. Same as when we were in high school. He'd be all over something. He formed this great band, the Orange Slices. Next thing you knew *pfft!* The Orange Slices were cold as yesterday's mashed potatoes."

This did not sound encouraging.

"I thought if Bennie saw you and remembered the old times with Bill. Well…." She shrugged.

"You thought he might honor Sonny Floyd's contract? And we'd keep getting monthly checks?"

She slowly nodded. "Yes, that's right. I was afraid the monthly payments would stop. I should never have put you in such a situation."

"You didn't, Mother. The truth is, I wanted to come the moment I saw Big Doodle on TV."

"Lucinda, don't meet with Big Doodle. Stay on the train in Denver. Return immediately to St. Paul and be with Erick."

It was tempting. I could forget this nonsense and join Erick for his big moment. Maybe hook up with Augie earlier than we'd planned. But I couldn't run away from one more thing. If I did, how would my life ever get back on track?

I laid my hand on hers. "Thank you, Mother, for letting me off the hook. But I've got to do it. I've got to set things to rights."

*

Rahtz and I were on the Winter Park platform, standing in the middle of coming and going people. I had been walking with him into the station, but he'd stopped me here, probably afraid I'd try to bolt and come with him.

"You look lovely," he said. The lamppost cast a ring of light upon us.

I'd slipped a red tank top underneath my lavender cardigan. I topped it off with a knitted cap Pooh had made for me. Underneath the snug cap, I'd combed out my hair—time to move on in all things.

"You don't look so bad yourself." I fingered the suit jacket he'd thrown over the pink golf shirt, charcoal with those chalky white pinstripes that are so thick they don't even deserve the name. "Be nice to have you on my arm when I confront Big Doodle."

"I'm not worried. You're not shy." Rahtz's eyes were watery, maybe from being crossed the way they were. "And, Mae?"

"Yes?"

"With or without me, you must face the ultimate question."

"I'm afraid to ask."

"You *must* ask. You must ask yourself how you can get along with your Mother. Otherwise, you've never going to be able to discover the *h* factor."

"My happiness."

"Yes."

"You're probably right. Could you maybe give me something easier to solve for?"

"There's nothing else worth the effort." He lifted his suitcase from the train platform, adding it to his bundle, as unsteady as an ant carting around a grasshopper.

"Please wish Erick the best of luck in his competition," he said. He stretched toward me, and I leaned down, offering my cheek for a kiss. As he gave me a peck, he released his suitcases so he could slip his hand into mine, palm against palm: dry, fleeting, a promise given and immediately withdrawn.

Then he was enveloped in the night, the last thing visible his tuft of hair sticking straight up.

*

Back on the train, I found Mother and Clyde in the dining car, dirty dishes from their supper pushed aside. A man and woman stood at their booth.

"I noticed your accent earlier, and I have to ask," the woman said. "Are y'all from Mississippi?"

"We are!" Mother exclaimed.

The couple was from Mississippi too. They introduced themselves: Rhymers (the woman) and Gentry (the man). As soon as the introductions were uttered, all four began calling out "do you knows" the way Mississippians do, running the lineage, until they land on someone they shared in common—"He's my double first cousin, once removed"—like the begats thundering through the Bible.

Mother and Clyde were reveling in the moment, grinning ear to ear, oblivious to how *Mississippi* they were being. I was cringing inside when Clyde scored a hit, naming a woman Rhymers knew. Mother clapped her hands, so pleased, and Clyde goosed her, so proud.

Aw, what the hell.

"What about Pammy Stevenson?" I asked Rhymers—Pammy's spa circle of influence might well spread across the state.

"Why, yes!" Rhymers exclaimed. "That name does sound familiar."

"There you go, dolly," Clyde said, and raised his palm for a high-five.

Hesitating a moment, I slapped his hand as the couple excused themselves. Could Clyde and I possibly ever get along?

I was crunching into the dill pickle on Mother's plate—she never eats her pickle—when a ruckus arose further down the dining car closer to the kitchen. Clyde craned his neck into the aisle but couldn't tell what was going on. A man wearing a napkin as a bib came rushing by. The man at the next booth swiveled around and said to Clyde, "Heart attack."

I was wondering if they had any emergency care on the train when Clyde hitched up his pants and sauntered down toward the action. In a moment he returned, shaking his head.

"What?" Mother asked.

"Heimlich maneuver. Everyone's rubbernecking so I popped the steak from the man's mouth. Big ol' hoss, twice as big as me. Took some squeezing to get it done."

"What about the doctor?" Mother asked.

"Man in the napkin? Rubbernecker, same as the rest of 'em."

But not all of them.

While everyone else stood transfixed by the prospect of a man choking to death in front of them, a guy slouched in the corner of the dining car, working a toothpick between his teeth. The man in the mirrored sunglasses. He hadn't taken his eyes off our table. The drug ring goon, I was sure of it. The reason, as Little Davey said, the ring knew my every move.

"I think we're being followed." I winced at how dramatic I sounded.

"What?" Mother's gaze shifted from the clump of rubberneckers to me.

"A man. He was in North Dakota with me. He cornered Rahtz and me in the stairwell. I'm pretty sure I saw him on the Golden Gate Bridge. He's at the end of the car right now, staring at us."

"Where?"

"Don't look," I hissed as her head began to swivel.

"Man in the sunglasses?" Clyde grimaced. "Tall, lanky fella?"

"Yeah, that's him."

"I seen him slinking around. Doesn't look FBI to me, not with that ponytail. DEA maybe."

"A Fed? You think?" That hadn't occurred to me, focusing as I was on the criminal angle. "They're tailing us?"

"What's this 'us'?" Clyde asked. "You got a mouse in your pocket?"

"He's following Lucinda?" Mother began scooting from the booth.

"Now, now." Clyde grabbed her arm. "I'll take care of it."

"What are you gonna do?" I don't know if I was more afraid of being followed by a goon or of Clyde's "taking care of it."

"Not me. Us." He slid from the booth. "Quick, he's getting away."

CHAPTER 19: Sleuthing with Clyde

We found our quarry in the sightseeing car with its glass bubble top. He was seated about half-way down, reading a magazine.

"Damn rocking train," Clyde halted, swaying with the motion of the train. He whistled softly through his teeth. The train zipped through an intersection with its waiting traffic. A yellow and green tractor sign lit up the night.

"What are we doing?" I whispered.

"Considering. Cain't run up to the man say, 'You following this gal?'"

I shrugged—that's exactly what I would've done.

"You go down there. Tell him you've noticed him. Y'all traveling the same path, blah, blah, blah. Act a little flirty if you can."

He paused. I offered no encouragement.

"Then I walk up and you introduce me. We'll see what he says."

It wasn't much of a plan, but it was more than I had.

Making my way down the aisle, I glanced out the window—we had entered the Rockies and patches of snow lingered on the ground. Who would've thought I'd be walking by a train window casually observing such beauty? Who would've thought I'd be on a clandestine sleuthing mission with Clyde?

When I approached the man, he craned his neck, staring up at me.

"Hi," I said. "Remember me? From the stairwell?"

The man nodded and scratched his cheek, careful to avoid his drooping mustache, which made me wonder if it was fake.

"You were in North Dakota, too, right?" I persisted. "And on the Golden Gate Bridge, perhaps?" Then I remembered Clyde's suggestion, and I fiddled with the buttons on my sweater, drawing attention to where my cleavage would be if I had cleavage.

No response.

"Sunglasses in the train," I noted. "Even at night."

"Fluorescent lights. Hard on the eyes if you're sensitive to light." He stood, a long, drawn-out process as he rose higher and higher. The train rounded a curve and a fake fern above the service bar swayed, clicking against the windowpane. The man loomed over me.

"Standing in the presence of a lady, aren't you a Southern gentleman." I gazed up at him. "Can't help but notice the accent. We stand out in these parts. Where are you from?"

"Can I buy you a coffee?"

"Now?" I was wondering where that durn Clyde was. "Caffeine keeps me awake at night."

"Maybe you wanna be awake. Tonight." Holding onto the back of his chair, he crossed his legs at the ankle. "Maybe I wanna be awake too."

I blinked. All I did was fiddle with a few buttons. Must've been the right ones.

"Lucinda!" Clyde clapped me on the shoulder. "You making friends?"

"I am." I gestured to the shaded one. "This is…."

"We were going to the canteen for a drink." The man straightened, squaring his shoulders. Beneath his checked shirt, he wore a t-shirt with loopy writing on it. If he was DEA, they needed to pay their guys better so he could buy some decent clothes.

"Canteen's closed this time of night, partner." Clyde took a step forward.

The man swiveled his gaze to me. "Didn't know you came with a bodyguard."

"Don't mind Clyde." Laughing, I lightly touched the man's arm, which was hard as steel. "He and my mother have unexpectedly joined me on my trip. I'm on my way to an important sit-down with the famous Big Doodle Dayton, perhaps you've heard of him?"

"You're what?" Clyde asked.

I forged ahead. Whether he was DEA or a drug goon, maybe I could sort this out. "Don't know if you've heard, but Big Doodle's Chicken Palace Emporium is, shall we say, *embroiled* in a drug scandal. Apparently, Big Doodle believes my dear dead daddy was running the drug ring, when I'm the one responsible for this mess. I intend to clear up the misunderstanding and hopefully convince Big Doodle to show a tad more respect toward me and my family."

I held out my hand, which the man shook like an automaton. "Clyde and I will leave you to read your magazine in peace. How you do that with those sunglasses on, though, is beyond me."

I pivoted to face Clyde, who stood stock still. '*Go*,' I mouthed.

He glared at me before conceding his spot.

The dining car was almost empty, and we slid into a booth. Mother must have already decamped—I'd given her and Clyde my berth for the night since they'd not thought to get reservations.

Across the table, Clyde gazed out the window. "Wherever you're at, there's a Walmart, ain't there? Satellite dishes too. Everywhere you go." He leaned and watched as we passed a truck stacked full of logs. "Pulpwood hauler."

"What is it?"

"You told that man you were the drug kingpin. You aren't the drug kingpin, are you?"

"I did no such of a thing!"

"Yep, you did. What am I gonna tell Rita Rae? 'I'm standing right there and your daughter tells a man who's probably a federal of some sort that she's responsible for the drug mess'?"

"Not the drug mess. I'm responsible for the misunderstanding."

"Not what I heard, dolly. I'm betting it's not what he heard either. He's probably calling the po-lice right now to put protection on Big Doodle."

"What do you mean?"

"You told him you were heading out to Big Doodle's to threaten him."

"I said I wanted him to show some respect...." I trailed off.

"You did an impressive mob moll imitation, girlie, I gotta give you that."

"Should I go back, try again?"

"No, no. I wouldn't do that." He returned his gaze to the window. "It's probably no big deal."

Clyde's trying to be nice made it even worse.

"I screwed up, huh?"

"Don't worry about it." He tapped the windowpane. "Funny how all the towns are on one side of the railroad, isn't it?"

It was something I'd noticed, too, as if a giant farmer had walked along the tracks dropping town seed from a hole in his pocket.

I rested my chin in my hand. "I saw a sod house in North Dakota."

"A house made of grass?"

"Looked like grass. It backed up against a stand of trees. Kind of forlorn."

"Mice live in the grass, I bet."

Then I told him about the mice and the railroad staff and the battery-chunking in the club car.

"Bored," he said disparagingly, twirling the bottom of the salt shaker on the tabletop. "Men dream up bad things to do when they get bored."

The train made a sharp turn, and the shaker spilled salt on the tablecloth.

Clyde brushed it off then laced his fingers behind his neck and stretched. "Not used to being on a lo-co-mo-tive."

"Y'all didn't have to come, you know."

Clyde shook his head. "Rita Rae wouldn't have it any other way. She was worried about you. She kept talking about the time you broke your arm and she wasn't there to take you to the hospital. It seems she had to hear about it from your granny, over the phone. You were okay, but...."

He scratched behind his ear as the train slowed and blew its whistle for an intersection: two longs, one short, and a final long. "She wasn't happy with that, not being there when you were hurt."

I remembered the visit to the ER, the odd smell of the place, being relieved to get home to my mom. "She bought me a stuffed dolphin. Everyone signed it instead of my cast. She didn't want the cast to get marked up."

"Your mom has her ways. But she's worth it. Worth every damn minute of it."

The train came to a stop at a small station. A few people hurried away from the platform, ready to be back in their warm houses. Within a stone's throw from the station, a barn was lit up like a carnival. Several cows were standing in a spotlight in the corral.

"Cows should be in the barn this time of night." Clyde peered close to the glass, seeing the world through his Mississippi eyes. "Must be about to time to hit the road to the slaughterhouse. You know, a cow's body temperature adjusts to the climate," he said, giving me some Learning Channel wisdom.

He saluted the passing cows and turned back to me. "Dust under the wheels now. Don't worry about what you said to that man, dolly. Rita Rae won't tell me what burr Bennie Dayton's got under his saddle over your family, but he's making life hell for y'all. Talking bad about your dad, sic'ing the Feds on your mom. For some reason, he's slipping the noose over y'all's necks."

He eased from the booth. "Off to bed for me."

"Good night."

"You, too, dolly."

Pulling away from the stop, we gathered speed. The echo of a train whistle ripped before fading in the distance.

In a blink, I realized: it wasn't another, fast approaching train.

It was us.

*

When I awoke around seven o'clock the next morning, I was momentarily confused as to my whereabouts. Then I recognized the maroon and navy upholstery of the train seat. The breakfast announcement repeated from the loudspeaker.

As I padded down the aisle in my fuzzy socks, I ruminated on how far I'd fallen since the days of my pink fur jacket and silver lamé pants. My hair must've been a fright, and my back was kinked from the night's contorted sleeping. Entering the dining car, I tripped on the threshold, and it occurred to me I might be on my last leg.

Mother, on the other hand, looked quite sporty. Wearing a lime-green suit with a belted jacket and a lime-green silk tee underneath.

"Where's Clyde?" I sat.

"Sleeping in a bit. He came in and fell right in the bed. Didn't have the energy even to tell me what happened." She lifted her coffee cup, raising her eyebrows as she sipped.

I was about to launch into an explanation of my conversation with the maybe-DEA-maybe-drug-goon guy when she said, "Lucinda Mae, about your meeting with Big Doodle."

"What about it?"

"Bennie is getting on up in age."

"He's your age," I objected.

"Yes, well. Even I'm having trouble keeping my facts straight every now and again. Plus, Bennie never took care of himself—never watched what he ate, exercised, none of it. I can't believe Bill Watkins, who was always careful with his diet and had such a positive attitude, left this world before Bennie. Anyway." She waved off her distraction. "Bennie gets easily confused. Look at his comments about your father. If he says anything that doesn't quite make sense to you, I want you to attribute it to that."

"What kind of things? What are you afraid he might say?"

She cut her eyes to the window. "Things about me. Things you might not admire."

"What kind of things, Mother?"

She turned her face to me, her look impossible to read.

Then the Moffat Tunnel swallowed us up.

CHAPTER 20: Bill Watkins's Girl

The taxicab began its long ascent up the mountain.

Pine trees slipped by the window. A chipmunk on a bolder raised its paws, sniffing. Craning my neck, I tried to find the top of the mountain. White fluffy clouds scuttled across a blue sky. Which Big Doodle would I find up there? A man who would ruin his best friend's family to save his own hide? Or the good-natured Big Doodle I remembered from my childhood?

Impossible to predict, really. Big Doodle might have high-tailed it out of the Chicken Convention to avoid me. But when he'd heard my voice in his office, he'd immediately told me to come on over. But that was before my screwed-up conversation with the goon. What if the man was a federal agent, and he'd done what Clyde said, calling Big Doodle to warn him I was on the way? What if I was greeted by a squad of police, guns cocked?

I settled back, and the plastic seat covers of the cab crackled. I'd never been involved with the law before. Other than the time Pammy went to conduct a spa and walked in on a dead couple sprawled on the bed. Fortunately, the time of death (carbon monoxide poisoning from the space heater) occurred when Pammy was with me. I went to the police and set them straight. It was a terrible ordeal but nothing compared to this.

When the phone rang showing Pammy's number, I stared at it a minute. Karma, the bitch, was beginning to scare the crap out of me. The cab made a sharp turn, and I leaned to the left. The phone rang again. The driver and I locked eyes in the rearview mirror. I answered the phone.

"You owe me, girl."

"You found something?"

"I sure did. I went ahead and used my bank connections—what's a little jail time between friends? How do you put up with that trust officer, Lucinda? The man has a major stick up his ass. But that fact works to our advantage, as such men rarely get attention from cute females such as *moi*."

"You sweet-talked Gunther Armstrong?"

"I did. Very productively too."

"No shit?" Making headway with Gunther was as hard as riding a bicycle on gravel.

"Know what he said?"

"How can I know when you won't tell me!" I glanced out the window. If the angle of the tree line meant anything, we were halfway to the top of the mountain.

"Gunther makes a deposit in your savings account every month."

"I know that. Sonny Floyd, who bought Daddy's business, is paying on time. He sends a check each month."

"The money's not from Sonny Floyd."

"It's not?" I paused, remembering the Feds vague reference to "money changing hands."

"Guess where it's coming from?"

Silence.

"Big Doodle Dayton!"

"Big Doodle?"

"Yep. Gunther thought you might be Big Doodle's hometown squeeze, but I set him straight. Not his mistress. His *daughter* perhaps."

"Is this a joke? Because I'm not laughing."

"I know, right? Who would ever believe you'd bang Big Doodle? You can do a *lot* better than that old coot, even if he is rich."

"Pammy, was Gunther serious about the money coming from Big Doodle?"

"Dead serious. We went through two bottles of wine trying to figure out why Big Doodle would be paying you money. 'Daughter 'was the best answer I could come up with. You have a better explanation?"

Pammy was jabbering on, but I was remembering Mother's words: "I need to talk to you about your father, and it's not a conversation I intend to have on the phone." Could my mother have possibly kept such a thing from me? I didn't want to believe it, but I felt again the shock of walking into the ICU and realizing Daddy was dying.

The cab took another hairpin curve, and my stomach lurched. I thought I might throw up.

"I don't know if I can take much more of this," I said, referring to the winding roads, the unexpected curves in my life. I knew a quest would test your fortitude, but what the hell?

"It's a mess, it truly is, girl," Pammy said. "But look on the bright side. Your dad might not be your dad, but he's not a drug lord, either."

I focused on the road—that always helped me with carsickness, a trick my dad had taught me when I was a little kid...at least I thought I'd learned it from my dad. "Oh God, Pammy. What were we talking about?"

"Who's your daddy?"

"Okay. Let's say Big Doodle was my father"—the very idea made me wince—"so he starts supporting me after Daddy dies. But that doesn't explain the money on Daddy's tax returns."

"I have a theory. You want to hear it?"

"Does it involve money laundering?"

She was silent.

A tiny rodent of some sort ran into the road, causing the cabbie to swerve and sling me against the door. "Sorry," the driver called over his shoulder. I couldn't bear to look behind us to see if the poor little bugger lay squished in our wake.

"Are you okay?" Pammy asked.

"Yeah, I'm great now that we've figured out my daddy isn't my daddy *and* he's a drug lord."

"I've made things a lot worse, haven't I?"

"Join the crowd." I hung up a little more abruptly than I should have.

Big Doodle giving me money? Why would he do that? I tried to come up with a sensible explanation, but my mind was suffering from information overload—so now Big Doodle wasn't the one putting us in the poorhouse; he was the one keeping me out?

I caught myself rubbing my forehead. Mother did that when she was overwhelmed. I forced myself to be calm. Why had this trip gotten so convoluted? The answer drifted down like a slow pop fly released by the Universe: you and your mother need to talk.

Mother had been wanting to talk for a while. All those annoying pregnant pauses in our conversations. Why hadn't I told her to say what was on her mind?

Probably the same reason I hadn't talked to her about what was on *my* mind, which was, why hadn't she told me my daddy was about to die?

"We're here," the driver announced.

We emerged from yet another switchback, and there was Big Doodle's mansion—white columns, wraparound porches: Tara in the Rocky Mountains. Big Doodle's house was right where a normal person would hate to have a house. Every car coming round the mountain would flash its headlights into your living room. The driver agreed to return in one hour and sped off.

I took my time walking to the front door. My stomach was in knots. If Big Doodle blurted out something about him and Mother while I was trying to talk to him about recanting, I would probably hurl on one of his miniature horses. I took a deep breath and exhaled. I rang the bell.

The porch where I waited was deep as a double-wide. It held a sofa and two side chairs and a table with a lamp—an entire set of living room furniture, complete with straw rug. Pammy was right: Big Doodle was rich. If I was Big Doodle's daughter and I could get my hands on some of that money, I could use it to save my family.

What family?

The door opened.

Standing there, holding on to the doorknob, Big Doodle looked smaller than I remembered—without the chicken suit, I guess. Must have been early in the day for his household because he was still in his bathrobe. The hem of too-long pajamas pooled on the parquet floor.

"I'm Lucinda Mae Watkins," I was saying when Big Doodle erupted.

"I swanee, if it isn't Bill Watkins's girl," and he flung open the door.

"Yeah, I'm Bill Watkins's girl," I repeated as tears started in my eyes.

"Now, now." Big Doodle waved me inside. "It's been a long time, it sure has. You come on in here. It's always good to see hometown folks."

I wiped my feet on the mat and peeped into the foyer. As I entered, Big Doodle patted me on the back. "You sure do favor your daddy. I mean in the face. What did you say you go by? Didn't sound quite right somehow."

Big Doodle acted so genuinely happy to see me, repeatedly naming me as my daddy's child, I almost hugged his neck. "It's Lucinda, but you might remember Daddy calling me Cindy Lou."

"Cindy Lou. That brings back memories, it sure does."

A woman hovered in the hallway. She had to be Big Doodle's wife, but I had not one whit of memory of her. Mrs. Big Doodle had a long, skinny neck and big, gawking glasses. I swear to God she could have been the cartoon chicken lady who was always trying to trick Foghorn Leghorn into marrying her. Unlike Big Doodle, she was dressed for the day, an apron over her flowered shift.

"Miss Sissy." Big Doodle motioned her to join us. "This is Bill Watkins's girl. I told you she was coming."

Miss Sissy nodded curtly—probably figured me for an Edison hobo looking for a handout from the famous

Big Doodle Dayton. Or maybe she was aware of the allegations against my daddy and was put off by the drug scandal. In any event, I was glad when she excused herself to get a tray of iced tea.

A chicken strutted through the foyer, a real live, sparkling white rooster.

"Prophet, say hi to missy."

The rooster halted in its progress and blinked its beady eyes at me.

"Another Prophet?" The rooster was a regular ol' chicken, not a Naked Neck. "Did you get the photo I sent of us, Big Doodle? The one I sent to the Convention?"

"Prophet the Twelfth," Big Doodle said, as if he hadn't heard my question. "This one thinks he runs the place." To the chicken, he said, "If you're going to be rude, then git!"

Prophet slowly turned his look on Big Doodle, giving him the once-over as if he could see Big Doodle's future and it wasn't pretty.

"Chickens," Big Doodle said as Prophet strutted on by. "Got the manners of weasels."

We exited the foyer—the house was big enough to hold the mythical bowling alley, but there wasn't a miniature horse in sight—and Big Doodle ushered me into the library.

"What brings you to the Rocky Mountains, little lady?" He and I sat in matching leather chairs.

"The train. From Jackson to Chicago to North Dakota—"

"I mean, why are you here, child?" Big Doodle lightly tapped the arm of his leather chair. The chairs

were overstuffed, with big arms that reached around
Big Doodle and dwarfed him in their luxury.

"I went to the Convention first, but you weren't
there."

He waited.

"I sent a message? Through the website?"

"Messages headed my way have to wind their way
through lines long as rides at Disney World. What was
it you wanted to see me about?"

"I need to talk to you about the drug scandal."

"You want some breakfast?" Big Doodle popped
out of his overstuffed chair right as I was noticing that
Miss Sissy never returned with the iced tea.

"Why sure." Probably best to adopt a go-along, get-
along approach.

Big Doodle led me through a wallpapered hallway
into a small, tunnel-like cut-through that dumped us
into an enormous kitchen. "My blessed mama, she
loved that song 'Midnight in Jamaica.' She longed to go
to Jamaica, stick a flower in her hair, stroll on the beach
in the moonlight. She never got there, so I put the goat
on the menu in her honor. Never expected my mama's
goat to be hijacked by dopers."

He wandered around his big ol' kitchen, opening
and closing drawers. "They shut down the Pancake
Shack, the breakfast spot where my Wednesday
morning men's group met. Claimed it failed the health
inspection. Stormtroopers with clipboards ran us out of
there. Wouldn't even let me finish my waffle. Now I
gotta eat my breakfast at home."

He retied the knot in his striped bathrobe. The man
was a dresser after my own heart. His red fuzzy slippers

matched the bright red stripe in his dragging pajamas. "Miss Sissy don't eat before noon."

"Probably how she keeps her figure," I said as he retrieved a packet from the fridge.

"Sometimes she'll make me some French toast if I ask. Won't eat it herself." He poked a hot dog into one of those rotary hot dog cookers. When he plugged it in, the coils glowed orange. "There's chocolate milk in the fridge if you want." Then he added, "How *is* your mama?" as if the connection between his statement and mine were women who kept their figure.

"She's fine." I watched the hot dogs rotate in the cooker like a miniature Ferris wheel. "Worried about Daddy's reputation, of course."

Big Doodle's head had disappeared into the open refrigerator. Butt in the air, he pulled things from the fridge, left and right, and slapped them on the countertop. Mayonnaise, ketchup, mustard, relish, and he was still going.

"What's Bill Watkins gotten himself into this time?" He looked up at his mess of condiments and slapped down a package of cheddar cheese.

Now that set me back.

"Your chicken scandal," I said sharply.

Big Doodle slowly turned from the fridge. His eyes were wide. Big Doodle had pale blue eyes, almost no eyelashes, and pale skin that didn't offer much support to his overall looks. "Bill Watkins is involved with the dopers? How is that?"

Then it hit me: Big Doodle didn't know my daddy was dead. He couldn't be putting money into my account to support his orphaned daughter because he didn't know I was orphaned. Big Doodle, in fact, had not a clue what was going on.

"My daddy is dead, Big Doodle. The newspapers are saying he was involved in the Edison Chicken Palace Emporium doper scandal because *you* said the culprits were the local investors. You've been maligning the dead, Big Doodle."

At that Big Doodle sat his tailbone down on the kitchen floor and ran his hand through his straggly hair. He hiccuped, and his cheeks wobbled with emotion. "Bill Watkins is dead?"

His heartfelt reaction restored my faith in him.

"The big C," I said, because that's the way my mother would've said it, and since she wasn't there, the burden fell to me. "He didn't last six weeks."

"When?" Big Doodle was practically sprawled on the floor, which I was glad Miss Sissy wasn't there to see. I intuited she wouldn't approve of discussing death while sprawled on the kitchen floor.

"Two years ago this month."

"And you've come all this distance to tell me personally that Bill Watkins passed from this earth? I swanee." He was getting sappy, his pale eyes weepy. "You know, he was my best running buddy at the Academy. Bill Watkins pulled my nuts out of the fire more than once. Excuse my language, little lady, Air Force talk. But I owe that man my life."

Then Big Doodle laid his face in his hands and boohooed.

It touched me, even though I suspected Big Doodle was prone to weeping at the drop of a hat. Still, I patted his shoulder, consoling him for my own daddy's death, and told him to stay seated while I put his hot dog together. The hot dog reminded me of my encounter with the man in the mirrored sunglasses. If the man had warned Big Doodle I was a dangerous mob queen, Big Doodle had obviously not listened.

He pointed to the relish, the mayo, the mustard, and I handed him his dog. "Here you go, Big Doodle."

"Sit with me, child." He patted the tile. "Let me tell you some stories about your daddy."

Any questions I had about my parentage evaporated as Big Doodle launched into a series of fond recollections about my Daddy—all of which were off-color. Big Doodle had not a hint of nervousness, and his memories of "that ol' buzzard Bill Watkins," were warm and genuine. Several times I asked him to repeat a detail about "my father," and he obliged without blinking. I was trying to decide if I should ask him why he was depositing money into my account or wait until I'd gotten him to agree to withdraw his statement about the investors, when Miss Sissy wandered in. She was wearing a tennis outfit, carrying a tennis racket.

"Big Doodle?" Miss Sissy asked, because we were eating our dogs jumbled there on the floor in the middle of a pile of napkin remains.

Big Doodle wiped his mouth, crawled over to his wife, and threw his arms around her calves. "Bill Watkins is dead!" he wailed, exposing all kinds of half-eaten hot dog parts.

If I hadn't been with him this entire time, I would've sworn he was slobbering drunk.

Miss Sissy looked at me. "Your father?"

"Yes, ma'am." I was relieved to find no doubt in my mind about the truth of it.

"You going to the funeral, Bennie?"

"He's been dead, Miss Sissy." I pushed myself off the floor. "I came here to ask Big Doodle to rid my dad's name from the taint of the Chicken Palace Emporium doper scandal. Big Doodle implied my dad was involved in the mess."

"Did you say that about this girl's father?" she asked Big Doodle.

He wrung his hands. "I might have, I surely might have. You know how those PR folks shove stuff in my face, ordering me to read it to the buying public. I could've said something bad about Bill Watkins and not even known it." Tears seeped from his eyes.

"You gonna fix it, Bennie?" Miss Sissy lifted Big Doodle's chin with her palm. "You going to do that for this girl? It'll make you feel better."

Big Doodle nodded his head in her palm like a heavy-jawed bulldog.

"What'll it take?" Miss Sissy turned her gaze toward me.

"We can settle on what he should say." I examined the perfectly good kitchen table going to waste. "We can write it out here."

And that's what we did, me and Big Doodle and Miss Sissy at that beautiful oak table, Miss Sissy taking dictation, me and Big Doodle negotiating what to say.

While Miss Sissy scribbled, I considered how to ask Big Doodle to re-instate my daddy's "be kind to chickens" philosophy. I had concluded the request was too much and might crater the whole deal, when Prophet wandered into the kitchen. The chicken's toes tapped on the tile.

"Why don't you add a sentence or two commending Prophet, Big Doodle?"

Big Doodle glanced across the room. The rooster was circling its scrawny neck like a feathery Mick Jagger. "You want me to commemorate that old bird?"

"Prophet, and my childhood chicken Peck, and Poppa Dean's chicken Hunt. The chickens in our lives. It's one of the values our families share, yours and mine. Loving our chickens. Daddy would appreciate that."

"Okay. Whatever you say, little lady."

As Big Doodle inserted my addition, I secretly crowed. I'd planted in his statement the ticking bomb that would explode into a revolution of fried chicken chain management. If nothing else came of this, at least I'd done one thing right.

When we finished with our work, Miss Sissy fixed her own dog. "Oh, what the hey. It's a special day," and she bit in.

*

Big Doodle had canceled my taxi, insisting on taking me to the train station himself. I hadn't had time to mention my family was traveling with me, and frankly, I was hoping we could avoid that scene.

The train station was full of hustle and bustle, Mother and Clyde nowhere to be seen. Big Doodle hugged me goodbye, patting me on the back.

"Life is a mystery," he sighed.

"Thank you, Big Doodle. For everything."

He fished the slip of paper with the public statement from his pocket. He examined it. "Can't imagine Bill Watkins involved in anything illegal."

He chuckled.

I chuckled back.

He fingered the paper. "What if he was?"

"Mr. Dayton, he wasn't."

"But what if he was? What if the PR people knew what they were talking about?"

"They didn't."

"Seems like I have a duty to find that out for myself before I go exonerating him."

He was folding the paper in half, stuffing it in his shirt pocket. The train whistle blew.

I grabbed him by the arm. "Mr. Big Doodle, I've got to go. Give me your word you'll read that statement to the public and exonerate my dad. Let the rest take care of itself."

He shook his head in sorrow. "Don't nothing ever take care of itself, child."

"Benjamin Dayton, why you mealy-mouthed, no-good, son of a—"

"Pooh!" I exclaimed. "Pooh!"

And there she was in the flesh. My grandmother's lumpy self in her lumpy dress with a black pocketbook big as Noah's Ark slung across her arm. She glowered at Big Doodle, who rounded his mouth into an O.

I gave Pooh a big hug, pulling her off balance and causing a hairy nose to pop from the top of the pocketbook.

"Ikie!"

Ikie yipped his pleasure, at which point Pooh stuffed his little head back in the pocketbook.

"Hide yourself, Mister," she scolded. "You remember what we talked about."

I clapped my hand over my mouth. "Ikie is a stowaway!"

Big Doodle was saying, "Nice to see you again, Mrs. Varner," while Pooh was saying, "Don't sweet talk me, you traitor. It's 'cause of you that I'm standing on this platform right now."

"Me?" Big Doodle echoed my own question.

"Don't have anywhere else to lay my head, now do I? Thrown out on my keister."

"They took the house?" Surely not even the long arm of the law could move that fast.

"Those nogoodniks took possession of the house. Skippy Van Zant calls it 'protective custody.' They're turning it inside out, looking for incriminating evidence."

"What have you done, Mrs. Varner, to lead you to lose your house?"

"Me?" Pooh jerked her neck. "What rock have you been living under, Bennie Dayton?"

The train whistle blew.

"The train is leaving." I glanced at Big Doodle, who was patting the pocket where the precious paper hid—if need be, I would stay right here on this platform until he agreed to do what he said he'd do. Turning to Pooh, I asked, "Are Mother and Clyde already on board?"

Big Doodle stilled. "Your mother? Rita Rae Varner is on the train?" His eyes bugged out like a teenager who'd been told his crush was downing shots of tequila at the next table and wanted him to join her.

"Rita Rae *Watkins*," growled Pooh.

Big Doodle climbed the train steps. "Let's take our seats. Sometimes they serve Squench's corndogs on this train."

"Where are you *going*, Big Doodle?"

"I can't let you down. Can't let me down, either." He saluted the conductor. "I'll be buying my ticket on board."

He must have been well-known in these parts because the conductor let him get on board, and I skipped up after him.

"I'll make some calls, clear this up, get off at the next stop. No big deal."

Behind me, Pooh huffed, "You better keep your paws off her, you decrepit old charlatan. She doesn't need you canoodling with her fancy again."

Which dynamited a hole in my certainty about who my father was.

CHAPTER 21: Mother's Greta Garbo Pose

Leading Big Doodle to his berth, I made him promise to make his phone calls to his PR team ASAP. Pooh hovered behind us in the hallway, keeping her beady eye on Big Doodle. I had to practically shove him into his berth—the man would not stop talking about Mother—but I finally got the door closed.

"That man is slipperier than a greased pig." I exhaled.

"Don't believe a word he says." Pooh stroked Ikie's head. "He's craftier than a crocodile."

"He likes Mother."

She bopped Ikie back into her pocketbook. "Tell me something I don't know."

We found Mother and Clyde in the buffet with Rhymers and Gentry, the couple from Mississippi. The group was laughing and joking, happy as all get-out.

"Rita Rae," Pooh humphed into their gaiety.

Mother's face fell, wary of what was coming next. I felt so bad for her. Even though Rita Rae was almost sixty years old, she was still her mother's daughter. I guess at any age, criticism from your mother didn't sit well. I flashed on Rita Rae's relaxed, happy face when she was telling us the story about North Dakota and the oil fires. The change was dramatic, and it made me sad to think I might be seeing the future between Mother and me.

Mother stood, introducing Pooh to her new friends. "And this is Rhymers and this is Gentry."

At which point, Ikie poked his nose from the handbag and yapped.

Pooh stuffed the dog back into the pocketbook like a Jack-in-the-box. "He's a service dog." She smiled sweetly at the Mississippi couple.

"Yes, my mother is almost blind." Rita Rae grabbed Pooh's arm as if she were about to walk into a wall.

"Service dog, my—," Clyde began, but Mother must have kicked him under the table because he said, "Ooph!" and shut up.

"Look." Mother pointed to a young girl at the buffet counter. Tattoos inked up and down the girl's arms. "That child is covered in tattoos."

It gave them something to exclaim over until Rhymers and Gentry said their goodbyes. Pooh followed them out to find her berth, stowaway Ikie bouncing along.

"Big Doodle is making his phone calls," I assured Mother...right as the door at the end of the car sucked open and Big Doodle appeared.

I wanted to holler at him, "Get back in your berth!" But I couldn't be ugly. All of my hopes hinged on Big Doodle, however emotionally unhinged he might be.

Big Doodle joined us, mooning greetings to Mother and barely acknowledging Clyde.

Mother shifted sideways. She crossed her legs where Big Doodle could see them. "We're going to St. Paul. They got an Elvis polka band in St. Paul."

She turned her profile to Big Doodle and raked her fingers through her red hair.

I gaped at her. That was Mother's Greta Garbo pose—her body language saying "I vant to be alone," but her dramatic hair raking saying, "come hither." The Greta Garbo pose came out whenever Mother wanted to flirt with deniability. Deniability she now required, what with Clyde sitting right beside her.

"The Gminski family is engaged in an oompah band competition," she explained to Big Doodle. "It should be quite the spectacle."

My mother was inveigling Big Doodle into coming to Minnesota with us, using the Elvis oompah band as bait!

As if the big galoot needed any encouragement.

Big Doodle cocked his big old head. "Elvis polka band, is that right? Can't say as I've ever seen an Elvis polka band. I've seen a collection of harp-plying Elvi, most talented Elvi you've ever seen. The Heavenly Graceland Elvi. Never an Elvis polka band, though."

"I hear the Gminskis can hold their own," Clyde chimed in. "Fierce competitors."

It made me feel sorry for him, trying to get his snoot back in the tent. The world must have turned upside down for me to be rooting for Clyde, but at least Clyde was Clyde, no surprises there. My mother, Big Doodle—I did not want to contemplate what might be swirling in those murky depths.

"Big Doodle? Have you made your phone calls to clear up the confusion over your drug scandal?"

"Not yet, but I will." He patted my hand.

"You need to get on it *now*."

"Have you ever known me to go back on my word, child?"

"You abandoned my daddy's 'be nice to chickens' philosophy."

"That was different." He glanced at Mother as if worried about her reaction. "That was *business*. This is personal, friendship and all."

"But you haven't called," I pointed out.

"Phone reception's worthless on trains. Should've remembered that. Soon as we get near a big city, it'll be fine."

"A big city such as Chicago? It's on the way to St. Paul." Mother was cool as a cucumber. Her hot pink fingernails stroked the tabletop.

Big Doodle stared at the slowly stroking nails. "Chicago would be great."

Clyde said, "I'm sure there are lots of big cities between here and Chicago."

"You think?" Mother asked.

I couldn't speak on behalf of Clyde, but I hadn't a clue what lay between here and Chicago, other than many, many fields of wheat. "Let's keep our minds, and cell phones, open."

"'Scuse me." Clyde indicated he wanted to leave, and Mother rose. He slid out of the booth. "Got something I have to check on."

If he had an ounce of sense about him, he would be checking on the train route, looking for big cities, getting ammunition against this interloper.

"Be careful, dear," Mother said, half-hearted, and retook her seat.

Which left her and me and Big Doodle, who was staring at Mother, his face a big glop of romantic goo.

Maybe it was Mother's crossed leg. Or Big Doodle's eyes glued to Rita Rae's well-turned ankle.

Whatever, I hightailed it out of there. Yeah, I'd said no more running away. But never did I expect to witness my mother picking up Big Doodle Dayton on the train. Best to preserve my sanity, even if it did make me a coward.

*

"Mama's flirting with Big Doodle." I leaned against Pooh's sink in her train berth.

"I'm sure she has her reasons." Pooh, who'd been laying down when I knocked on the door, was trying to mush her hair back into shape. Ikie wiggled from beneath a bundle of clothes on the sofa. From the neck down, he was bald as a rat.

"Ikie!"

"He dove into the duck pond and got his hair all matted. Little girl at Stanley Park took one look at him and said, 'Squirrel!'"

"A squirrel? You not a squirrel. You a sweet dog!" I rubbed noses with the pup in case he had any lingering shame. The dog shook all over and scampered around, yapping until Pooh shook her finger at him, and he curled up on Pooh's sweater. "He looks fat," I studied his plump tummy lapping over his hind leg.

"He is fat. The vet put him on a carrot diet, but I don't know how well that'll work on a train." She lifted a plastic bag from her pocketbook. "Treats to keep him quiet."

"Mother's talking Big Doodle into coming to Minnesota with us."

"Could be."

"I have reason to believe they have history."

She snapped a treat in two and fed it to the dog.

"Senior prom," she finally said. "Your mama had to choose between Bennie Dayton and Bill Watkins."

"And she chose my daddy?"

"Never looked back. Even though Bennie had a rock 'n' roll band that your mother found very attractive."

"Big Doodle and Daddy were friends," I repeated what I'd heard all my childhood. "Didn't they both play in the marching band?"

"Pure coincidence. The only thing they had in common in high school was being sweet on your mama."

"They went to the Air Force Academy together," I argued. "They both moved back to Edison and went into the chicken business. Their lives have pretty much tracked."

"They weren't friends until senior year in high school after your mother chose between them."

"But they *were* friends?"

"They were friends. Thick as thieves at the Academy. Each other's best man in their weddings. Nothing separated them until they disagreed on the mistreatment of chickens. I can understand why Bennie admired your dad, but Lord knows why Bill admired Bennie."

"Maybe because he built the biggest fast-food chicken chain in the Southeast?"

"Don't be smart."

"They both married women with chicken legs."

"Your mother has fine legs." Pooh picked up a brush, but instead of taking a turn at her hair, she went at Ikie's mane. He preened his neck and almost purred.

I toyed with the cord on the blinds. "Pooh, is it possible Big Doodle was giving me money for some reason?"

She stroked the dog's long, silky mane. "Have you had a chance to talk to your mother since she arrived?"

"Not yet."

"You might want to do that."

"How can I when she's spending all her time flirting with Big Doodle?"

When she didn't answer, I said, "I'm glad you're here. Things are a terrible mess. Each time I try to fix it, I make it worse. I had such high hopes for my quest. I even thought I could make Big Doodle reinstate Daddy's "be kind to chickens" philosophy."

"That would be wonderful, Lucinda. It would make your dad happy."

"Yeah, I tricked Big Doodle into putting a hidden message into his public statement. I've planted a bomb, but I don't know how to light the fuse."

"Something will come to you."

I opened and closed the blinds like an SOS. "Did you really get kicked out of the house? Or were you just saying that to make Big Doodle feel guilty?"

"I was told to vacate the premises—leave that blind alone. Peggy Margaret offered to put me up, but with the rest of you out here, it seemed the better choice."

"A man might be following me. A goon."

"That man Augie?"

"No! How does everyone know about Augie?" It had to be Erick who'd told them, but why would he share that with my family?

"Erick told us. He was trying to reassure your mother, telling her you were having the time of your life. I don't think he wanted her to actually come check on you."

"Mother doesn't have to worry about Augie. He's a great guy. I'm seeing him when we get back to St. Paul." I didn't tell her about Augie's warnings—why did she need to know that?

"Be that as it may, you're prone to diving into the lake before you check to see how deep the water is. Sometimes you hit your noggin on the bottom, and wind up mad at the lake."

"Grief made me marry Stirling. I met a man on the train who was really nice. He helped me see that. I was distraught over Daddy dying."

"You've always had an exuberant personality, Lucinda. Grief simply got you confused about where to put that exuberance."

"I'm gonna fix this thing, Pooh. I swear I will."

"I don't doubt it. I didn't change all those dirty diapers for nothing. Remember: you don't have to fix everything yourself. Others are there to help."

"Trust Big Doodle, you mean? He's a tad flighty, Pooh, to say the least."

"No. Trust your mother, who loved Bill Watkins more than anyone can imagine."

She leaned back to assess her work. Ikie yipped impatiently, and she went back at it.

That dog's mane wasn't tangled. He wanted the attention. And Pooh gave it to him because she loved him more than anyone can imagine.

"Okay," I said.

"Okay what?"

"I'll see how it goes."

Of course, my entire caravan was hurtling forward on a train that wouldn't stop for love nor money. No turning back either. That was one thing about trains: no second-guessing. Decisions made were decisions made.

Even if they turned out to be wrong.

CHAPTER 22: Mr. Potato Heart

I couldn't pry Mother away from Big Doodle with a crowbar. During the long trek to Minnesota, all of Mother's time, attention, and feminine wiles were trained on "Bennie dear." Who knew if Big Doodle was making phone calls to exonerate Daddy or if he even remembered why he was on the train? His puppy dog eyes never left Mother. He jumped up when she walked into the dining car. He grinned when she said the least clever thing, such as, "Pass the salt, please." Then he jumped up when she walked out of the car. He was a puppet on Mother's string, and as a result, I didn't have a moment alone with her. After hounding me about "needing to talk," she had entirely lost interest. Try as I might, she rebuffed my every overture. Even though her attitude made me want to snatch a knot in her tail, all I could do was what Pooh had advised: trust her.

I was so glad to see Minnesota arrive, I almost wept. Finally—Mother and I could have a private confab at the Gminski's.

Crazy me.

Ten o'clock on a Saturday morning and everyone in the Gminski household was drunk.

Maybe it was better that way. Here we were, the Southern contingent, showing up in full force when Karen Gminski wouldn't spit on a person from Mississippi if their hair was on fire, and we were all shouting with our very beings, *Mississippi! Mississippi!*

Robert Gminski was slapping Clyde on the back and leading him to the bar. Karen, her halter top barely containing the snuggling whales, stroked Mother's lime green suede jacket—had Mother brought nothing but lime green on this trip? The twins popped hands over surprised mouths at Ikie tucked into Pooh's pocketbook. Big Doodle was deeply engaged in a conversation with a man with a burr cut, something about an El Camino with no license plates. In the background, a loud thumping song played: "Smoke on the Water," oompah style. In the chaos, someone belted out, "Wreck of the Edmund Fitzgerald!"

Well, it's true what they say: you can't go home again, even when it's not your home. Everything in the room had changed. The trophies had disappeared from the end tables, replaced by platters of food. The floor tambourine, baby tuba, and accordion were missing. In their place, four TVs were stacked on chairs, each television pointing in a different direction: north, south, east, west. On screen, a group of five-year-olds gyrated in silver swimsuits. Dr. Detroit, the druggie bird, was nowhere in sight.

I felt adrift, the billowing tent dress I'd chosen for the day not helping. I wove in and out of folks I didn't know and ended up in the dining room. The table was dotted with potato pancakes, barbecued cocktail weenies, and, of all things, tomato aspic. Rita Rae was gonna be flabbergasted to learn they ate tomato aspic up North—bet they didn't put it on a soda cracker with homemade mayonnaise though. In the middle of the table was a big bowl of ambrosia, flakes of canned coconut, canned mandarin oranges, and bottled maraschino cherries. At least the grapefruit was fresh. There was also a chocolate dessert that looked suspiciously like Pooh's Katherine Hepburn brownies.

We Watkins women don't travel far without our brownies.

I was filling a Styrofoam bowl with ambrosia when Clyde sauntered in, twirling his drink with his pinkie the same way Mr. Gminski did—the man absorbed everything around him. Pooh's transistor radio rode his belt like a tool belt. He took a swig of his drink and grimaced, stretching his mouth across his big dentures as he surveyed the room. "I heard talk of Elvi. I don't see nary an Elvi."

"You gonna fight for her?" I asked.

He squinted at me. "I'd rather be in Hell with my back broken than let that little gal get away from me. Problem is, Rita Rae's got a mind of her own. You never know what she's up to."

We watched as Mother sashayed our way. She clapped a hand on Clyde's arm and drug him off to meet a couple who were wearing green-and-white leis. I peeked around the corner, where I spied Big Doodle. He was not on the phone. He was talking to a woman who was popping chewing gum like a truck driver. She, too, had huge bosoms. It made me wonder if they just grew them bigger up north—maybe the cold climate.

I was moving to interrupt them when Mrs. Gminski appeared at my elbow. She nodded toward the mantel. The twins had freed Ikie from Pooh's purse and were holding him in front of an eyeball-shaped video camera perched on the edge of the mantel. "The *Save the World* show is filming all of this. If Erick wins, it'll cut to us, live."

As we watched the twins jiggle Ikie in front of the camera, she said, "Nice family you've got. Who is that Big Doodle, though?"

"He's the pot-in-every-chicken man."

She stared blankly at me.

"You know, the politician's promise, a chicken in every pot, except the drug scandal is stuffing pot in chickens?" I felt a little stupid: it's not much of a joke if you have to explain it.

Finally, I conceded. "Family friend. Sort of."

She nodded, not even smiling when one of her daughters crossed her eyes and waggled Ikie for all the world to see. "You know, it's important to Erick to win this thing." She gestured at the TV, where the five-year-old dancers had been replaced by a lady displaying a toilet seat that looked to be coated in something waterproof. The lady dribbled water on the seat; it ran off. "He doesn't let on, but what that judge said hurt him badly. If his invention wins, he'll get a chance to prove the judges wrong."

I hmmed, pretending to know what she was talking about, even though Erick had never told me exactly what the hateful French judge had said to him. On screen a man in a long, white beard appeared, holding a plaster copy of the Ten Commandments. The Commandments blared, "Thou *Shalt* Not Steal. Thou *Shalt* Not Lie."

Oh, to hell with it.

"Karen, I feel terrible about running off right at Erick's big moment. But I had to find Big Doodle. The Feds slapped a lien on the money from the Chicken Palace, and Mother relies on that chicken money. And they took Big Blue, that's Mother's Cadillac, and they made Pooh leave the house. Mother thought they might even take her fur coat. Well, it's squirrel, and it's really ratty, but it's the only fur coat she owns."

But Karen was hardly listening because of a conversation Clyde was having next to us. Talk of "tanning bed" and "delicate parts" and "shock" drifted our way.

"Listen, honey. I'm not the one you owe an apology." Karen swept up my discarded ambrosia bowl and turned to sail off.

"Wait." I grabbed her arm. "What did the judge say that hurt Erick so badly he traveled all the way to Minnesota to go on a tacky TV game show—our cool-as-the-other-side-of-the-pillow Erick?"

She was grim. "That judge told him he danced with his heart, not his legs. To a trained ballet dancer, there's no worse slap in the face. From that judge. In Mississippi."

"He's on! He's on!"

The twins were jumping and shouting.

I squirmed through the crowd to get a better look. Erick was gorgeous—cool, calm, and collected. Only his left eye twitched a little. If you looked closely, you could see the "Wave If You Knew The King" button pinned on his shirt.

When the emcee nodded, Erick held up an anatomically correct heart about the size of a potato. Legs sprouted from the bottom of the heart. Erick set it on the demonstration table, the little heart standing tall on its plastic legs.

"Mr. Potato Heart?" someone said, and was immediately shushed.

With a delicate touch, Erick lifted the valve on top of the heart, and the legs began dancing.

To "I Left My Heart in San Francisco."

Except it was the oompah version: "I Left My"—oompah-pah—"Heart in San"—oompah-pah—"Francisco."

The heart's little legs kicked up and down, but when the song hit "oompah," the heart rocked, back...and forth.

It was the cutest thing I'd ever seen. Who cared if it made not one whit of sense? How could a three-inch-high, kicking heart save the world?

"Well, I'll be danged." Clyde whistled. "That boy has talent." This from the man who once called Erick my too-too friend: "He's just too *too*, that boy."

"He won *my* heart!" Robert sang out. He hugged Karen by the neck, dragging at her shirt and almost releasing one of the whales. "That's my wifey singing inside that heart!"

"And me on tambourine," Ingrid or Debbie crowed.

Then Erick was gone, vanished from the screen.

"That's it?" I cried, stricken.

"That was taped." Debbie ran up to me.

"When they finish showing all the semifinalists, they'll go live," Ingrid said.

"At the mall. To pick the finalists."

"If he wins, he'll be in the finals."

"And we'll all be on—"

"National TV!" they screamed in unison, holding hands and jumping in a circle. Then a girl ran over and pulled them onto the floor. They all crumpled in a giggling heap, scattering everyone around them.

I stepped aside and almost backed into Pooh.

"Sorry, sorry." I balanced against her arm.

"No matter." She fed Ikie ambrosia from a bowl. His little pink tongue lapped and lapped. A piece of coconut stuck to his nose.

"Come here." I lifted the dog's chin and snagged the wayward flake. "Gotta look your best if you're gonna be on national TV."

"What do you think of his bow?" Pooh had tied a tiny scarf with paw prints into Ikie's topknot, and she leaned back to admire her handiwork.

"I like it. Trez chick," I added. Which is what Daddy always said instead of "tres chic." Whenever Mother or I would prance out in a new dress—sundress, cocktail dress, velvet Christmas dress—"Trez chick," was always his response.

"Second time I've seen you tear up since I arrived." Pooh tucked Ikie in the crook of her elbow. "What's gotten into you? You pregnant?"

Both she and Ike looked at me, all ears.

"No. At least, I don't think so. It's just that I have messed things up so badly." I removed the barrette from my hair and stroked my bangs, combing through the tangles, trying to get everything back in place.

But it wasn't easy.

"I disappointed Erick after he let me come on his trip with him. I slept with someone I probably shouldn't have." I spied Big Doodle hunkered in the corner, phone to his ear. Mother was standing next to him— much closer than necessary. "And I might have brought Big Doodle back into our lives when I shouldn't have."

Pooh hiked Ikie on her hip. "What did I tell you to do?"

"Trust my mother?"

Out of nowhere, Debbie popped up and snatched Ikie. "It's Erick and the toilet lady!" She danced Ikie in a circle.

"In the finals!" Ingrid squealed while Debbie kissed Ikie smack on the nose.

Behind them, Mother slipped through the kitchen door, unattended.

Ikie set up a barking the likes of which you've never heard of.

I hurried after Mother.

*

I found Mother standing at the butcher-block table in her lime-green suit. A coffee pot gurgled on the counter. She busily sliced pats of butter onto wax paper, ignoring the stool beside her, hunched over like a crone.

"Whatcha doing?"

"Butter to dab on the apple cobbler. They don't do enough fat up here."

On the counter was the butter carton, sporting the little Indian maiden. "Well, we are in Minn-e–so-ta."

"Don't make fun, Lucinda."

I watched the knife slice through the butter.

"I took money from Bennie Dayton." Her words came fast and clean, each word punctuated with a *whack* of the knife. "I set up an account with his money, and I didn't tell you about it."

"You what?"

She turned, leaning against the butcher block. "I told you, Bennie cheated your dad out of his interest in the Chicken Palace chain. A men's breakfast group Bennie belongs to convinced him to make amends.

Bennie calculated how much Bill would have made if Bennie had given him stock in the chain."

"Rather than ownership in the Edison CP?"

Mother nodded and went back to work on the butter. "Bill didn't want the money. By that point, Bennie had dropped Bill's natural growing methods, and Bill thought the money was tainted. Bennie sent it anyway. Of course, Bill didn't use it for himself—he bought me the house. The rest he gave to ETC, which ticked Bennie off big time."

"The charity Daddy set up."

She hesitated for a second and resumed her slicing. "He did. He wanted to support growers who were using ethical techniques." She looked at me from beneath her eyebrows. "Ethical standards are all well and good, but they do not make a lot of money."

"But Big Doodle knew Daddy supported being nice to chickens. Why did the donation tick him off?"

"Could be the kids filming fake commercials at Chicken Palace locations. On the public sidewalk, where they couldn't be run off. Their videos were all over the internet. Kids in chicken costumes moaning over their lost chicken childhoods."

"I never heard of such a thing."

"Bill hadn't either, but Bennie wouldn't listen to that. Personally, I think Bennie was mad because he had made this grand gesture, and Bill rejected it. When Bill died, I waited to see if the checks would come. They did."

"Because Big Doodle didn't know Daddy was dead."

Mother turned to me, her knife raised. "What are you talking about? Do you think your daddy died, and I wouldn't let Bennie know?"

"He told me he didn't know. He was very upset when I broke the news."

Mother snorted. "Blubbering like a baby? That's nothing more than bad acting from the former president of our high school drama club."

"Why, that dog." I watched as Mother slid another stick of butter from the carton and unfolded the waxed paper. "Why would he pretend he didn't know Daddy was dead?"

Mother raised her palms. "Who knows? I told him he better not breathe a word to you about the money. I wanted to tell you myself. Maybe overacting was the only way he could hide his lying. Bennie has always been a bad liar."

"You were talking to Big Doodle?"

"Lucinda, I could not let you go into that meeting without trying to protect you as best I could. I'm sorry for showing up on your trip, but when Bennie told me he was in Denver, I talked Clyde into flying to Reno. I had to be there on the train with you in case Bennie did something crazy. Sometimes Bennie gets these wild ideas that seem brilliant at the time, but they're not."

"Soooooo, you were planning all along to use your charms against Big Doodle? You knew he had a crush on you, and you showed up in person to make sure he did what you wanted?"

"You give me too much credit, Lucinda. I saw Bennie and thought, better with honey than vinegar." She shifted her feet. "Anyway, when Bennie's checks kept arriving after Bill died, you were floundering, not sure about a job, and dating Stirling. I knew trouble was on its way. I took the money and created your account."

"What about the money from Sonny buying the business?"

She waved her knife. "Sonny finished his payments long ago."

"But the only reason Big Doodle was sending the money was to pay Daddy back?"

She nodded, laying each butter pat against the previous one, building a domino line of butter.

"No other reason?" I had to erase all suspicions Pammy had raised.

"Guilt money, pure and simple."

If I was sorting all this correctly, I had money coming in, but Mother didn't. "You're giving me all of Big Doodle's money? Why don't you take half for yourself?"

"Pooh asked me the same thing, but, good Lord, it was bad enough accepting it on your behalf. Every time I endorsed that check and deposited it in your account, I felt Bill Watkins glaring down at me from Heaven, shaking his head and saying, 'Now, Rita Rae, you know that's not right.' Oh, Lucinda." She stilled. "When you said Bennie was gonna sever ties with the Edison operation, I panicked. I thought he might end your checks. I sent you off on a wild goose chase, figuring if he saw you in person, he wouldn't do that. I've brought all this trouble on our heads. I should have never taken Bennie's tainted money." She bent her neck, cupping her forehead with her palm.

"No, no, Mother."

She straightened, yanking her jacket into place, and picked up the butter pats, doling them onto the cobbler, which she shoved in the oven. "Bennie Dayton and I had a come-to-Jesus last night. I told him all this foolishness about accusing Bill had to stop."

"Mother, that might be my fault. I left a garbled message at Chicken Headquarters that made them suspect Daddy was involved."

"Pshaw!" She flapped her hand. "We woke up some corporate suit and had him play that message for us. If Bennie had taken the time to listen to it, he'd have recognized it for what it was: a proper expression of sympathy. He let those corporate types use it as an excuse to point the finger at Bill."

"He knew he was accusing Daddy?"

"Bennie wants to have his cake and eat it too. Always has." Opening and shutting cabinet doors, she found a flowered china plate for the remaining butter slices. "He wouldn't let them name Bill directly, out of so-called friendship. Told them to make some vague reference to local investors. As if that would solve the problem." She set the plate on the table a little too forcefully.

"Is he going to clear it up, then?"

Mother concentrated on arranging the butter pats in a circle. "I did my best."

The grim set of her mouth made me ask, "But you didn't do too much, right?"

She kept at her work. She had knifed up enough butter to give the whole party a heart attack. Her frenetic work indicated how nervous she was—about our talk or the path she'd taken with Bennie, I didn't know.

"It's okay, Mother. Whatever you thought was best. The money, whatever. It's okay."

Actually, it was more than okay. It was pretty damn amazing. She had handled Big Doodle's guilt money and negotiated with him to clear up the scandal, all on her own. Here I was thinking Daddy's death had undone her.

"Mother." I pulled a stool from the butcher block and sat. "You know I cherished the last week I had with Daddy, right?"

She glanced at me. "Of course."

"I'm grateful to have the memories I do."

Mother abandoned the butter, sliding onto a stool by my side.

"What is it?" she asked.

CHAPTER 23: Show Your Heart

I traced a scar etched deeply into Mr. Gminski's butcher block table. A man wearing lederhosen sauntered into the kitchen, opened the refrigerator door, and removed a pitcher of beer. Upending the pitcher, he took a gulp, wiped the back of his hand across his mouth, burped, and returned the pitcher to the fridge. Then he noticed Mother and me sitting at the table, and beat a hasty retreat.

"Lucinda, what's on your mind? You can tell me, whatever it is." Mother crimped her hands on the table. Her ring finger was knotted with arthritis, the knuckle swollen. If she'd still been wearing a wedding band, she might not have been able to get it over that knuckle.

"Daddy was a real trooper, wasn't he?"

"Your dad was a fighter."

I fiddled with a slotted spoon lying on the butcher block. "Why didn't you tell me he was so sick?"

Mother sighed. "It was a mistake, Lucinda."

"But why?" I asked, undeterred by her saddened face.

She reached for my hand and gave it a squeeze. I gently withdrew it.

"When we first heard he might have cancer, Bill didn't want to tell you. You were so happy at college. Finally in your element, carefree. He didn't want to worry you until we knew there was something to worry you about. Then." She glanced around the room. "It got bad so fast. I...I didn't..."

"I'm sorry, Mother." I laid my hand on top of hers. "I shouldn't have asked."

"I am so sorry." Her jaw trembled.

"It's okay. You had no way of knowing."

"I didn't *want* to know. If I told you, I had to admit to myself: Bill Watkins was dying."

"I understand."

"Then, Bill's death. I got so afraid of everything. I'd hear myself talking and cringe at how much I sounded like Louisa Jennings. But I couldn't help it. I was frightened by this horrible thing that had come out of nowhere and ruined my life."

She didn't need to know I had thought her closed-mindedness was due to her hayseed boyfriend.

"This trip, it's been good for me. To let go a little." She stared, her eyes red-rimmed. "I didn't think it was possible, Lucinda. I didn't think Bill Watkins could actually die."

"Me neither," I whispered. "Sometimes I still can't believe it's true."

"Well. It better be." Her face crumpled into a laugh as she wiped away her tears. "If it's not, Bill Watkins is gonna be mad as a wet hen when he comes home to find Clyde Higgenbotham in his bed."

I laughed, relieved to be able to do so. Why did death have to be so hard? I thought of the boring readings we'd picked for the funeral. "Daddy looked after us so well, Mother. I wish for his funeral we'd used that Bible passage about Jesus watching over us the way a hen protects her chicks."

Mother shot me a look. "You know what was happening during that speech, right?"

"Sure," I lied.

"Jesus was riding into Jerusalem. To his death. On an ass. When was the last time you read your Bible, Lucinda?"

I shrugged. "When I found out the flock wasn't chickens?"

Mother stared.

"'Tending their flock by night'?" I quoted from the Christmas story Pooh read to me each year when I was little.

"You thought the shepherds were tending chickens?"

"Stevie Barnett said it was sheep. I thought maybe the chickens had been stolen."

She waited.

"By the shepherd's crook?"

Her lips twitched.

"To make chicken dinners. For the last supper," I concluded, and Mother shook her head while I giggled.

The laughter from the Gminskis' party drifted into the kitchen. "I think Daddy would be okay with Clyde, Mother. Even if he wasn't on the list."

"I hope so." Mother pressed her palms on the table, preparing to leave, but I caught her arm.

"Mother, can we keep talking this way? Real talking, not snipping or complaining?"

She pulled away, crossing her arms against her chest. "If I am hard on you, Lucinda, it's only because—"

"You're *worried* about me. I know. But maybe you can worry less?"

She gave me one of her looks, and I thought she was going to say, *I will if you give me less to worry about*. Instead, she said, "It's been hard since your dad died. You've been spending so much time in Jackson doing crazy things. But I guess you haven't gotten yourself killed…yet. So, okay. Maybe I can worry less."

"And you'll quit banging on my choices? My clothes, my hair, my not being Kim Stratton?"

"Kim Stratton is a beautiful girl, but she's not you, Lucinda. She's marrying that son of a bitch when everyone in town knows what a worthless husband he was. You might be…susceptible to a good-looking man, but Kim Stratton doesn't have the sense God gave a rock."

"Thank you." I patted her hand. "Tell me something. Where do you think Daddy saw me, say, ten years from now?"

"Divorced from Stirling. Planning to move to Jackson. Hyped up on your new career." Her answers came swift and sure.

"What new career?" It felt strange using my mother as an oracle, but she knew so much more than I'd given her credit for.

"Fashion designer." Her gaze wandered back to her butter work, appraising. "Fashion coordinator maybe."

"Was I happy?

"Happy as a June bug."

Which I was: a June bug, a girl born in June.

"Your daddy always saw you as happy." She bent to inspect the apple cobbler in the oven, and she could've been Pooh checking on Ikie, butt in the air.

"Mother, I…."

I wanted to tell her I was worried about this thing
we had set in motion. What if Big Doodle did what
came naturally and weaseled out of admitting he'd
made a mistake?

As if reading my thoughts, she said, "We have to
have faith, Lucinda."

Faith, I thought, plus a little action.

*

I returned to the party, where Karen Gminski stood
in the middle of the room, her chest heaving like an
opera singer about to burst into song. While I surveyed
the crowd, I asked how the oompah competition was
going.

"Fine. We're in the finals tonight, against an Elvis
band. The Teddy Beers."

"Erick told me about them. Your fierce
competitors." (Or was it the Tuba Whos?). "He assured
me y'all would win," I added, sucking up.

Pooh, who'd arrived at my side, rolled her eyes.

"They can't carry a tune in a bucket," Karen said.
"But they've got that visual thing going. It gives them
an edge."

"Have you seen Big Doodle?" I asked Pooh.

She pointed across the room, but a cousin named DJ
or PJ ducked through the doorway, a huge bouquet of
balloons blocking my view. "How 'bout our Erick!"
DJ/PJ shouted.

Each balloon was heart shaped.

"Did everyone in the world but me know about
Erick's idea?"

"It was a group effort," Karen said. When the
balloon guy walked by, she stopped him, flattened a

palm against his jaw, and kissed him hard on his cheek. "TJ makes novelties. He pressed the heart. I sang, and the family played. Erick designed the different legs."

I thought back on the performance. "The legs seemed the same to me."

"Those were the ballet dancer legs. He's also got fireman legs, policeman legs, farmer legs, all kinds of legs."

"Laigs," she pronounced it, her vowels slanting in all the wrong directions.

"And different legs because…?"

"Because that's what it takes to conquer the world. Showing your heart."

"Save the world," I corrected her. "*Your Idea Can Save the World.*"

It was her turn to roll her eyes.

Clyde wandered over, and the crowd parted, revealing Big Doodle talking on the phone. "I don't trust that man," Clyde said. "In fact, I smell a rat."

"Maybe. Or maybe it's the sauerkraut. Excuse me. Big Doodle!"

Glancing at me, he clicked off his phone and slipped it in his pocket. "Lucinda! Just who I was looking for!"

"You knew my daddy was dead!"

Big Doodle looked nonplussed. "Why, yes. I did."

"Then why all the caterwauling?"

"You were being so dramatic, I wanted to play along. You know, like when we made the chicken angel costume way back when." He flapped his wings.

"And you ran off when you knew I was coming to Chicago."

"You sent that photo of a Naked Neck."

"You knew it was me, and you left town?"

"Who else knew about the Fearsome Foursome? I mean, anyone who wasn't a chicken. The way you said it, I couldn't help but think you were looking to blackmail me."

"Blackmail?" I was incredulous. "I began this quest thinking this entire mess was my fault, but now I see the truth: you've been taking advantage. You knew my daddy wasn't part of the drug ring. You just wanted someone to blame."

"Now, now." He held up his hands, waving his fingers. "I knew no such of a thing. I pay a pile of money to folks to sort those things out, and they were talking about insider tips and gang passwords and big money flowing around where it shouldn't have been."

"That was the money *you* were sending Daddy."

Big Doodle's flapping hands gradually slowed. "Uh, a jailbird was singing?"

I stared at him. "Big Doodle, you cared about my daddy. You sent him that money, trying to make amends."

"And he flung it in my face!"

"He did not. He flung it at the Ethical Treatment of Chickens."

"Ten times worse," he humphed.

"You cared for each other, Big Doodle. You can't let people believe something about him that isn't true."

He puffed himself up. "I am Big Doodle Dayton. I can do whatever I damn well please."

"You *are* Big Doodle Dayton. The question is, which Big Doodle Dayton? The one my daddy admired? The one who was so passionate about his chicken business he sewed a homemade chicken costume and made a fool of himself on TV? Are you the Big Doodle I loved with all my child's heart?" I searched his eyes. "Or are you a calculating businessman who sits at the top of the pyramid and looks down on the little people who made you who you are?"

His look was skeptical, and I plowed on. "Big Doodle, you caused an avalanche of problems by letting folks believe something about my Daddy that isn't true. That puts karma on your tail. And believe you me, you'd much rather be dealing with me than that bitch karma."

Suddenly, the crowd shifted, flowing closer to the TV. Everyone except Big Doodle, who pivoted, ducking down the hallway.

"Big Doodle!" I stamped my foot.

"Lucinda!" Debbie grabbed me by the arm, dragging me to the front of the crowd.

Erick was on the screen with the toilet lady.

"Who wants a waterproof toilet?" a middle-aged guy asked.

"*Everybody* wants a waterproof toilet," the woman next to him retorted. "Pee beads up on it. You see the pee and don't sit down on it, get pee on your legs." She shuddered.

The toilet lady was on screen babbling something about germs and decency and why can't bathrooms be more civilized, but the camera kept cutting back to Erick, probably because he looked so damn handsome.

I felt for him. Putting it on the line, letting everyone know how much it mattered—letting them see his heart.

The toilet lady finished her yammering. It was Erick's turn. He was on national TV.

And Oh! My! God!

He danced.

He did the most perfect whirling turn. And he kicked his leg to the ceiling. And spun around, scissoring the air—snip, snip—and landing right at the table with the dancing heart.

Never missing a beat, he said, "To save the world, we must be willing to show our hearts."

He lifted the valve.

As Mr. Potato Heart danced its goofy dance, Erick danced with him, tapping his feet, then—oompah-pah—rocking back and—oompah-pah—forth.

I know I said the little heart was the cutest thing I'd ever seen, but the two of them dancing together, that truly was the cutest thing I'd ever seen.

And if nothing came of it, if Erick didn't win the *Your Idea Can Save the World!* competition and if instead, we trudged back home to Edison, Mississippi, where I joined him at the diner every morning for sausage biscuits and orange juice, it was worth it.

Because at least he'd gotten to dance. No one in the ballet world would ever again believe what the French judge had said about him.

Once again, the show cut to a commercial.

A Big Doodle Dayton Chicken Palace Emporium commercial.

Except, instead of being in his chicken suit and flapping his wings, Big Doodle was appearing as himself. His own big head and big eyes. Such sad eyes.

Someone yipped in the background of the commercial.

It was Ikie. I would recognize his yip anywhere.

I turned to catch Pooh scooping up the dog and clamping his mouth shut. Big Doodle was posed in front of the camcorder set up to broadcast the Gminski family's living room frolics to the world.

Only it was broadcasting Big Doodle.

"My family, friends, and neighbors," Big Doodle said, very solemnly. "I must report some sad news, some of the saddest news in the history of the Chicken Palace Emporium and Museum. The tragic news involves my dear friend, Mr. Bill Watkins."

CHAPTER 24: The Prettiest Non-lying Blue Eyes

"Seldom does one have a friend such as Bill Watkins."

Big Doodle stared into the camcorder positioned on the mantel in the crowded living room.

"I'm talking about the type of friend you can go years without seeing, but you know the world is a better place because he's in it. But he's not in it anymore, not in this world." Big Doodle wiped a tear from his eye.

"Bill Watkins was my partner for many, many years. Without him, there would be no Chicken Palace empire. Now the museum, Bill had nothing to do with that. I oughta make that clear, 'cause that idea's always been a little creaky." Big Doodle waved off his own distraction. "Anyway, many years ago, when we first started out, I did Bill Watkins wrong. He didn't recognize it, but others did."

"Sure did," Pooh humphed next to me.

"I tried to make amends, which he did not take well. Maybe it was too little too late, but it didn't heal our friendship as I'd hoped. Next thing I know, this drug scandal pops up. I did not want to believe Bill's resentment of me would lead him to dealing dope in the Chicken Palace, but you never know about human nature. I have since made diligent inquiry to ascertain the truth."

"He made a few phone calls," I grumped, tired of Big Doodle's drama—he needed to get to the point.

"I want to make this clear." Big Doodle paused and stared into the camcorder, which someone in the crowd jostled, knocking it cattywhompus.

For a minute, the camera cast its eye across the room. It caught Mother, her jaw set; and Clyde, anxiously watching Mother; and Pooh, frowning while she petted Ikie's head. All of us from Mississippi, on national TV. Except for me. Briefly, I wondered what I would have looked like. Anxious to hear what Big Doodle was about to say? Or calm, knowing I'd done everything I could, let the chips fall where they may? Then someone righted the camera, and we were back on Big Doodle, his face serious.

"It's hard as pulling hen's teeth to get me to say I'm sorry. But a little lady recently reminded me of something I was threatening to forget. I loved Bill Watkins like a brother. He made me a better person. The Big Doodle I want to be is the one Bill Watkins would admire.

"Whoever was responsible for the scandal rocking the Chicken Palace Emporium, it was not Bill Watkins. Anyone who says otherwise will have to answer to me. I will not allow anyone, myself included, to sully Bill Watkins's great name. Oh, and I've been given something to read."

He reached into his jacket and retrieved a pair of reading glasses which he settled on his nose. Fumbling in his pocket, he withdrew the slip of paper with our notes on it. "Let's see what we've got here."

Scanning the paper, he read: "Chickens are like family. We recommend them for the happiness they bring us. Prophet is good, but there's a limit to what we can allow. Prophet will no longer be allowed to rule the roost. Our hearts remember what Bill Watkins loved: to see chickens Hunt and Peck in the yard. In honor of Bill

Watkins, I Big Doodle Dayton recommit to our shared value of loving and being nice to our chickens."

He glanced up from the paper. "Read out loud, it sounds like I'm saying something I didn't know I intended to say."

Frowning, he caught my eye. He looked annoyed but something else too. A jiggle in his cheeks, a twitching at the mouth. His gaze wandered from me to Mother. "Seems a mother/daughter duo are gonna make sure we quit being mean to our chickens and treat them with the proper respect they deserve. Quit shooting them full of hormones. Let them run around when they want to, peck in the yard in the sunshine. In honor of Bill Watkins's, I hereby reinstitute his 'be kind to chickens' philosophy. Let that be his chicken legacy. That's all."

He snapped off a salute, and the screen faded to black—because Ingrid was slowly draping a black t-shirt over the camcorder.

Except for the Mississippi folks, no one in the room knew what Big Doodle was talking about, but it didn't matter. Big Doodle was theirs, and the place erupted in applause.

"Walk-off home run, Big Doodle!" I went to hug his neck, but he demurred.

"I cleared up what I could, child. The rest is up to the Feds."

"You said Daddy was innocent."

Big Doodle took my face in his hands. "Those phone calls didn't tell me a damn thing. I don't know whether your daddy was a drug kingpin or not. I don't care. You were right to remind me of our friendship, your daddy's and mine. That's all that matters." He kissed the flat of his thumb and wetly pressed it on my cheek. "I've done my part. Now you have to decide for yourself what's most important to you, little girl."

I remembered what Daddy had told me beside the cotton fields: Decide what's important to you and hold it close to your heart. Otherwise, you'll get lost. "My Daddy told me the same thing a long time ago."

"Where do you think I learned it?"

Standing there with his eyes searching mine, Big Doodle looked so *familiar*, so much the man I'd known as a child. "Big Doodle, why did you ignore the Edison Chicken Palace? Why'd you let it go to rack and ruin? Were you trying to cheat my daddy? Or did you not care about us anymore?"

He drew back. "Ignore it, child? I let it *be*."

"What do you mean?"

"Do you know how often those corporate types have tried to get their mitts on the Edison Chicken Palace? 'Modernize it, synthesize it, bring it in line with the corporate look.' If I've had to put the quietus on a blueprint for a wraparound drive-thru lane once, I've had to do it a million times."

"They wanted to update it?"

"Update it and exploit it. At one point they wanted to turn the original Big Doodle Chicken Palace Emporium"—Big Doodle threw his hands in the air and waggled hallelujah—"into a theme park. I couldn't let them do that. What would happen to the museum? What would happen to Cecil Everette Clay?"

What indeed?

"No." Big Doodle shook his head. "I have to listen to those suits talk all day long about corporate responsibility to shareholders. But the Edison Chicken

Palace belonged to me and Bill Watkins. I made sure of that from the very beginning, formed a corporation to keep the chain separate from the Edison place. I vowed to always protect the original Chicken Palace and, by gum, I wasn't about to let those widget-makers talk me into ruining the one thing that meant something to me. I know, I know. I admit now that my greed might have corrupted my original intent a tad. But my feelings are real. The Edison Chicken Palace is some kind of special. Why"—his pale eyes grew wide—"the Edison Chicken Palace is *sacred*."

"Benjamin Dayton."

Mother walked right up and nudged me aside. "We're not done here."

"What else you needing, Rita Rae?" Bennie wrung his hands.

"Turn over the management of the Chicken Palace Emporium Museum to the Watkins family. Instruct Cecil Everett Clay to restart the video on humane chicken management methods. Rename it the Bill Watkins Chicken Museum."

Big Doodle shrugged. "Why not? Miss Sissy never could lay an egg. Who better than Bill Watkins to carry on the name?"

"And all the museum profits go to us."

Big Doodle looked at her sideways. "Well, okay. If you insist."

At that, Mother gave Big Doodle a big smacking kiss on the lips. "Thank you, Bennie Dayton. My family and I thank you from the bottom of our hearts."

"Me too," offered Clyde, who was trailing behind.

I nudged him with my elbow. "She said family, didn't she?"

Squinting at me, he broke into a grin. "Well, I guess she did."

*

When the show resumed, it didn't take long for them to announce the winner.

Of course, Erick won.

What? Did you think they were going to give the *Your Idea Can Save the World!* prize to a toilet seat?

Soon after Erick took his congratulatory bow—him holding the oversized million dollar check (!) while some babe-a-licious Vanna White kissed him on the cheek, (not much of a thrill for Erick)—he was in the Gminski's living room, live and in person.

"What are you doing here?" Erick worked his way through the crowd toward me. "I thought you had a date with Augie."

"I do, later." I wormed my arm around his waist. Up close, he smelled like baby powder. "You think I'd miss your show?"

"Did you see I won?"

"Of course I saw you won! You're the only person in the world who could bring class to a game show." I stood on tiptoe and gave him a kiss on the cheek. "I might run out on you, but I wouldn't miss your big moment for anything."

"I'm glad you made it back."

"I did make it back, didn't I?"

"I couldn't stand it when I thought you wouldn't make it. I even asked Rita Rae to help ensure you got here." He made his *eek!* mouth. "I wanted to surprise you with my idea."

"You did surprise me. Mr. Potato Heart was the cutest thing I've ever seen."

"That's what you call him, Mr. Potato Heart?"

"Not me, I didn't start it." A man rolled a keg of beer past us. As he reached the middle of the room, a chorus of, "Roll out the barrel!" erupted.

"How did you know?" I asked.

"Know what?"

"How did you know you could follow your heart's desire and make all these people so happy in the process?"

"Not sure I did."

"Your idea *will* save the world!" I raised my fist in triumph.

Erick covered my fist with his, slowly bringing my arm to my side. "Not my idea. Yours."

"My idea?"

"You and your, 'love your heart, love your heart.'" He gently swung my arm back and forth. "I decided to embrace what that French judge said about my dancing and love my own heart."

And there it was on Erick's face. The serenity that came from a deep place of understanding. The place where you'd shaken that cur dog Life from your neck and dropped the hound on the floor and kicked it out the door.

"Ahhhhh. I see, said the blind man."

"What is it, Ms. Williams?"

"I may know the answer."

"Which is?"

"Same answer as yours. If you want to be happy, you have to love your heart."

"Mine was 'show your heart.'"

"Then it's my very own answer."

He raised my hand to his lips and kissed it. "Speaking of which, guess what?"

"What?"

He leaned and whispered in my ear, "I've got mine."

I grabbed his hand and drug him into the hallway. "Tell it."

"He was a choreographer for the awards show."

"Sweet." We were nose to nose, eyeball to eyeball, my beautiful friend Erick who loved me through thick and thin, back with me because I was back with him, sharing.

"He used to be a dancer."

"Even sweeter."

"His name is Fulton. He loves Elvis." Erick took a deep breath.

I pressed my palm against my cheek, waiting.

"Guess what Fulton's favorite city is?"

"San Francisco?"

Erick nodded.

"Hot damn! I knew you would find someone on this trip. Of course, I thought it would be Sampson, but then that's me: swinging at the first pitch." I beamed, then dropped my jaw. "Goodbye, J.J.!"

"How depressed was I to take up with that loser? He just about ruined this trip, calling every five seconds, griping." Erick studied me. "Ma was right. Losing the competition derailed me. I had to take a break, but I was afraid if I moved someplace brand new and started completely over, I would give up dancing altogether, and I didn't want that to happen. Staying in Jackson meant I had to drive by the auditorium and remind myself to find a way to get back in the game."

"When you came downtown to watch the pretty men strut, you drove by the auditorium." For some reason, this realization brought tears to my eyes— Erick, driving by the scene of his greatest failure, hoping to find a way to heal. Drenched as I had been in my own sorrow, I hadn't noticed his.

Erick fiddled with my shirt collar. "Just think, Ms. Williams, I would never have met you except for the Chicken Palace."

"What do you mean?"

"The day I was driving to Vicksburg and saw the sign for the Chicken Palace Emporium and Museum, I thought, any town silly enough to have a chicken museum could make room for me. GIve me some space to lick my wounds without making too big a deal of it."

I laughed. "The Chicken Palace brought you to Edison!"

"Who would've ever thought I'd be sorry to leave the Chicken Palace behind?"

"Leave?" I said then the truth slapped me upside the head: Erick wouldn't be returning to Mississippi. "You've been leaving Edison from the minute you boarded the train, haven't you? Entering the contest, getting all your family involved in making your invention, reconnecting with them."

"The timing was right for me to give moving home a shot."

"You were in transition."

"A turning point." He executed a perfect pirouette.

I clapped and hugged him and wished him the best of luck, and he held on to me and hugged me back, and finally, knowing it was time, I whispered, "Love your heart," and he melted into the welcoming arms of his family.

Then my phone chirped, and I was on the line with Augie.

*

Augie said he'd seen Erick on TV and was all excited about the win. He might have mentioned something about my dad and Big Doodle too, but I was having a little trouble hearing because the party around me had revved into high gear.

"Hold on a minute." I maneuvered into the hallway where it was somewhat quieter. In the living room, the Gminski relatives were squealing and thumping and singing. I could see the TV screen, which switched to a replay of us, the celebrating family. The twins held Ikie aloft beside Pooh and Clyde while Big Doodle patted Mother's rear end.

"Ikie says hi," I told Augie.

"And who might Ikie be?"

"My grandmother's dog."

"Is he there?"

"He and Pooh…and Mother and Clyde. I've been back on the train since I last saw you." From the living room came a cluster of dragging noises followed by the tinkling of a floor tambourine. The party was transitioning from congratulatory celebration to competitive preparation. "Gonna kick Elvi butt!" someone who sounded a lot like Robert yelled.

"We've got a bad connection," Augie said.

"No, it's noisy here."

"Okay. We can talk tonight. Straighten out some things between us."

That was quick—I was about to find out if I'd made yet another stupid mistake, sleeping with a practical stranger before I should have because I thought he had the prettiest, non-lying blue eyes.

"Hello?" he asked.

"I'm here. I'll see you tonight. Seven o'clock. Just as planned."

Except it wouldn't be just as planned.

With Important Revelations swirling in the air, I wouldn't be able to bring myself to wear the dress.

*

The dress fit like Mylar. A sea foam green with plunging halter neck. The pleats in the halter hid the fact that I had no boobs, the scoop back dipped so low it sat on the shelf of my ass. Four-inch gold high heels and gold icicle earrings completed the effect.

You could not wear such a dress to meet someone who might possibly—or probably with the way Life rolled for me—ruin your image of him forever.

As I rummaged through my much-worn clothing selection, I considered the possible outcomes of the evening. Strains of oompah drug music thumped, the family practicing for the big competition.

Outcome One: Augie would confess an inconsequential truth about himself—such as he actually couldn't stand pleather—and I would laugh and tell him that was ridiculous; then I'd run home to change into the dress and we'd go out to dance the night away.

287

Outcome Two: Augie would share an unpleasant fact about himself—he had a criminal record, maybe, something he was desperately trying to put behind him—and I'd be so impressed with his fortitude of character we'd immediately begin planning a trip to New Orleans for the weekend.

Final Worst Outcome: Augie would tell me something so unexpected it would upend my view of him in such a way that I could not bear to finish the meal and would storm out of the restaurant, teary-eyed at what might have been.

Which, I wondered, was Life going to send my way?

In the side flap of my suitcase, I found a leopard bra I had forgotten I'd packed. As I'd said, "You can't run away from leopard." You put on a leopard bra, you expect someone to see it.

What the hell. I slipped on the bra. "Live wif abandon," as Rahtz would say.

Having found one unexpected thing in a side flap, I decided to try the other. Aha! I unrolled a cotton top Pooh had given me, red with black Yorkies on it. I studied the shirt.

It was so awful as to be cute.

Plus, Augie and I were at a dogleg in our relationship, no doubt about it.

That is, if we had a relationship.

I slipped on the Yorkie top and buttoned it up the front, leaving the last three buttons undone. Sure, all it showed was a ridged collar bone, but give a man a peek, and he'll think there's something worth peeking at.

I plopped onto the bed in my doggie top and
panties. I was diverting, trying desperately to ignore the
issue at hand. Why did I want it to work with Augie?
As soon as the thought formed in my brain, I heard the
answer: the man's sense of serenity. He knew to hold
on to the things important to him—his nieces and
nephews, his mama's cooking, his city—and let the rest
roll away. I was almost at that place, I could feel it.

I sighed. When I looked back at the beginning of
the trip, it was as if I were looking through the wrong
end of a telescope. My angry self and Erick's cool self
were as small as itty-bitty, arm-waving robots. We'd
only been gone, what? Five days? But our past selves
looked far, far away. And not that important.

I'd done my part to set my daddy's legacy back on
the right course. Granted, for everything to work out,
the Feds had to agree to back off, but Big Doodle had
cut the head off the snake. Plus, I'd finally cleared the
air about Daddy's death. Maybe I could even move to a
place where I didn't resent Clyde so much. A
relationship with Augie would be mere icing on the
cake. That's the way I should think of this evening with
Augie. We would laugh and have fun, or we wouldn't.

I unrolled a black mohair skirt from the suitcase,
and the bag of Pooh's Katherine Hepburn brownies
tumbled onto the bedspread.

So that's where they'd been hiding.

I wiggled my fingers into the bag, unstuck a
brownie from the clump, and munched on it. Gooey,
almost caramel-y, but I knew the recipe had no brown
sugar in it. I'd stood on the kitchen stool no bigger than
a pea-mite and watched Pooh beat the hell out of the

batter. That was the secret, I think. Beating the hell out of it.

Nothing in this life came easy.

I nipped the bottom of the brownie, saving to the last the sheen of pure, sugary icing, which I quickly licked from my fingers.

*

Life being Life, my equilibrium was immediately tested when I emerged from the cab to see Augie loitering at the front door of the restaurant. A blond bombshell was standing next to him. Big-boobed and curvy, Mae West to his Sam Spade. She threw back her head and laughed. Then she leaned, whispering something in his ear.

Augie stuffed his hands in his jacket pockets and, glancing down, smiled at the sidewalk.

CHAPTER 25: An Unnecessary Fork

The blonde swung her hair behind her shoulders, instantly transporting me to the tenth grade, a stick-skinny teenager in a world of voluptuous girls.

But only for a second.

Yanking my too-short skirt into place, I strode up to Augie and gave him a full kiss on the mouth, then tucked my arm in his. "Who's your friend?"

He stared at me. "Who?"

"Her." I inclined my head.

"Oh." To the blonde, he said, "Sorry, I didn't catch your name?"

"Katherine." She flashed me a fake smile.

"Lucinda Mae Watkins," I rejoined.

"Well, don't the mag-nol-ias drip from your lee-ips?" she said with an exaggerated drawl.

"You bet your sweet ass they do." I turned to Augie. "Ready?"

His eyes twinkled. "Whenever you are, *cher*."

The interior of the restaurant was dark and discretely lit, with a suit of medieval armor by the hostess stand. The maître d' weaved us around the tables until we arrived in the far back corner. A pewter candelabra in the center of the table cast wavering light.

"Isn't that lovely?"

Augie pulled out my chair. "Guy I work for recommended the restaurant. He said to ask for Jude."

The waiter—a tall, slim Black guy who was undoubtedly Jude—nodded and handed us each a menu.

When Jude had taken our order and exited, Augie became very busy with his napkin. Beneath his blue blazer he wore a pink golf shirt like Rahtz's, right down to the tip of his collar pointing straight up, grazing his cheek, like Rahtz's jaunty collar.

The events and people of the last week—Big Doodle's scolding Prophet the rooster, Coletta singing in the pond, Rahtz squeaking his highlighter across his textbook, Clyde high-fiving me in the dining car, the Bruised Magnolia trailing her suitcase, Erick studying the Mall of America maps—it all clacked through my mind as blurry as boxcars whizzing by while you're sitting in your automobile at the intersection, waiting for the train to pass, you looking in.

Except I wasn't looking in. I'd been on the train, riding. I'd taken this trip the same way the folks in Edison were known to "take the Fourth": a no-holds-barred, all-day-long, doing-it-up-right, hope-you're-alive-in-the-morning celebration of Independence Day.

The sheer exuberance of it made me want to shout with joy. I didn't, though, because Jude was serving our salads. The candelabra cast golden light on Augie's sublime face. He was clearly nervous.

"Well…." he said. "Great news about Erick."

"Erick deserved it. He'd been done wrong." I told Augie about the International Ballet and the French judge eliminating Erick from the competition.

"You have an International Ballet in Jackson?" Augie was mostly moving his lettuce around on his plate with his fork. At our plates was another, smaller fork, which didn't seem necessary but what did I know about fancy forks?

"Jackson, Oslo, Moscow, and somewhere else. It rotates. Don't ask me what it's doing in Jackson."

"I don't much go to the ballet."

I set my fork down on my plate and moved the large candelabra to one side. "Are we waiting for the entrée to start talking for real?"

"No." But he studied his uneaten salad.

Another bad sign—unless he wasn't eating the salad for the same reason as me: hates balsamic vinaigrette.

Jude, the famous waiter, returned, whisked away our uneaten salads, and set a tiny steel cup down at each of our plates. Inside a dab of sherbet melted.

"Life's too short. Eat dessert first." I peered into the cup.

"To cleanse your palette before we serve the entrée," Jude said.

"That's why I brush my teeth." But I dipped my tiny spoon into the tiny cup and took a tiny, cold bite. The cup and spoon would make great souvenirs, but I was afraid Jude would notice if I slipped them in my tote.

Our spoons clinked against the steel cups.

Augie cleared his throat—and said nothing.

"Look." I buttoned the top buttons on my Yorkie shirt. "We had fun on the train. Some laughs, some good memories. Let's don't make it into a bigger deal than it was." Across the room, a woman let out a tinkling laugh.

"I work for the Feds."

The room went silent. "What?"

"I'm a federal agent." Augie looked up from his salad. "Five years now. The New Orleans division of the DEA."

"DEA? You mean like drugs?" Then it hit me. "You mean a goat-doping, chicken-smuggling drug scandal in Edison, Mississippi?"

"Sort of."

When I glared, he said, "Exactly like that. But let me explain."

I didn't want to hear any such explanation. "The DEA? Not scouting at all. You knew I loved baseball, so you told me you did too." I flashed on Stirling telling me he loved the same book I did. "Using something close to my heart to entrap me. That's…entrapment."

"I do love baseball. I—"

Waves of enlightenment rolled over me. "You slept with me to get information on the *drug* scandal?"

"No. No, I didn't."

"My lousy husband cheats on me with everything that moves, and the very next guy I meet lies to me to get *information*?"

As Jude cleared our sorbet cups, the realization of what Augie had said sunk in: He'd made it up, all of it, from the very beginning. I lowered my head into my hands. Right when everything was clearing up, sunshine and bright skies ahead, la-di-da, I'm so happy—Life throws me a total curve ball. "Aw, crap."

"I didn't intend it, Lucinda. If someone had told me I would start something up with a woman I couldn't be completely honest with, I would have told them they were crazy. I never—."

"You said there was something about you I wouldn't like. You didn't tell me everything about our relationship was a lie."

"I couldn't tell you. My job—"

"No, no." I raised my eyes. "It's not your fault. It's mine. I'm snake bit. We're not talking a bit of bad luck. I'm so snake bit, I have a rattler permanently attached to my ass."

"It's all my fault. I crossed a line."

"When did you start following me? I would've noticed you in Edison."

"I told you, I'm based in New Orleans. The smuggling was happening at our port. That's why they put me on the case. Because of my port connections. We heard you were planning a train trip out of town—"

"You 'heard'?"

"One of the team was on your mother."

I thought back. "The only lady in the Clandestine Book Club who wasn't pushing eighty."

"I had you. When y'all all jumped on the train, Fred Gentry had Clyde. Debbie Rhymers had your mother."

"Rhymers and Gentry?" The Mississippi couple Mother and Clyde had met on the train. "You were following all of us? Like we were a white trash criminal clan? Were you the one who sic'ed the man in the sunglasses on me?"

"I'd already told you the St. Paul banquet story, then you went on the move again. I couldn't jump on the train and run after you. We had to put someone else on you. He said you confessed to being the drug lord, by the way. I didn't believe him."

"But you believed I was a criminal?"

"You were jumping on and off the train like a cat on a hot tin roof. I thought you had a meet with someone in Chicago to drop off a packet hidden inside your coat."

"In the Great Hall? When you told me to take a turn?"

"To make sure I was wrong."

"And the white dinner jacket?"

"Short notice to board the train. I was in Jackson, debriefing the team, when I got the word. The only shop that was open downtown was a costume shop."

"The jacket was rented?"

He nodded. "Someone was kind enough to leave a flask in the pocket."

"Ugh!" I wanted to spit—my lips on a stranger's flask!

He smiled. "Don't worry, *cher*. You had plenty of alcohol to kill the germs."

I crossed my arms. "Y'all had a lotta resources committed to a know-nothing Mississippi hick."

"Well, we had eyes on the others too. James Tolbert, of course. And a guy they call Stew."

That made me pause. "Lives down by the interstate exchange?"

"Yep."

"And James Tolbert is Erick's J.J.?"

"Tolbert was the Boss Man. He used the manager at the Chicken Palace to coordinate everything, a David Lester Cox."

"Little Davey."

He hesitated. "You were mixed up with all these guys, Lucinda. Then you and Erick took off like scalded dogs soon as the story broke."

I thought about what Erick had said about J.J. calling him the entire trip. No doubt, Erick had been telling J.J. what was going on with me. The drug ring really had been keeping tabs on me.

"Lucinda." Augie was studying me, worried.

I stared at him. "How was the sex, really?"

His face was as blank as an oyster shell shucked clean of its oyster. "Are you kidding me?"

"I want to know if you were faking that too."

"I…I made a mistake. At first, I was going with the flow."

"'*Laissez le bon temps rouler*,'" I said, sarcastic. "And, of course, I told you it was all just for fun."

"That's not it. I knew what I was feeling wasn't professional. But the kiss in the station, you clapping at my stupid dance in the moonlight."

I felt myself caving, giving in. "You *suspected* me."

He leaned forward. "Don't tell me you didn't wonder, if only for a minute, whether your daddy was actually involved in the doping."

"My mother and I untangled a scandal that you people blew all out of proportion."

"Me, I exonerated your dad by catching the real perps."

"You were spying on me when you called on the train. Not being attentive at all. Being…spying." I narrowed my eyes. "Did you sic the Feds on my mom? Did you tell your goons to threaten to take her house?"

He sighed. "If I'd known then what I know now, I would never have let them go there."

"And if pigs had wings, they wouldn't bump their asses when they flew."

We stared at each other until he leaned back. "Ask me anything you want. Anything."

"Are you married?"

"No."

"Were you married?"

"Yes."

"Why'd she leave you?"

Augie took a sip of water. "Like I said, I coached Tulane baseball. Rode the train all over the southeast checking out recruits. I got tired of it and switched to the DEA. When I quit traveling and we were together all the time, turned out she didn't much care for me. Your...happiness at meeting me was really nice."

Jude appeared at Augie's elbow and presented his entrée, a beautiful lamb dish with the leg bone sticking straight up. "Grilled lamb." He set down the plate. "For the man getting grilled. And for the lady." He swirled the plate in front of me. "Pompano in a bag."

He looked at me significantly as he set down the plate, but I didn't catch his drift—was he calling me a windbag?

"Sorry," Augie apologized after Jude left. "I didn't know the waiter would be so opinionated."

"Fancy restaurant, snooty waiter." I was only half paying attention, thrown off by my dinner.

I had no idea the fish would still be in the bag.

"Do you know how to eat this?"

"Open the neck of the bag."

When I did, steam billowed free. I peered inside. The speckled fish sat on a bed of spinach, four tiny shrimp perched on top.

"Should I cut open the top of the bag...or shovel the fish out?"

"You want me to call Jude over and ask him?" Augie teased.

"No!"

Augie gestured with his knife. "Slit the top of the bag."

I stabbed it with the knife, then cut along the fold, exposing the fish. "You probably get fish like this all the time in New Orleans."

"The cuisine capital of the world. Look, I'm really sorry."

And in the candlelight, shadows pooling in the worried planes of his face, I could see the truth of it: he was sorry.

"It's been bothering me a lot. I did believe your dad was guilty, initially. Then you gave that impassioned speech about him and his morning coffee on the porch. I sent the boys back to Little Davey, told him we knew your dad wasn't involved, and he folded like a cheap suit. I've been anxious to tell you the truth. It was only a couple of days of keeping quiet."

He was right about that; it only seemed like a lifetime.

"I'm fond of you, Lucinda. I would never have put myself in this position if you hadn't been cuter than the flying horses at City Park. Your pink jacket. Your…enthusiasm in the tree house. In fact, you kind of snuck up on me and stole my heart."

"You liked my pink jacket?" I poked the fish with my knife.

"I did. But you know my favorite thing about you?"

"My pleather suit?"

"Your enthusiasm. The way you run at life like a winner at the race track."

"My exuberance? I like your serenity. It really bothered you, that you lied?"

"Of course it bothered me. It bothered me you might not care that it bothered me because you wouldn't be able to get past the fact I'd lied. What'd you think? That I was a jerk who seduced women to wring information out of them, laughing all the way?"

"Last question." I was directing with my fork, a much better use than eating the mud-ugly fish. "If the Cubs and the Cardinals were in a race for the pennant, who would you pull for?" If he were a real Cubs fan, he would never root for the Cardinals. If he said Cardinals, then I'd know he'd lied about liking the Cubs *and* he was sucking up to me now.

"I cannot lie to you, *cher*." He laid his hand over his heart. "Being a lifelong Cubs fan, come hell or high water, I could never pull for the Cardinals. Take me as a Cubs fan or not at all."

"I don't know if a Cubs/Cardinals couple could ever stand a chance." My turn to tease.

But he didn't laugh. "Can I have one last question?"

I flinched, waiting for it.

CHAPTER 26: Only a Chicken would Refuse

Augie sawed away at his lamb chop as I waited across the table. "I was wondering. That ex-husband you mentioned."

"Yeah?"

"How over him do you think you are?"

"Oh, that." I stabbed a shrimp with my fork. "I figured that out on my trip."

"Wanna share?"

"Sure." I set the fork down. "I met this guy on the train. He was a math guy. I'll tell you all about him later. Anyway, what happened is, I'm grieving for Daddy and I run into Stirling. *Pow!* I think I'm in love. I see Mother sitting at the kitchen table with Clyde and *pow*! I'm all alone in the world, and I marry Stirling. Each time, I should've asked, what is really happening, Lucinda? Do you truly love Stirling? Aren't you actually glad your mother found someone? But I didn't ask myself those questions, and it got so tangled up I had to go around the world to figure it out. Well, at least across country and back."

The candlelight on the table flickered. Beneath the present-day reality—the restaurant, the table, the tablecloth—I felt the rhythm of the train gathering under me, the even-keeled rocking, the anticipation. As sure as day follows night, this whole trip had been intended to take me to this moment, laying down the tracks for me to follow into my future happiness.

"Lord knows I can mess things up quicker than shit running through a goose. But my dad, when I saw him sitting on our front porch, what I saw was the ordinariness of it. What he was actually doing was using that porch to connect with whoever walked by. Early in life he had learned his most important thing was to care about people as individuals. It's gonna take all my energy to focus on my important thing, but I'm determined to do it."

"And what's your important thing?"

"I'm not sure, but it's got to do with the way my heart soars when I find something special. A first kiss. Or an amazing book. Or a new friend."

"The exuberance?"

I laughed. "Yeah, I guess so."

"And what gives you that joy?"

"Right now? The candlelight reflecting in your eyes. Teensy cups of sweet sorbet. Tomorrow, I might love something else. The trick is to keep seeing what your heart loves."

"That's nice, *cher*."

Jude slid up to the table and handed us each a dessert menu.

"Separate menus for dessert," I said. "Will wonders never cease."

"You folks aren't from around here, are you?" he asked.

"No. Augie's from New Orleans. I'm from Mississippi."

"Mississippi? No shit? My old man's from Mississippi. Engineer. He built the platform at the Jackson train station. Put a roof on it so you don't get rained on while waiting for the train."

"I boarded the train in Jackson."

"My old man loved the train. Made a lot of money off the train." He folded his hands behind his back—

Jude didn't carry a notepad; he memorized orders. "Ask me about the desserts."

"Is the crème brûlée any good?" Augie complied.

"Not the best." Jude leaned over, pointed on my dessert menu. "I'd get the Double Chocolate Unrepentant Sinners Cake if I were you." When he straightened, he added, "Tell me it's your birthday, and I can get it to you for free."

"It's my birthday," I complied.

"My pleasure," he replied and whisked away the menus.

After he left, Augie asked, "We good?"

"I'm good. You good?"

"Good as finding the baby in the king cake."

"Is that good?"

"Doesn't get any better. Maybe...." He reached over and unbuttoned my top buttons. "Now. That's better."

I had to admit: he was right.

*

The next day at the airport, Mother had dressed up for the flight the way people used to do, wearing a smart tweedy suit in the lime-green family and low-heeled pumps. She'd found a vendor selling Ben and Jerry's ice cream. Scooping up the last bit of ice cream with a plastic spoon, she tottered over to the trash. "Now I've eaten ice cream up North." She threw the cup away. "Just like a real Northerner."

They were flying commercial, even though Big Doodle had offered to send his company jet over. Mother thought that would be unseemly, arriving back in Edison on Big Doodle's jet when she was engaged to Clyde.

Yep.

They'd become official.

Maybe the competition with Big Doodle had made Clyde see the light. Or maybe the trip made Mother realize how much she'd come to depend on Clyde. Either way, they were on the calendar for June 19. "A proper June wedding," Mother said. "Nothing jumped-up, like Ms. Kim Stratton," she added, and for Edison, a two-month engagement was, in fact, not jumped-up.

I kissed them all goodbye, one by one. "Now, Pooh, you have a safe flight. When I get back, we'll chat on the glider."

But, Ikie under her arm, Pooh was already underway, headed through the glass doors.

"Old people." Clyde took off after her.

I wouldn't be going inside. I couldn't stand walking down those long corridors and waiting at the window while the plane flew further and further away. No matter how far I'd come, some things didn't change.

"Well…" Mother said. "I don't suppose you want me to tell Mary Martha you'll be ready for a new job Monday?"

"Stall her for a week. I'll be back by then, I hope," I added because we had agreed to be more truthful with each other. "If you could, thank Pammy profusely for me, that would be great. Since you're the Chicken Museum manager now, maybe you could set up a spa at the Museum for her? Cecil Everett Clay probably wouldn't mind."

Mother fiddled with the strap of her pocketbook. "Anyway, I need you to know."

Uh oh. Not again.

"I got Bennie to cooperate using sweet-talking. Nothing more." She gave me a significant look.

I smiled. "I never doubted you."

"Plus, Clyde thinks we should license a Big Doodle Chicken doll. Sell it at the Museum. The revenue would be ours too."

I laughed. "Look at you!"

She raised an eyebrow. "I pressed an advantage. Remember that. It'll serve you well."

"Oh, Mother. Thank you so much for coming to check on me." I hugged her close. It brought her off balance, tottering, and I stepped out on a limb.

"I love you."

"I love you too, Lucinda Mae."

She turned, a little wobbly on her heels.

Then she stopped.

Over her shoulder, she said, "But you might want to think about changing that dress."

*

I had on the Mylar dress.

Sea foam green stuck to my body. Gold high-heeled shoes and dangling gold earrings.

I was on my way to meet Augie at the train station.

When I arrived, a woman was standing on the platform, crying at the empty tracks. Behind the platform, a switch engine was running forward, backward, forward. Around it, ten or twelve tracks crossed and crisscrossed. Finally, the freight train chose a track and pulled away.

As I watched it depart, I thought about Augie and me, imagining our trip to Jackson and then on to New

Orleans. Things might work out for us so well one day we'd create a big happy family, the kind that got into fights at Thanksgiving, throwing pumpkin pie and all.

Or we would enjoy a fun week in New Orleans, date a few more months then decide great sex and a love of baseball weren't enough to build a relationship on and fondly call it quits.

It didn't matter.

What mattered was the chance to find out. The ability to move forward without the baggage of the past weighing me down. Either way and in all ways, the decision would be mine.

In the middle of my musing, from down the track, the train appeared.

The sun glinted off the steel. The platform shook with anticipation, and for a moment, I couldn't tell if the train was coming or going; whether this was the beginning or the end. Until suddenly the picture shuddered into focus and I saw myself: I was standing clearly in the middle, looking at myself watching the train.

A hand circled my waist.

I looked up.

"Why you crying, boo?" Augie wiped away the tears that had started.

"I love the train."

"You are beautiful." He ran a fingertip down my naked back.

"Trying to distract me, huh?" I dabbed my fingers under my eyes, careful not to smudge my mascara.

"If at all possible." He turned me in his arms and kissed me as the train shuddered to a stop at our feet.

"All a-booaaaard!" the conductor shouted.

Augie released me, lifting his bags.

I held the image of the train in my mind for a moment and stepped onto the stairs.

As my feet hit the steel, the train let out its lonesome whistle whine, issuing its invitation to join in the ride.

I stepped on board.

After all, only a chicken would refuse.

THE END

ACKNOWLEDGEMENT

TRACKING HAPPINESS has been years in the making. I am grateful to the many readers who have assisted in its creation. I thank the members of my long-ago RUMP writing group that got me through early versions of the novel, especially Rick DeStefanis who has hung in there with my writing over the years. Also thanks to readers Blake Burr, Sybil MacBeth, Virginia Van Hecke, Corinne Sampson, Joe Hawes, and Suzanne Henley. Thank you to Bel Shofner, a supporter and creator of the phrase "Edison, Mississippi, fried chicken royalty." Special thanks to the Sudbury sisters who believe "no one here is mean to their chickens."

Listen to Ellen Morris Prewitt's CAIN'T DO NOTHING WITH LOVE, an award-winning collection of delightfully edgy and decidedly Southern short stories, at scribl.com

Coming soon by Ellen Morris Prewitt:
MODEL FOR DECEPTION: A VANGIE STREET MYSTERY

Vangie Street is older—thirty-two to be exact—when she takes up modeling. She loves showing fabulous clothes almost as much as she loves her pound-puppy, Retro, her kooky neighbor, Lankford L., and her hunky new boyfriend. Her post-divorce life in Memphis is perfect—until a very expensive earring shown by her modeling partner disappears. When Heather herself disappears, Vangie's "clothes whisperer" intuition tells her all is not as it seems. Why does Heather's doctor husband sport a tuxedo beneath his lab coat? What's up with his sexpot office manager's ugly black watch? And why does Heather's replacement show up in a green leather miniskirt? Vangie must puzzle out the revelations these and other clothing choices tell her about the people involved in the crime if she wants to discover the truth . . . and keep her own self out of trouble.

Made in the USA
Lexington, KY
09 September 2018